The Life

Liberation Classics

Notes of a Native Son James Baldwin
A Long Way From Home Claude McKay

The Life of the Automobile

By Ilya Ehrenburg

Translated from the Russian by Joachim Neugroschel

Pluto Press

London and Sydney

First published in Russian by Petropolis Verlag, Berlin
Copyright © Petropolis Verlag 1929
This translation first published in 1985 in the UK by
Pluto Press, 105a Torriano Avenue, London NW5 2RX
and in Australia by Pluto Press, PO Box 199,
Leichhardt, New South Wales 2040, Australia

Translation copyright © Urizen Books 1976

7   6   5   4   3   2   1

89   88   87   86   85

Printed in Great Britain by Guernsey Press Company Limited
Guernsey, C.I.

British Library Cataloguing in Publication Data available

ISBN 0 916354 07 5

Translator's Note

The Russian text of Ilya Ehrenburg's The Life of the Automobile
*(10 H.P.) was printed by the Petropolis publishing house in Berlin
during 1929. It was never reprinted. Soviet editions of the Ehrenburg
canon offer butchered and retitled versions with some additional later
material.*

*Unfortunately, the original Petropolis version is full of typographi-
cal errors.*

*A German translation, based on the Russian manuscript, was pre-
pared by Hans Ruoff and put out by the Malik Verlag that same
year, 1929. The German rendering helps to clear up most of the
problems in the Russian text. Furthermore, it contains many words,
phrases, even sentences having no equivalent in the Russian original.
There is no way of determining whether these omissions were due to
the author's editing or the typesetter's sloppiness. Ehrenburg's
memoirs have only one reference to the book and none to the German translation.*

*My own feeling is that the German version is by and large correct,
since the words and phrases in question are generally crucial to the
book. I have translated all of these omissions from Hans Ruoff's
German text and included them here in the proper places.*

Joachim Neugroschel

Author's Note

This book is not a novel; it is a chronicle of our time. The heroes are not imaginary; the story was not invented by the author. However, the author felt justified in offering his own explanations for the actions of the characters rather than relying on official versions by any of the heroes.

In a few rare instances the author felt it necessary to replace real names with fictitious ones. This was done only for people whose lives can in no way be regarded as public.

In the chapter entitled *Stock Exchange* and in parts 2 and 5 of the chapter entitled *Roads,* the author took the liberty of rearranging certain details, blending several figures into one, and concentrating events. In the other chapters he made a point of not deviating from the raw material: new items, minutes of meetings, court records, as well as memoirs, diaries, private letters, plus personal observations by the author.

Paris, June 14, 1929

Contents

Chapter One

The Birth of the Automobile

1

Charles Bernard at first dealt in cigarette paper. Then he sold the paper depot and simply began living. He lived slow and wise, like a turtle. He read the *Almanac of Nature Lovers*. The almanac explained which clouds were a sign of rain and which of wind. It also explained when the swallows and linnets came back, and how to raise rabbits, and where to pick fragrant lavender. Bernard didn't have rabbits. He had never seen a linnet. He lived in Paris, on narrow Rue Estrapade. Under his windows, the day smelled of red cheeses in the dairy, and the night of garbage cans.

Bernard read the Almanac, for he had a great deal of time. In addition, he had a dreamy heart and a small private income. After breakfast, he usually went to the Botanical Garden. There he fed the sparrows crumbs of yesterday's bread and smiled at the drooling babies who were squeaking in their carriages.

He could have lived quietly to a ripe, old age: turtles are famous for their longevity.

Bernard's younger sister, who lived in Perigueux, often invited Bernard to visit her. But he pleaded business or illness. He was afraid of the trip: stations, hurly-burly, whistles. After all, it was twelve hours to Perigueux! Bernard preferred the *Almanac of Nature Lovers*.

Little by little, though, disquiet started oozing into Bernard's life. It began with some stupid movie. Earlier, Bernard had only gone to the circus with the concièrge's children. Friends dragged him to a film. Bernard liked everything: a galloping horse, an Apache on the roof of a very tall house, the life of underwater reptiles. He took to going to the movies every Friday. A harmless entertainment: The movie house was on the next block, and it showed poignant melodramas. But it was there that the bad thing happened. In the dark theater, amid the smooching couples and the comforting rattle of the projector, Bernard unexpectedly started trembling: A car raced across the screen. The entire audience was racing in that car. Bernard suddenly felt that he too was racing somewhere. Everything else was quickly forgotten. Did it matter that the car belonged to a young soccer-player, that his lovely fiancée was waiting for him in a cottage, and that they both feared her father's curse? Bernard only saw the flashing bushes and dust. Even though the theater was very stuffy, his face felt a sharp wind. His skin contracted and burned. Bernard forgot himself to such an extent that he stood up. Behind him, people yelled: "Hey you! Sit down! . . ." Without waiting for the picture to end, he ran out into the street. Let them marry or not marry! It was all the same to him! He had come to realize a great deal. Bernard did not go home. He walked swiftly through the deserted streets. He wished that the houses could always flash by like the bushes. He was far away, perhaps in Granada or at the North Pole.

As of that day, he neglected the almanac. He bought an old guide to the Pyrenees, some maps, and a compass. Only he didn't travel anywhere. He journeyed, while sitting in his home on Rue Estrapade. He could still fight temptation.

Then a new serpent moved into his home. It hissed sweetly. It was the radio. Bernard's days still had an appearance of well-being. But at night he went crazy. He wore warm slippers with pompons. But he wasn't sitting at his fireplace; no, he was whizzing through the world. His lips moved suspiciously. He was looking for waves. Here was Barcelona. . . . Here was Karlsruhe. . . . The German word "bitte." Bach. Spaniards. A charleston. The winner of the race at Oxford. The Royal Dutch rates. An Italian lesson: forte, morte, cane-loni. The victory of the Conservatives in Sweden. The bells of the Kremlin: The *Internationale*. Another charleston. The world moohed, bleated, meowed. Charles Bernard whizzed through the world, in soft slippers with pompons, that same Charles Bernard who had once dealt in cigarette-paper. His thinny-thin moustache wriggled convulsively, his face turned lilac. He really looked fearful in the silence of

2

his musty room. No one saw him, however. He was still at home, on Rue Estrapade.

Then? Then the inevitable happened. It was not for nothing that tens of thousands of people bent their backs; it was not for nothing that the conveyor belt screeched; it was not for nothing that the fateful letters blazed night after night on the Eiffel Tower. The streets of Paris, swarming with automobiles, were covered with posters as cajoling and coddling as the hiss of the nocturnal serpent. Charles Bernard remembered the almanac and his sister in Perigueux. He would be able to admire the clouds, the various clouds from the *Almanac of Nature Lovers:* cumuli, cirri, strati. At last he would get to see those unknown linnets! And the lavender! . . . What a fine fragrance it must have!

The car wasn't cheap, however, and Bernard still vacillated. But then he recalled the evening at the movies. He ran to one of the dealers. The man received him, calm, friendly, as though he had known for a long time that Bernard, modest Bernard, the turtle-man, would come to him sooner or later.

Bernard purchased a marvelous car: ten H.P., eighteen monthly installments, a smooth drive, steel body, and last, last but not least, an electric lighter and a luxurious vase. That night he didn't even listen to the meowing of Barcelona. Nor did he sleep. He sat silent in the dusty armchair, throwing his arms up from time to time. He was probably flying. His eyes were moist like the green earth after the fall of man.

Every morning he went to driving-school. He learned quickly. Two weeks later he went to take the test. He was so careful—that ex-dealer in cigarette-paper! Long before reaching a crossing he would slow down and honk menacingly. He never tried to pass another car. He drove slowly and wisely, like a turtle, and naturally he passed all the tests.

Then he began preparing for his trip. He bought a knitted jacket, a first-aid kit, and a strategic map. He went to the Botanical Garden for one last time to feed his sparrows. Tomorrow he was driving to Perigueux. He was driving, more precisely, to his sister Louise. But he admitted to the sparrows: "Messieurs, I am driving to the linnets. Those are remarkable birds! . . ." There was only one thing he didn't admit to them. And he was afraid to admit it even to himself. His face was already burning, it was singed by the extraordinary wind.

And thus Charles Bernard, a man of private means, drove off to his sister in Perigueux.

At first, Bernard drove slowly and sedately. He knew that you mustn't drive a car fast for the first five hundred miles. That was what they had taught him at school, that was what the dealer had told him, that was what it said in the instruction booklet. Still, thirty kilometers an hour seemed like a furious flight to Bernard. He couldn't distinguish hills, trees, or people. Everything flashed by as in the movie-theater. He halted. He almost wanted to see if there were any linnets about. After all, he was already far away from Paris. But instead, he looked at the bolts in the wheels. Then he drove on. Forgetting himself, he increased the speed somewhat. The needle shot forward, and the wind suddenly became as huge as the world.

Aha, so they were all lying: the dealer and the instruction-booklet. You can drive a new car a lot faster than they said. Well, all the better! He hadn't bought a car just to creep along. He wasn't a turtle. Away with the Botanical Garden! But wait, Charles! What's the hurry? Louise had already waited eight years. She'd wait another day. Why, supposedly, you were driving off to see the lavender. Stop the car! Have a rest! Lie down on the grass! The grass must be downy here, like the fleecy cirri. That was Charles Bernard, the former cigarette-paper dealer, speaking. But Charles the second didn't reply. Charles the second knew only one thing: surge and wind. He squinted. He was drunk, as though he had polished off a bottle of cognac. He grinned. He was zooming faster and faster.

A train is faster than an eagle. But a fly, a teeny fly, can outspeed an express train. A swallow flies faster than a fly. But any swallow is outstripped by a car. Bernard had once read about that in the Sunday papers. But now he wasn't thinking about the swallow. He wasn't even looking at the needle: What did he need numbers for? The car raced for dear life. A long, straight highway. Perhaps he should slow down? . . . It was a new car, after all. . . . The first five hundred kilometers. . . . The man who had once dealt in paper muttered dolefully: Perhaps? . . . However, the car ought to know itself. After all, it was the car that was zooming. Bernard had nothing to do with it. He had merely bought it on the installment plan. . . . Besides, he was insured. . . . And his life? The sparrows? Too late to think. He had already stopped smiling. The wind struck his face painfully. His eyes stuck together. Bernard couldn't see anything. He turned off to the right. Perhaps it wasn't Bernard turning. Some people hollered: Yes! He didn't hear. Then—only one thought: What had happened to the car? . . . Oh well, it was quite obvious! Bernard even opened his eyes for a moment. Quite obvious: The car had gone crazy. Things like that happen. A chapter in the manual: "Illnesses of the Engine." Addendum: Mental Illnesses. White, incredible sun and wind. Better close your eyes. Here comes the end. The highway ended. The long, straight highway came to an end. School, cigarette paper, Estrapade, sparrows. Everything ended. Faster! Faster, faster!

Then a soft shriek. That's how children's balloons perish. Emerald-green or light raspberry-pink. The crazy car raced toward a slope. It was dreadful and simple. It no longer had a thousand parts, it only had one cruel will. It was ancient and human now. With the lofty joy of self-oblivion it flew downward, into a pitiful dale filled with dry juniper.

The linnets warbled, and the lavender was sweet and fragrant. Car No. 180A–74—iron splinters, glass shards, a lump of warm flesh— lay unstirring beneath the solemn midday sun.

2

A flickering candle revealed a peculiar shadow on the wall, a pile of technical drawings, instruments, a tiny kitten dozing among bottles and papers, and last but not least, a scrawny face blanched by many sleepless nights.

This was the home of our young dreamer. For quite some time now, the neighbors had been whispering that he'd gone out of his mind. Still, he was a nice guy and, needless to say, a patriot. Not being a patriot in these times would have been difficult and even dangerous. It was the year VIII of the united and indivisible Republic. There was also a portrait of the dashing Corsican in the room, that same man who was ruthlessly wiping out all enemies of the revolution: secret Chouans, emigrés, and Austrians.

When Philippe Lebon's neighbors told him about the new victory of the Republican armies, he naturally congratulated them, each in turn, particularly Citizen Marot, a Royalist and a spy for the Directory. Lebon rigorously observed the revolutionary calendar. He ate chicken not on Sundays, but on Décadi. His mind, however, was on other things.

When the revolution began, he was twenty. He quickly got used to vows of fraternity and Dr. Guillotin's contraption. The revolution became like the very air he breathed. He stopped noticing it. When he heard about the Ninth of Thermidor, he smiled in amazement. Again? . . . That day struck him as just the usual squabble of the two factions. Another five years went by. Did anyone care what plots Citizen Sièyes was hatching against Citizen Barras? The revolution had won—that was obvious to everyone—even Pitt. And the revolution had failed—they all realized it: the Jacobins, the Directory, and General Bonaparte. What was there to argue about? . . . The citizens had to fulfill their civic duties and button their lips in the cafés, where police agents hovered around every table. That was all. The reasons for Citizen Lebon's insomnia lay elsewhere.

Was he in love? After all, the Republicans were no less canny about love than the loyal subjects of the Capet (of blessed memory). Tallien, for instance, was supposedly wasting away in Egypt for lack of his Thérèse. And then there was that Corsican's woman, the Creole! . . . Phillip Lebon was thirty. Just the right age. Someone knocked. Was *she* at his door? . . . But in walked a physically solid citizen with a fleshy nose and a huge national cockade. He was a friend of Lebon's, a certain François Barré, ex-Jacobin, an orator at ten clubs, and the terror of Chaumont, but at present a peaceful official, who checked the new revolutionary weights at the markets of Paris.

"Still working?"

"As you can see."

"I envy you. You're engrossed in your own matters, and you don't notice a thing. Meanwhile, I think we can say the Revolution is doomed!"

Lebon smiled.

"Well, that's nothing new, brother! It's already been doomed fifty if not a hundred times! Either the revolution is immortal, or else it perished long, long ago."

"You and your sarcasm! But just look at what's happening! Fouché arrested 120 more patriots from the *Manège* Club. The Royalists are scheming out in the open. And do you know what the patriots are carrying on about? Beer! My word of honor! The signs say *March Beer,* and those jackasses are demanding that they change the name to *Germinal Beer*. Sièyes is plotting something. He's an old mole. Barras has got cold feet as usual. Now everything depends on the general. . . . Didn't you know? He's already landed in Toulon."

Lebon, who had only been half-listening to Barré, looked up.

"Aha! And what does this Bonaparte fellow intend to do? . . ."

"Damned if anyone knows! Some people say he's decided to disband the Directory and restore the true republic, *our* republic of '93. But other people claim he's reached an agreement with the Chouans. What do *you* think, Philippe?"

"Me? I don't think anything. I don't think about that stuff at all. I'm very busy."

"But what about your civic feelings?"

"Listen, the revolution is over anyway—with or without Bonaparte. What I'm doing now is making our old dreams come true. The things we used to talk about ten years ago. Don't you believe me?"

"No. You're wasting your time. It's an aristocratic diversion. We dreamt about something entirely different. We dreamt about the common good."

"Exactly! And that revolution never materialized. Some people have been ruined, others have gotten rich. The cards were shuffled. But the aces remained in the pack, and the kings, and the common deuces. Why? Because all men are afflicted with a curse: Work. That's one thing the priests don't lie about. People have to be liberated from work, not from the Capets. You saw the steam-mill on the bank of the Seine, didn't you? Believe me, that steam-mill is more important than any declarations. I've been working on this one thing for a long time now: I made up my mind to invent a self-propelled carriage. Let machines carry people. That's the real common good. That's the brotherhood of nations, too. How happy men will be when all they have to do is flick their wrists to go from Paris to Rome or Vienna."

"But these things are just dreams! . . ."

"These things *were* dreams. Marvelous dreams! Listen, let me read something to you: 'With the aid of the arts and sciences, man will be able to build a carriage that moves at a miraculous speed without horses or other draft-animals. . . .' That was written by Roger Bacon in 1618—180 years ago! . . . And now? Now these things are no longer dreams. Tomorrow, your Corsican may very well be riding in such a carriage. Do you know what, François?"

Lebon got to his feet. His eyes were now as yellow and as flickering as the candle. He spoke softly, constantly losing his breath:

"François, I've finished my work. Tomorrow I'm handing in the application. I'll get the patent. I can't go over all the details now. Though I can tell you one thing: People are going to be transported by air. But listen, not steam! Gas! This gas will be able to light up streets. It will run machines. First, a mixture of gas and air is compressed. Then it's ignited by special sparks. Right inside the engine. That's much more sensible than steam. The motor won't take up much space, and it will have tremendous power, more than a team of four horses. It will be able to pull an ordinary stagecoach with absolutely no inconvenience to the passengers. Now tell me—isn't that the true public good? Within fifty or a hundred years every citizen will own such a self-propelled carriage. Other machines will do away with poverty. My machine will overcome hostility, indolence, ignorance, languor. A human being needs food and clothing for his body. There's no doubt that people will soon invent machines for cultivating grain without having to do the gross drudgery of farming. But now man is satiated. His spirit requires perfection. He travels all over the world. He has no homeland anymore. His home is everywhere. He's as blissful as the gods on Mount Olympus. This pile of papers, François, is the guarantee of true welfare."

But Barré was a difficult sort. Congratulating his friend and, for politeness' sake, observing a minute of silence, he started arguing again:

"No, that's not what made our hearts beat in '93. We dreamt about a wonderful simplicity of morals. Why do people have to dash off somewhere? Just look at your kitten—it's dozing so peacefully! The Ancient Greeks knew nothing about carriages with motors; and were they unhappy? Machines will bring a new oppression of man. They will only stir up envy and competitiveness. I really prefer the drudgery of farming, which you condemn! It's so much closer to Truth and Brotherhood!"

Barré apparently forgot that he was just a minor official in the Directory. He imagined himself back in the club of the city of Chaumont. He waxed eloquent:

"We honest Jacobins are opposed to these machines! Phillipe, I love you, but Truth is higher than Friendship. We are opposed to your invention. It is no use your hurrying to take out a patent. The Revolution is in jeopardy, but it shall not be destroyed. If we win, then we shall annihilate these motors. Instead, we shall plant the groves of Jean-Jacques. . ."

To which Lebon, cheerfully grinning, answered:

"Well, you just don't understand. That Bonaparte *will* understand. Or someone else will. In a word: the future."

"But what about the Revolution?"

"Why, it was the revolution that kindled my desire for the general welfare and my new restlessness. The soul of the revolution is right here—in these drawings."

Barré left off arguing. He was fond of Lebon and didn't want to quarrel. Sighing, he went to a café to drink a carafe of wine, and he and the barflies could talk to their hearts' content about Citizen Sièyes's wicked machinations. The next morning, he calmly verified his weights. He didn't even recall that cunning, gas-propelled motor.

Meanwhile, Philippe Lebon, having exultantly blown the motes of dust from his hat, went to file for a patent in the stuffy bureau where goose quills were scratching drearily and clerks were murmuring with one another about General Bonaparte's arrival. Lebon heard neither the scratching of quills nor the whispering. The dreadful motor was roaring and hissing: it was his machine racing into the new century.

Philippe Lebon registered his invention on the 6th of Vendémiaire of the year VIII, or, according to the old calendar, on September 28, 1799. He had devised a gas for an engine with internal combustion. And thus, ninety years before the appearance of new and unprecedented carriages in the streets of Paris, the first suspicious tremors resounded in the womb of humanity.

3

"Darling, what a simply divine perfume!"
"Isn't it? It's the latest thing: *Fin de siècle.*

"Forgive me, Madame Gilbert, I like the style, but these puffs . . . aren't they just a bit too . . . outré? . . ."
"What are you saying, Madame Drouot! Haven't you seen the current issue of *Fashion? Every*one's having these puffs made, even the Countess de Montbéliar. That's *Fin de siècle.*"
"These newfangled dances are really bizarre. First, they're like a waltz, then they're like a gallop, and then, do forgive me, like a vulgar cancan."
"No, no! That's a new dance: *Fin de siècle.*

"Art is simply degenerating! Instead of paintings, the Salon is showing some smear by that madman Cézanne. There's no pleasant lighting, no spirituality, not even attractive colors. I shudder at the thought of writing about it. And as for poetry! . . . Haven't you heard about that new genius? Who else, pray tell, but Monsieur Stéphane Mallarmé! Some windbag explained to me that this Mallarmé is superior to Sully-Prudhomme. Just read him—he's interesting for a psychiatrist. Why, that's the title of his book: *Ramblings of Meaning*. In my opinion, this spells the end of art."

"I don't think so. It's just a fad—*fin de siècle*."

"What's Clemenceau trying to do? Anatole France has joined the Dreyfusards. Labori is ready to steal the documents himself. It's no longer a court trial, it's a European scandal. Millions of people are deranged because of the sword of some trivial officer."

"Psychosis . . . Craze . . . *Fin de siècle* . . ."

"Millerand is all set for a new Commune. I saw their demonstrations yesterday. That song by that bandit Pottier! Those mobs of arsonists! There's one particularly dangerous agitator among them. His name is Briand. And the government is busy with some idiotic exhibition. We must all unite for the battle against the new Huns."

"Mon ami, you're exaggerating just a wee bit. They're not bandits, just dandies. They'll sow their wild oats and then they'll settle down. In the past, we had the *mal de siècle*, now we've got the *fin de siècle*. Just a slight dizzy-spell, that's all."

"Did you see the bonafide automobile on Boulevard des Italiens?"

"Four automobiles! . . ."

"Eleven automobiles! . . ."

"An automobile exhibition! . . ."

"It's absolutely the end of the world! . . ."

"No. It's *fin de siècle*!"

Paris looked mockingly at the numbers on the calendar. Another century! . . . Paris was no longer capable of wild enthusiasm or severe censure. It had seen imperial cossacks and Garibaldi's shirt, Musset's sand-colored tophat, the corpses of the Commune; it had seen Balzac and Michael Bakunin, Monsieur Thiers and Ravachol, Alexander Dumas, the Shah of Persia, elephant meat during the Siege, and the tears of little Mimi. It had seen everything. What else could lie ahead but tiresome repetitions?

The Republic was hitting thirty. It had long since forgotten its boyhood pranks. Now it had settled down with a household of its own. Our dear Tsar would help us. Hoorah for the Tsar and high dividends!

Some people spoke of an empire of the machine! Well, machines had brought neither bliss nor doom. Stockings and cannon were cheaper, life was cheaper; it was a bit easier to make a fortune, and a bit harder to govern the state. But all in all: *Plus ça change, plus c'est la même chose.*

Let long-haired adolescents shout about a social revolution. At forty, they all become, if not ministers, then gouty civil lawyers, pettifoggers, and devotees of *pâté à la Strasbourgeoise.* On one day, indignant viewers hurled rotten eggs at a young artist's painting. The next day, the Musée de Luxembourg bought it. Life was orderly and stable.

In Parc Monceau, children were playing. They were playing wargames. They had wooden sabers, flags, and drums. Fifteen years later, they would have to hide in cellars and pull outlandish gasmasks over their faces. But for now, they were just children banging away on their drums. The nineteenth century was peacefully living out its last days. No one was rushing it. Let it leaf about in its albums of family photographs and babble about its stormy youth.

However, the horseless carriage refused to be kept waiting. With a disrespectful roar it leaped out into the sleepy boulevards. Old nags reared and pranced, and terrified ladies pulled vials of smelling-salts from their *réticules.* The automobile moved along in fits and starts. It hopped like a kangaroo. It would jam and then unexpectedly jerk forward again. The streets were filled with a horrible stench. The din was louder than a thunderstorm in spring. It was an ordinary phaeton, but with the horses unharnessed, and, obeying some secret explosions, the phaeton ominously whizzed through the outraged avenues of Paris.

It was customary to laugh at automobiles. What a silly contraption! Why, the engine was bound to break down, and the driver would sooner or later have to get horses. Besides, the carriage was hideous. A good team of horses is so much more pleasant and reliable!

People laughed at the automobile, but these hideous carriages wouldn't leave them in peace. What did the stars sing about in all the *cafés-chantants?* Why, the automobile, of course:

> *Gaston likes to lay it on*
> *In his horseless phaeton.*

Dance instructors taught their anemic young demoiselles new dance steps: Monsieur Simon's Automobile Gallop and Monsieur Salabre's

Automobile Polka. A young author was trying to think up an original way of ending his hero's life. François Coppée recommended: "You could let him die under the wheels of a car!" The *Magasins du Louvre* had a contest for devising a new form for the automobile. Why bother with a carriage if there are no horses? The prizes went to Monsieur Courtois for a royal coach with bucolic adornments à la Louis XVI, and to Monsieur Selmersheim for a two-story fortress with tiny bull's-eyes and a captain's bridge for driving. A certain Monsieur Mille, dissatisfied with all these things, constructed a Swanmobile. The engine was lodged in the bird's stomach. The swan pulled a straw basket, in which a person sits and guides the machine with iron reins.

Messrs Panhard and Levassor opened the first automobile factory; they manfactured internal-combustion engines modeled on that of the German engineer Gottlieb Daimler. At the latest race, Panhard's automobile covered the stretch from Paris to Marseilles in sixty-seven hours. The car—under especially favorable circumstances—could develop a speed of up to forty kilometers an hour. The newspapers called it "an infernal gallop!" Municipal authorities were quite unnerved. They issued strict ordinances: Within the city limits, the so-called "automobiles" were not allowed to drive faster than three kilometers an hour. It was a good thing there were so few of them. The factory of Messrs Panhard and Levassor was a tiny workshop. No one bought a car for business trips. And a pleasure-drive was a lot more pleasurable behind a pair of trotters than behind a stinking machine. The automobile required the tough heroism of youth. It demanded self-sacrifice. It attracted men who, by some fluke, had not gone off to discover the North Pole or to hunt for gold in Alaska.

The dreams about the common good were long since forgotten, but a romantic yearning still slumbered in the hearts of men. For visionaries and lunatics, Messrs Panhard and Levassor manufactured cumbersome machines full of enigmatic roars and mysterious shudders.

Horses reared, and journalists sneered: What a silly contraption! But then the automobile achieved some recognition: Impervious to danger, Émile Zola mounted a horseless carriage. The carriage trembled convulsively. But Monsieur Zola drove all the way to Versailles. The president of the Automobile Club rightly called Émile Zola "our most enlightened contemporary."

Zola had gray hair. But he was much younger than his era. Gasping with asthma, he tried to peer into the new century. His fellows of the pen were describing harems in Constantinople, love amid the antiquities of Florence, or the tears of an abandoned country-girl. Zola was busy with other things. He greedily listened to the roaring of the Stock Exchange, the sullen scraping of miners, the clanging of machines. For him, the drive from Paris to Versailles was not just a heroic picnic, it was a reconnoiter into the twentieth century, and smiling, he answered the president of the club:

"The future belongs to the automobile. I am convinced of it. At this point, it is difficult to measure the full significance of such an invention. Distances will shrink, and thus the automobile will be a new bearer of civilization and peace. In the end, it will doubtlessly heighten prosperity. . . ."

Philippe Lebon in 1798 dreamt about the general welfare. His engine was never built. Now, in 1898, Monsieur Émile Zola drove from Paris to Versailles. Émile Zola spoke about prosperity. Meanwhile, the automobile gnashed and stank.

Monsieur Hay was not Émile Zola. He was not a renowned writer and not a hero of the Dreyfusards. He was a mediocre lawyer. He lived in Poitiers, prim, boring Poitiers, with its relics of St. Radegunde and its sixteen poorhouses, Poitiers, where everything went to bed with the chickens, at the first hint of darkness, where an operetta was a scandal, and Monsieur Millerand the anti-Christ. However, Monsieur Hay had a progressive mind. He had been to Paris and seen the horseless carriage. Ever since, he had been haunted by a single dream—to buy one of those vehicles. The automobile whooshed along like a tempest. Now, Monsieur Hay had nowhere to whoosh to, and he knew he wouldn't get very far with an automobile. His friends jeered: "It's a toy, and, besides, it's dangerous!" But Monsieur Hay dreamt about an automobile the way schoolboys dream about the heroic death of Chief Hawkclaw.

An automobile carriage was expensive. Monsieur Hay had put something aside for a rainy day. He parted with his savings. Why wait? Rainy days come out of the blue. All the inmates of the sixteen poorhouses crossed themselves and hid in the pantries. The mayor issued an urgent decree. Monsieur Hay's friends were still trying to reason with the madman:

"Near Mehun, some cows attacked an automobile, and the owner was nearly killed. And not far from Triel, a bull pounced upon such a carriage, and the driver jumped into a ditch. Luckily they managed to pull him out. . . ."

Monsieur Hay only half-listened to these jeremaids. No one could stop him. One lovely April day, he and his wife took a drive in the country. The automobile zoomed full speed ahead: perhaps thirty kilometers an hour! The engine whined and strained itself to the utmost! It was brand-new, that motor, and new were the sparkling wheels. But the cruel joy in Monsieur Hay's heart was as old as the world: He was racing towards death.

At the first steep descent, the brake failed, and the bold couple landed under the wheels. Farmers eyed the corpses from a distance. They were scared of coming too close to that horrible machine.

No monument was put up for Monsieur Hay. He hadn't invented anything. All he did was buy a horseless carriage and take his wife for a drive in the country. Zola read a news story about the dreadful calamity. Unlike the journalists, Zola did not start cursing the automobile. No, the conclusion was obvious. They had to manufacture stronger brakes. Within thirty years, the blissful grandchildren would be amazed to hear about automobile catastrophes. . . . As for prosperity, it was sure to grow. Monsieur Émile Zola was a man of the new century, the twentieth, and thus, an optimist.

4

Barney Oldfield finished first in the automobile race. He used to be an ordinary cyclist, and he had learned how to drive a car just one week before the race. Luck helped him. Or perhaps not luck but the undeniable merits of the new 900 automobile constructed by a young engineer named Henry Ford. All the papers carried stories about this automobile. But it wasn't glory that Ford was after, it was dollars. He wasn't rich, and to make his dreams come true he had to acquire at least a small capital. Tomorrow, he would have the decisive meeting with the financiers. Henry Ford strolled along an avenue of beeches, rehearsing the dialogues. He began with that venomous tycoon, the one who didn't believe in anything—human morality, Mr. Ford's genius, or the ordinary motor.

"Aren't you barking up the wrong tree? . . . Doesn't the future belong to electricity? Maybe a convenient electric engine will conquer the automobile too. Why shouldn't we imagine reservoirs of electrical energy, at least on the main arteries of the country? After all, there will still be tiny distances, that is to say, first of all taxis. . . ."

Mister Ford scornfully moved the tip of his nose.

"The motor has to remain independent. Tiny distances are tiny matters. America is not an amusement park. America is a huge continent. Reservoirs of electrical energy are, if you'll forgive me, a mere fiction. Whereas the reservoirs of Standard Oil, with their fine gasoline, are a sure thing. We're not living in the 1890s, and we're not discussing a new invention. The internal-combustion engine has been recognized by all the experts. Let me cite the most outstanding man of our time, Thomas Edison. Who else, if not he, would be called upon to speak for electricity? And yet Thomas Edison has said to me: 'The demands of humanity are complex and manifold. The internal-combustion engine is light, independent, and at the same time powerful. It will indisputably find a place for itself.' "

The financiers listened attentively. There was satisfaction in their eyes, and a touch of disquiet: 100,000 dollars didn't grow on trees. Before handing over that much money, they had to weigh everything thoroughly.

Mister Ford went on:

"As you know, my *900* model finished the race first. Now we have to get down to business. The automobile can do more than just excite inquisitive minds. It can also bring dividends."

Mister Ford stood up. He spoke distinctly and solemnly like a Sunday preacher. He had a high forehead and a high calling. What was he prophesying? Perhaps, the fragrant groves of Canaan. . . .

"During the first year, we shall manufacture two thousand automobiles. The so-called Model A. Two cylinders. Eight horsepower. The construction of the machine will be as simple as possible so that the most inexperienced people can drive it, even women and adolescents. The price will likewise be reasonable: We are going to sell our cars for 850 dollars a piece. Within four years, we will produce 10,000 cars annually. Such self-confidence may seem staggering, but I foresee the possibility of turning out as many cars in one day as all American factories together now turn out in a whole year. It is a question of efficient organization. The automobile industry must inevitably move to first place.

"I myself like walking. More than anything in the world I like the chirping of birds and the smell of hay. But life is more complicated than my personal tastes, and I am counting not with myself, but with life.

"Allow me to read to you the draft of our appeal to the public: 'Five minutes of wasted time equals one dollar thrown out the window.' And this: 'Relax the mind and clean the lungs with the most reliable medicine—fresh air.' And finally: 'We have accommodated the automobile to the daily needs of the businessman as well as his family life. A sensible speed. A sensible construction. A sensible price.' "

"What allows you to set the price so low?"

"First of all—our farsightedness. We're not manufacturing ice cream, we're not afraid of rainy summers. We're restricting ourselves now. Tomorrow, our modesty will be repaid a hundred times over. We have to calculate many years ahead. It is wiser to sell cars at a loss or just barely at cost in order to conquer the market, rather than manufacture expensive automobiles that bring in a high profit each time but can never penetrate the great mass of buyers.

"Secondly: A proper organization of the entire process. Man is born of woman, that is to say, from another human being. Machines have to be produced by machines. As for the workers, they have to be transformed and accommodated to each type of machine. While working they will stop thinking. This is not a utopian fiction, it is the only sensible solution to the labor question. A man without mental functions is much more suitable for the production of machines than a highly qualified mechanic."

"But how do you intend to achieve that? Our workers aren't Negroes, after all. They're not as easy to deal with. . . ."

"I am starting out from the unshakable laws of life. As I have already said, I love the singing of birds, but I myself cannot sing: Unfortunately, I don't have the voice. The tenor Caruso, however, has an extraordinary voice, which, so far as I know, is worth hundreds of thousands of dollars. Equality is not only dangerous, it is unnatural. Workers cannot think while working, any more than I can sing. If, however, they do wish to show their originality, then their place is not in the factory. Some of them will become inventors, others beggars or criminals. We will comply with the workers. By simplifying all the processes, we will gradually free them from any strenuous effort, both physical and mental. The majority will be grateful to us; there are eccentrics everywhere, however. If you put me in front of a machine, I would go crazy in a week. Monotony goes against my grain. I am convinced that the creative principle is alive in you too. But there aren't very many of us, we are the brains of America. I am speaking, however, of the muscles of America. I am not by any means equating the workers with the Negroes of the South. On the contrary, I want to relieve them of the burden of drudgery. If they manage to adjust to exemplary machines, then their pay will go up, and the time will not be far when our very own workers will buy automobiles from us. . . ."

The financiers looked at one another. One of them even snorted. A sensible fellow, this Ford, but he was really getting carried away!

"I don't understand your surprise. I am not saying that the workers will sing like Caruso or govern the state. No, we can leave such ravings to the European socialists. But the workers *will* buy automobiles. It's just a question of price. I'm sure some of you can still remember the days when a bottle of kerosene cost a dollar. On my father's farm an oil lamp was considered a luxury.

"If you will permit me a slight digression, I would like to say that America is now starting on the road to true perfection. It is really God's own country. It has maintained a lucid mind and Christian virtues. I am not by any means an advocate of a caste society. I myself come from a simple though well-to-do family. However, democracy, as various visionaries comprehend it, is nonsense. Instead of genius: electoral arithmetic. Just look at the Old World. A doctor would diagnose the condition of some countries as paralysis. Neither arms nor legs obey the brain centers anymore. People of independent means keep their gold in stockings, transforming valuable thrift into avarice. This impedes the blood circulation. The workers go on strike day after day. The stock market runs after easy profit. Such a democracy cannot improve the roads, or build new universities, or put up museums. Culture is sinking. And there's no other possibility. On the lips of an idle dreamer, democracy is merely the sum of zeroes.

"An automobile race is true democracy. The best men win. If I achieve my goal, I will participate in ruling the country without having to bother with petty politics. I will build good technical schools. I will try to wipe out alcoholism and prostitution. I will devote myself to re-educating the working class, which is suffering from unrestraint and spiritual somnambulism because of the influx of immigrants. Finally, I will struggle for a simplicity of morals, for a hygienic way of life, a rapport between man and Mother Nature. As you can see, I have not betrayed my birds! . . .

"We are gathered around this table to found the Ford Automobile Company. Each man is entitled to dividends. I'm just a technician, a draftsman, a mechanic. I'm putting in one quarter of the fixed capital, the design for the Model A, and my labor. I hope you will not take it amiss that I wasted a few precious minutes of your time. After all, we're good Americans and good Christians. However, gentlemen, it is mankind who will receive the highest dividends. The automobile is the guarantee of universal prosperity!"

Mr. Ford's business partners blinked reverently, the way they blinked in church when the pastor spoke about the fragrant groves of Canaan. After all, they were all good Americans and good Christians. They understood the solemnity of the moment.

However, none of the business partners was present now. Henry Ford was striding all alone through the deserted lanes of the park, moving his lips very slightly. Birds were all around him. More than any other, he liked the black martins. Incidentally, the black martin flies at a speed of 180 miles an hour. Ah, but we'll outrace the black martin. . . . Ford smiled a tender and ghostly smile. Tomorrow, the agreement would be signed. Tomorrow, a new creature, loud, fast, and invincible, would roll into human life. Clear the way, everyone, clear the way!

Mister Henry Ford would get his way. The black martins, poetically chirping, soared off.

Chapter Two
The Conveyor Belt

1

Long ranks of workers. One group is tightening nuts, another is turning screws, a third is bolting fenders, a fourth is painting the rims of wheels, a fifth is stamping axles. A man lifts his hand and drops it again. He has exactly forty seconds for this small belt. The machine is in a hurry. There's no talking to it.

The worker doesn't know what an automobile is. He doesn't know what an engine is. He takes a bolt and tightens a nut. The wrench is waiting in the raised hand of the next worker. If he loses ten seconds, the machine keeps running. He'll be left with his bolt and a dock in pay. Ten seconds—that's quite a lot, and that's very little. In ten seconds, you can recall your entire life and not even catch your breath. He has to take a bolt and tighten a nut. Upwards to the right, half a turn, and then down. He does this hundreds, thousands of times. He does this eight hours in a row. He does it all his life. And that's all he ever does.

The chassis creep through the long workshop. Their path intersects that of the wheels. The wheels revolve in the air. The wheels hurry toward the chassis. A man takes a wheel and attaches it. One wheel. Another man—another wheel. His purpose in life is simple and solemn: he attaches the left rear wheel, always the left, always the rear.

He is used to bending his right knee. His left leg is immobile. He is used to tilting his head only to the right. He never looks left. He is no longer a human being. He is just a wheel—the left rear wheel. And the conveyor belt moves on.

The chassis are on the lower belt, the bodies on the upper belt. The body sinks into the hatch with an agonizing exactness. This is known as "marriage." But no human being could ever adjust to another one so exactly. The "marriage" takes exactly one and a half minutes. The man leans over: a nut, a tiny bolt. The conveyor belt moves.

It's not a silk sash. It's an iron belt. It's not even a belt. It's a chain. It's a miracle of technology, a victory of human intelligence, a growth of dividends. And it's an ordinary iron chain. It chains together a gang of 25,000 convicts here.

Pierre Chardain worked in the assembly division. He attached the rear springs. His hand held an iron shackle-plate. The chassis moved. Pierre Chardain had one minute and twelve seconds. He fastened the shackle-plate. He worked properly. After all, he had three children. His pay was four francs seventy-five centimes an hour. He wanted more. He wanted to buy a new bed. He even dreamt about a bright apartment: his windows faced a blind courtyard, and his youngest daughter, who was already four years old, still couldn't walk. He had a lot of dreams. He made an effort to fasten more rapidly, he wanted to gain ten or twenty seconds.

It now took only fifty-five seconds to attach a shackle-plate. That was certain. Now seventy chassis moved past Pierre every hour. He still received the same four francs seventy-five centimes. He didn't buy a bed. His daughter still hadn't learned how to walk. He would come home, dismal and mindless. He was always silent. He seemed to have forgotten how to talk. All he knew how to do was fasten a shackle-plate. In fifty-five seconds. He would die five years ahead of time. But now each automobile was six centimes cheaper.

Jean Lebaque worked in Suresnes. He made joints. He had an old mother and two children. Like Pierre he had a lot of dreams. He was paid four francs per hundred joints. He forgot about living. He went berserk. He was no longer Jean Lebaque who played dice and made fun of his buddies. No. He was an American machine. Instead of 120 joints, he produced 220. He would do something nice for his family! But no. A car has to be cheap. If Jean Lebaque produced joints faster, then the piecework pay would have to be changed. Instead of four francs, he now received two francs eighty per hundred pieces. He pushed himself to work even faster. Two hundred thirty. but no, he wasn't an American machine after all. He collapsed, exhausted. The doctor said he had the flu. He himself knew it was despair. No matter how hard he drudged, he wouldn't earn more than the established rate. There was nothing to hope for. He simply had to hurry, hurry for hurry's sake.

The workers rushed. The engineers rushed. Monsieur Citroën rushed.

In the spacious offices, the typists were clattering away. Lucie Neuville. Number 318. Faster! Putting in paper—44 seconds. A letter—three minutes nineteen seconds. Checking it—50 seconds. Putting the carbon in the box—4 seconds.

The chronometer man hurries from workbench to workbench. He has a stopwatch, a clipboard. He keeps count of the seconds. He looks at his wrist and at the dial. He takes notes. These aren't death sentences, these are just cheaper cars.

The engineers rush. They think up a new model. Greater speed. More comfort. Lower costs. The engine has to use as little gas as possible. A Ford does twenty miles on a gallon. Ah well, Americans have both gasoline and dollars. A Citroën has to be content with less—0.63 gallons for the same distance. The buyer is a snob, he demands six cylinders. The buyer is high-strung, he demands a noiseless engine. The buyer is thrifty, he doesn't want to pay very much. Everything has to be thought out: the oil filter and the shape of the jump-seats. There he was, the unknown buyer, standing at the display window of the store. He gazed at the different brands of cars. The engineer took the subway home. He didn't own a car. But the unknown buyer had already stopped at the window. The engineer was in a hurry. The new model had to be ready for the next auto show. In a few months, this model would be out of date. The engineers would then come up with a new one. They wouldn't leave this place alive. This was the belt, after all, moving and moving.

Monsieur André Citroën frowned. He had his share of worries. Peugeot was expanding production. Peugeot was turning out a model with a Cardan shaft. Old man Ford had reopened his factories. Ford, too, had engineers. They also sat and thought. New markets! More publicity!

Monsieur Citroën worked, just like Pierre Chardain. Did he still remember life?

Automobiles hovered before him. Fords, Fiats, Peugeots, Renaults. Millions. Hordes. And the earth was so small! So easy to encircle!

The Japanese didn't use cars. They used people. What barbarians! A man could do only five miles an hour. A Citroën could do fifty. Why be so slow! Another Japanese could outstrip you! But the Japanese were stubborn! Ford was well off. All his workers had their own cars. The Citroën workers dreamt about a bicycle. Why, if Citroën could raise production to three thousand a day, his workers might start dreaming about a car. What happiness—for them and for him! He had to increase production. But first, increase demand! Publicize air: If you don't take a drive to the country on Sundays, your life expectancy will be shortened by a third. Publicize life: You only live once.

Sinister wheezes from Fords and Peugeots, Renaults and Fiats. Their wheezes were constrained. They were noiseless, after all. They even had oil-filters. And the earth is so small! A revolution in Russia. The Chinese slaughtering one another. And the Africans—they simply climbed up trees.

Everyone knew that Monsieur André Citroën was a gambler. His passion was Baccarat. He held a four or a five. He had to buy more cards: Who could say, Ford might have a nine. The game went on and on. Sometimes Monsieur Citroën broke the bank, sometimes he lost. He lowered prices. He turned out new models. He risked everything. But speed was of the essence!

Pierre Chardain occasionally thought of Monsieur André Citroën. He thought that Citroën must be awfully happy, he not only had a bright apartment, he had a radiant life. If Pierre Chardain had only known that Monsieur André Citroën never even had a chance to catch his breath, that Monsieur André Citroën was shackled to him, Pierre Chardain, with an iron chain, the one that never stopped moving! . . .

The Citroën factories were marvelously equipped. They had not only imported machinery, but also central heating, powerful ventilators, and glass roofs. Monsieur André Citroën was an enlightened manufacturer. Was it his fault that people had thought up the automobile, that they were in a hurry to live, that there were such things as chemistry and poverty in the world, that buyers became more and more demanding every day? Monsieur Citroën was a servant of his times.

The Citroën works had twenty-five thousand employees. Once, they had spoken different languages. Now they kept silent. A close look revealed that these people came from different places. There were Parisians and Arabs, Russians and Bretons, Provençals and Chinese, Spaniards and Poles, Africans and Annamites. The Pole had once tilled the soil, the Italian had grazed sheep, and the Don Cossack had faithfully served the Tsar. Now they were all at the same conveyor belt. They never spoke to one another. They were gradually forgetting human words, words as warm and rough as sheepskin or clods of freshly plowed earth.

They listened to the voices of the machines. Each had its own racket. The giant drop-hammers boomed. The milling machines screamed. The boring-machines squealed. The presses banged. The grinding-lathes groaned. The pulleys sighed. And the iron chain hissed venomously.

The roar of the machines deafened the Provençals and the Chinese. Their eyes became glassy and vacant. They forgot everything in the world: the color of the sky and the name of their native village. They kept on tightening nuts. The automobile had to be noiseless. Engineers sat and thought. How could they build a mute engine? These valves here were still trying to talk. The valves had to be silenced. The buyer was so nervous! The men along the belt had no nerves. They only had hands: to tighten a nut, to fasten a wheel.

Citroën's ad men publicized the sea and the mountains, the banks of the Loire, Alpine passes, pine trees, ozone. Citroën's workshops were filled with the foul breath of machines. Noxious gases, the stench of hot oil, sharp acid fumes, alcohol, gasoline, paints, enamels. Metals were etched with acids—the workers had eczema. Metals were cleaned with sand—the workers would be ambushed by consumption. Metals were painted with automatic sprayguns—the workers were being poisoned by the vapors. In the foundries, the eyes of workers teared from the oil and sulphur. Little by little, they could no longer bear the sunlight. But there was no sun in the workshops. They continued carrying away the frames. Why have eyes, ears, or life? They had hands, they stood at the belt.

A newcomer asked Pierre Chardain:

"You coming to the meeting tonight?"

Pierre shook his head. No, he wasn't coming. The newcomer was still green. He still didn't know anything. He believed in books and discussions, in self-education groups, and in the world revolution. Pierre no longer believed in anything. When he was young, he had worked quietly and calmly. He had worked ten hours a day, but nobody pushed him. He had loved his tools and the iron. He relished the work. He mastered his trade. In those days, he read books and went to meetings. He believed in the victory of labor and in the brotherhood of man. But then it turned out that his mastery was useless: The milling-machine worked with an accuracy of one one-hundredth of a millimeter. Pierre no longer ran the machine, the machine ran him. Now he attached shackle-plates. He forgot about the brotherhood of man. He understood only one thing: Nothing could possibly change. The conveyor belt moved. Against that, all arguments were powerless. If he hollered, they would kick him out. They would hire someone else—an African or a boy. Anyone could attach those shackle-plates. . . . Pierre no longer went to meetings. He avoided his comrades. What good were other people? To keep silent with? . . .

His wife—she still had dreams:

"If we're lucky, we'll move to Vanves. . . .The air is clean there. . . ."

Pierre kept silent. Lucky? Shackle-plates would always be shackle-plates. If they gave him five sous more an hour, the price of butter would go up. Clean air in Vanves? Maybe. But from there it was an hour to the factory—and an hour back. And he was so tired. A weird kind of tiredness. He felt as if he could chop up a whole load of wood or run half a mile without stopping for breath. His body wasn't tired. It was his mind. Quick! The shackle-plate—before the car goes by! . . . He forgot the names and faces of his friends. He didn't understand what his wife asked him. He just waved her off sadly: Leave me alone! . . .

Sometimes his wife took him to the movies. He sat there, leaden and sleepy. In the darkness, he could barely keep his eyes open. It was hard to grasp why that banker was so friendly to that insolent guest. . . . Nearby, amid smoke and beams of quivering light, the reddish, stuffy air swarmed with the gloomy thoughts of the other viewers, men who carried axles or men who fastened bolts. Thoughts without legs, without fins, without wings. Writhing like earthworms sliced by a space. They weren't even thoughts, they were a mechanical chain of half-forgotten images, they were the dreams of a caveman, the garble of a deaf mute, and they were the delirium of a calculator: instead of wallpaper, instead of lips, instead of medicine, only rows of figures. It seemed like an ordinary audience, sitting in the theater. Each viewer had paid a franc or two admission. They watched a society melodrama permitted by the censors. This was art, the culture of the lower classes, this was Paris, the "light of the world." Thoughts writhed, legs went to sleep, eyes were dazzled by the mother-of-pearl screen. The projector whirred. The belt kept moving.

And all at once, a roar. It was the laughter of a hundred throats, loud, gross guffaws, like the noise of a valve, a laughter of "o"—ho-ho-ho! The theater roared. On the screen, the insolent guest had fallen while dancing. He had tumbled down and smashed his monocle. Look at him crash! Look at him sprawl! Look at his flailing leg! How he wiped his nose! Ho-ho! Ho-ho! For a minute, the caveman raised his paws and growled. His eyes glowed with a desperate merriment. Then the electric lights flashed on and the eyes dimmed out.

Monsieur André Citroën could relax. Pierre Chardain would be attaching shackle-plates until his dying day. He would never make a revolution. He wouldn't even try to brawl on a holiday. The machine had done its job: It had taken the man apart and then reassembled him. His hands moved faster, his eyelids blinked less often. On the outside he looked like an ordinary person. He had eyebrows and a vest. He went to the movies. But you couldn't talk to him. He was no longer human. He was merely a part of the belt: a bolt, a wheel, or a screw. Unlike others, he didn't live simply to eat, sleep with women, laugh. No. His life was imbued with profound meaning. He lived in order to produce çars: ten horsepower, noiseless engine, steel body.

Pierre was silent all the way home. His wife tried to talk:

"That was an interesting movie. I guessed right off that the dark-haired guy was a rat. Didn't you? . . ."

Pierre didn't answer. His wife had been working all day: she had done the wash, carried coal, scrubbed the floor. The small of her back ached. Her shoulders ached. She ached all over. But she hadn't stood at the belt. She could still talk about some dark-haired guy. Pierre, however, remained silent. He undressed in silence. He lay down in silence. He was thinking about something, hard, earnestly. The dark-haired guy? A car? Death? No, he was thinking about a stain on the wallpaper right near his pillow. That stain was just like a head with a pipe! How disgusting! And there was the smoke! . . . He thought about it for a long time. Then he said:

"Listen, we ought to hang something here. . . ."

His wife was still darning socks. Pierre gaped wide-eyed at the electric bulb. He gaped without blinking. The cold light streamed into him. He mulled for an instant: the head with the pipe, the dark-haired guy, the way he fell—funny, quick, put on the shackle-plate! . . . Pierre's hand rose out of habit, the right hand; the left lay there immobile. Pierre fell asleep. The hand on the blanket stirred convulsively. The breath shifted to its nighttime rate.

His wife looked at Pierre. How haggard and pale he'd become! That goddam factory! . . . His wife sighed softly, very softly—for Pierre was sleeping now. He was sleeping, but his fingers just barely winced. He must have been attacking shackle-plates: till morning, till night, till death.

2

Monsieur André Citroën, judging by the society pages, was the darling of the casinos. Without him, a game just wasn't a game. He had a fine talent: He knew how to lose. He lost with nonchalance and beauty. The green cloth was not crude profit; it was, more than anything, the poetry of sleepless nights, swallowed sighs, carefully concealed sweat, atrophy of the fingers, a duel with destiny, and the shadow of a smile quickly wiped away with a silk handkerchief, like beads of sweat on the temples.

Monsieur André Citroën was a gambler by nature. His factories were chips in his vest-pocket. He owed his success not to obstinacy, not cunning, and not genius—but to gambling. True, semiofficial biographers speak of a rack-wheel invented by André Citroën, a young engineer and a graduate of the Paris Polytechnique. But aren't intelligent engineers and even new rack-wheels a dime a dozen? . . .

In 1915, Citroën opened a factory in Paris. Naturally, he manufactured goods that were in season: projectiles. There was no lack of orders. Patriotism and profit went hand in hand. But the war ended. Monsieur Citroën had American machines and an uncertain future ahead of him. Some wagered on a new war, others on a long depression, still others on a revolution. Monsieur Citroën put his money on America. He realized that the old era was past, the era of poetry and landaus, meetings and decadence, horses and love. The stay-at-home, dreamer, dunderhead of yesterday will convulsively snatch at a clock tomorrow.

In its first year, the Citroën factory turned out 3,300 cars. All around there were strikes, riots, soaring prices; the workers were electing delegates to Parliament; Dadaists were screaming about doomsday; prudent patriots were transferring their accounts to London banks; all around, there was fear and hope. Citroën was gambling on good highways and a fierce struggle for survival.

He was figuring how to combine American know-how with European poverty. He had to make low-priced cars. These cars had to consume very little fuel. These low-priced cars had to look very smart. The European was poor, but vainglorious, he was so proud of his thousand years of culture! He would put up with a feeble engine, but not ugly proportions.

Two years later, the Citroën factory produced its thirty-thousandth automobile. That was no small number, but Monsieur Citroën only liked a high ante. A car wasn't a pearl necklace or a Stradivarius violin. The automobile was the new divinity. Everyone had to kneel and worship it. Ergo: The costs had to be lowered. Monsieur Citroën bet on a new card. He overhauled his workshops. He publicized his new model: five horsepower. Within everybody's reach. Happiness at half-price! Happiness on the installment plan! The factories turned out two hundred cars a day. Sales were going up. The streets of Paris became dangerous. Now, petty tradesmen and farmers dreamt about an automobile.

Iron was costly. Coal was costly. Paint was costly. But the debit column induced one item to which Monsieur Citroën paid particular attention. You can't lower the cost of materials, but you *can* lower the cost of labor. The year 1919 was past. The workers' committees were disbanded. The strikes had failed. Monsieur Citroën showed his workers a new toy from overseas: The belt, the moving conveyor belt. Let the workers groan, their grumbles would be drowned out by the noise of the new presses. Citroëns were cheaper than ever. Monsieur Citroën had broken the bank again.

But now the game no longer interested him: the stakes were too small. Five horsepower didn't bring in enough. The gambler threw caution to the winds. He dumped the 5-H.P. chips. Everyone was perplexed. Second-hand 5-H.P.'s were sold for a song; the factory stopped producing them. Monsieur Citroën gambled on the enrichment of some, on the rashness of others. You can't live without a car: This was a proven fact. Ergo: Customers would pounce upon the new model—10 H.P., B 12. He himself tightened his belt. His workers tightened their belts. Let all of France tighten its belt. People could drink fewer aperitifs; people could go to the movies less often; people could wear their overcoats three years instead of two.

The buyers didn't give in right away. A pause means bankruptcy for a businessman. For a good gambler it merely means beads of sweat on his temples and a silk handkerchief. He hastily wiped his brow. He broke this bank too. The new model was a lot more profitable. Dividends soared. The gamble was worth the palpitations.

"You buying?"

"I'm buying."

An eight. The player had bought and overbought. The others smiled discreetly. The cards crackled discreetly. The chips shone discreetly. And again:

"You buying?"

And again, discreet smiles. The ocean roared beyond the drawn blinds. The game could never end. Sometimes the player lost, sometimes he recouped, but he never left. He wanted to win. Finally, he did win. But he still didn't leave. He wanted to win more. Now he started losing again. It was like ebb and flood. The game was constant. The player didn't want to win. He only wanted to play. Weren't these ivory chips just like children's toys? No, he didn't even feel like playing. He was all worn out. The suits dazzled him. The nine shriveled into a meagre four. He wiped his brow. He was pale and sad. He didn't feel like playing anymore. However, it didn't matter whether he felt like it or not. All they asked him was:

"You buying?"

He had to play. It was no longer a game, it was a belt, an iron belt. His smile was more forced now. The excessively long cigar-butt was tossed more hurriedly into the ashtray. But the voice was smooth:

"I'm buying."

But then the dawn started seeping in. At that time, there was a change of shifts in the Citroën plants. The workers' faces were immobile and gray, as if they weren't flesh. The gambler's face was even more immobile, even grayer. It wasn't a face, it was a gambling chip.

"So you've lost four million. . . ."

The player understood nothing. His hand reached for the pack, but the pack was gone. The casino was closed. His hand chanced upon a branch completely wet from the customary pity of daybreak. Before the player lay the ocean. Its movements are lawful and fixed. First it beats against the rocks, then it dashes back. The player and the ocean remained alone. They contemplated one another with a slight distrust that gradually turned into indifference. Both were tired and both had to continue their work. Neither had time for complaining, and philosophy was a thing of the past. The tide started coming in. The player was thoughtful although he wasn't thinking of anything. He was brought to by the beeping of an automobile. Four million. . . . Just two more weeks. . . . Just twenty or thirty more years. . . . Obedient, the player stepped aside for the car. It was the latest Cit-

roën model, six cylinders, ten horsepower, B 14. The player smiled.
His smile was meaningless, like the dew on his cheek.

3

Citroën had five thousand sales representatives. They scoured
towns and villages. They had the energy of Mr. Hoover and keen
noses. They were as wise as the Biblical serpent. Shrewd, resourceful, and patient. Some were excellent orators: Gambettas, Henry
Roberts, Briands. Some could be called marvelous psychologists.
They divided humanity into several categories: those who buy a car
on the spot; those who buy in six months; and finally, those who buy
within a year. As for people who never buy a car—that was beyond
these salesmen's wildest imaginings. They believed in human happiness and progress. This farmer sold his peas at a good profit; he
could buy a car right away. Now, this young doctor was just getting
his first patients—six months from now he'd be ripe for a charming
little automobile. With the baker, however, they'd have to wait till
next spring.

Five thousand salesmen spread the new ten-horsepower happiness
and clouds of silver dust throughout happy France. They sent reports
to Paris. They eulogized the endurance and lightness of the automobile. They only asked for one thing: Cheaper! Cheaper! The baker
just couldn't afford it! And it was hard for the doctor. After all, he
only got ten francs a visit here. France wasn't America! . . .

Monsieur Citroën knew that France wasn't America. And in that
golden America, a car was twice as cheap. But what could he
do? . . . Costs were curving up as fast as ever. Lollipops and violets
were also getting more expensive. Monsieur Citroën was burdened
with a mission beyond his strength: He had to supply everyone with
a car. That wasn't an assignment. It was a vow.

For publicity, Monsieur Citroën sold toy cars. They were given to
children for Christmas. Wooden horses were long out of fashion.
Children were playing change of speed. But children also grow up.
They get tired of their favorite toys. Soon they would turn to one of
the five thousand. If they couldn't buy a car, they would become
misanthropes or—horror of horrors—Communists. Monsieur André
Citroën had to save young France from a ruinous disappointment.

Clerks posted white notes in the workshops: "Sacrifices are indispensable. The management has understood this. Now the workers must understand it as well. . . ." Monsieur Citroën was filled with self-sacrifice. Soap and thread could go up—they're time-honored veterans. They enter a person's life with his very first words, together with ripped pants and a warm sponge. They are universally recognized, like the sun or the police. Manufacturing soap or thread is certainly respectable, but it's so boring! Monsieur André Citroën was the apostle of the new covenant. He kept saying that the automobile was more important than resting. Five thousand salesmen gave converts so-and-so many tons of iron and so and so many grains of restlessness. He was willing to make any sacrifices for this. He was willing to wait a bit for income. Yes, he was willing. Now it was the workers' turn.

To sell cars, you need salesmen. To rule the world, you need poetry, chemistry, and selectiveness. You have to give shoulder-straps to a few warriors. You have to decorate a Socialist with the ribbon of the Legion of Honor, you have to make out a few tactful checks at the right time. Monsieur Citroën never got involved in politics. He didn't dream of a deputy's seat, he didn't subsidize the right-wing press, and he didn't organize a League for Civic Unity. He was beyond that. He was above that. He manufactured series of cars. For him as for the Almighty, they were neither Hellenes nor Judaeans. In his factories, sensible patriots worked cheek by jowl with dyed-in-the-wool Communists. Monsieur Citroën was concerned with only one thing: speed. For sales, he had created agents; for production, "demonstrators." A demonstrator might himself be demonstrated at fairs or university hospitals: "A highly interesting specimen! A live machine!" He doesn't supervise. Nor does he stand at the belt. He only demonstrates. He demonstrates how easily any man can forget he is human.

Joseph Lepont was an excellent demonstrator. He instructed the workers in the assembly department. How much time did that guy waste installing a hand-lever? Four minutes? Lepont tackled the job himself. Quickly he fitted the bolt and quickly he tightened the nut. One minute forty seconds. The manager decided: For an average worker, two minutes are enough. Next, the demonstrator went over to the belt. The demonstrator demonstrated. In one hour, he installed thirty levers. Then he went away—to demonstrate other things to other workers. The worker remained with the levers. What the demonstrator had done for one hour, he would have to do eight hours in a row, eight long years, perhaps for the rest of his life. The worker looked at Lepont's back and furiously whispered:

"Scum!"

Lepont was despised by everyone. Citroën was far away; he was practically a myth; he was something like the Good Lord or a cabinet of ministers. It was hard to hate the engineers. They were a special case. Did they know what it was like tightening nuts all day long? . . . Lepont, however, was one of them, a worker, he got only one franc more an hour than the others. He was the cause of all the trouble. The cause of the belt. The cause of the seconds. The cause of that goddamn stupor at night that kept you from laughing, from arguing, even from falling asleep.

Officers are given honors. Actors get their names on marquees. A good engineer keeps getting called in to the director's office. Joseph Lepont lived among the workers, and the workers despised him. He worked just like them, perhaps even more. He set new records. He staggered the engineers. He could stand in one place without moving for ten hours at a stretch. He could work all day without visiting the latrine. He could go without food or sleep. Instead of fingers, his hands seemed to have chisels, tongs, pliers, drills, braces; inside, an engine had replaced his heart. He couldn't remember his childhood. His human origins were attested to only by a birth certificate and a birthmark. He was as new and as godly as an automobile. But that was where the injustice began. Everyone dreamt about a car. Even workers, upon leaving the factory, glared enviously at the cars belonging to the chief engineers. Even workers worship the automobile. But when they ran into Lepont, they spat in disgust. Lepont, as it turned out, was still imperfect. He not only had an engine inside himself, but archaic feelings as well. He could feel hurt and make a face.

He had just come through the gates. He called over to Durand the handyman:

"Why don't we have a drink?"

His treat, of course. But Durand murmured:

"Another time. I'm in a hurry today . . . "

Durand loved rum, but he was afraid his comrades might see him with Lepont. And Lepont understood. He cursed under his breath. Sadly, he walked down the street. No need to hurry now. It was evening, he didn't have to demonstrate sleeping, everyone knew how to sleep. He looked into a mirror by a bakery. An ordinary face. A red moustache. Freckles. A cap. Ah well, he *was* a very ordinary person. But whenever he approached a worker, the man's pupils widened in horror, as though death were approaching. Lepont had noticed it more than once. So what! A cheerful job: playing death.

He entered a tavern. At the bar, there were workers he didn't know. He started a conversation. He stood a round of drinks. Deeply moved, he shook hands with everyone. He swallowed the rum, slowly, dreamily. He tried to say something pleasant to everyone:

"Looks like spring is here. . . . It's really warm. . . ."

He pointed at a girl passing by:

"What a hat!"

He complained:

"I'm tired. . . . Well, with all my work! . . ."

But then he heard one of the drinkers say:

"That's the demonstrator from the assembly department. Everyone knows what a pig he is!"

Lepont flung the money on the bar and left silently. He walked along the deserted quais. The water glittered hostilely. This was where people jumped in. But windows were lit. It was cozy up there—a gramophone and cards. The hell with all of them! They could all jump in the Seine. Could rum cheer him up? If he went to another tavern, they would drink with him and then curse him. If he found a girl, she might do the same thing: "You . . . demonstrator!" And then, he was so tired! He had to sleep. Tomorrow he would be demonstrating how to attach a shackle-plate in thirty seconds.

But he didn't turn right. He didn't head home. He didn't go anywhere. He stood on the bridge and gazed down. The water still glittered maliciously. Joseph Lepont was an ordinary person. He couldn't live. He was miserable.

A policeman noticed a person on the bridge. The policeman knew that no one catches fish down there and that there are no barges to unload. There was only cold water. The policeman had been stationed at the corner for four years. He knew very well why people there gaze so hard. With familiar steps, he strode over to Lepont.

Monsieur André Citroën read: "Our enterprise, as we foresaw, is developing to our full satisfaction. In fact, during the current year, our sales reached a total of 1,210,000,000 francs with a total production of 73,802 cars, as against 1,005,000,000 francs the previous year. . . ."

Monsieur André Citroën breathed heavily: because of the bad air and the figures. It was a hot June day. Outside, thousands of cars were howling, screeching, snorting, rattling. Their wheezing contained everything: the night of miners in Lovraine, the scorching heat of rubber plantations, the oppressive stench of oilfields somwhere, far away, in Venezuela, and the grinding of the nearby iron belt. The wheezing of the cars contained the agony of millions of people who lived and died for just this one purpose, to produce these cars. The wheezing contained the halting breath of Monsieur André Citroën and the consumptive, whistling breath of the grinder. The automobiles outside the windows strained to the utmost.

Catching his breath, Monsieur Citroën dispassionately continued: ". . . and as against 872,000,000. . . ."

4

The farmer had gotten his car long ago. The doctor bought a convertible before Easter. Yesterday, finally, the baker gave in. He signed the contract laid before him by the eloquent salesman. And he smiled enigmatically, just like Faust. Yet he was merely an ordinary baker from the little town of Montreil.

Monsieur Citroën was manfully carrying out his mission. Soon, the consumptive grinder would also own a car. Dying, the poor wretch would comprehend why he had lived in the first place.

But the longer the gambler played, the further his luck retreated. In France, there was one car per forty-two inhabitants; in America, there was one per five. The gambler took a new card. Once again the apostle went among the obstinate heathens. He had no miracle cures, no claps of thunder, no stigmata. But still, he was resourceful and stubborn. More than anyone else, he knew how to praise his new God.

Supposedly, Paris has the Chamber of Deputies and the Venus de Milo, the Egyptian obelisk and Paul Valéry, remarkable tailors and the wise Sorbonne. A foreigner arriving in the city at night, when both the Venus and the professors of the Sorbonne are fast asleep, will see only one word: It blazes in giant letters on the Eiffel Tower. Monsieur André Citroën's calling card. The great name shines. All around it, lightning crackles, and the tongues of a mystical flame dart from earth to heaven. Those are 200,000 electric bulbs and ninety kilometers of wiring. It is also a new revelation, the tablets of Mount Zion: Come to your senses! Join us! You must buy immediately—ten horsepower, a new model!

Monsieur Citroën explained: That wasn't advertising, that was a valid participation of the Citroën works in the International Exhibition of Decorative Arts. Advertising was all right for soap or cigarettes. But the owner of an automobile plant was a champion of culture. Thus, Monsieur Citroën had built a car with a caterpillar track. The impious claimed that these caterpillars were in preparation for the next war. They whispered about Polish orders. They forgot that, more than anything, Monsieur Citroën was an apostle. His caterpillars crept across the sands of the Sahara.

That was such a romantic safari. Upon seeing the Citroën cars, the lions and natives fell to their knees. Writers wrote remarkable books. Painters brought back exotic canvases from Africa. All the movie houses in the world presented *The Black Trek*. Monsieur Citroën even took this film along to the Chamber of Deputies. On the screen, lions and natives fell to their knees. On the screen, the sacred name flickered: Citroën, Citroën, Citroën.

Monsieur Citroën invited the simply delighted deputies to visit his plant. The honorable legislators, Radical Socialists and Social Radicals, viewed American presses, and even the remarkable belt. That was much more complicated than introducing a bill or having a second ballot. The deputies realized that Monsieur Citroën was really a grand citizen: He didn't give speeches, he silently manufactured cars. Incidentally, in honor of the so eloquent guests, Monsieur Citroën offered a small toast. He offered it, of course, during dessert, with the traditional glass in his hand:

"I dare say that he who is called upon to govern our country, who is called upon to maintain a harmonious equilibrium of all her vital forces, would not be uninterested in getting to know the efficient organization of an automobile factory. . . ."

One of the deputies, a Radical Socialist or a Social Radical, recalled the long ranks of workers and squinted in fear. Was that Citroën fellow proposing that the whole of life be transformed into a conveyor-belt system? For instance, he, the deputy, would speak on the rostrum, another would, at the same time, introduce amendments, a third would vote, a fourth would appeal to the nation, a fifth would stand at the buffet and drink lime tea, a sixth. . . . However, the sensitive deputy may have been squinting from the overly ample breakfast. . . .

Monsieur Citroën's toast was answered by Monsieur Le Trocqueur, a former minister of Public Labor and Monsieur Citroën's classmate at the *École Polytechnique*

"Ah, this is not a chain for enslaving man. Nay, it is the road to social perfection! . . . Permit me, dear friend, to wish you the very best. . . ."

Monsieur Le Trocqueur's speech, as well as his portrait, immediately appeared in the *Gazette Citroën*. Underneath were the words: "New prices! Eighteen monthly instalments!"

Was there anyone who didn't visit the Citroën factories? Students from Bucharest and the Organization of Automotive Machine-Gunners of the 5th Cavalry Division, Polish ice-skaters, the Press Club, sopranos, boxers, delegates of glee clubs, members of the diplomatic corps, and even Mardi Gras queens. Like the hostess of a society salon, Monsieur Citroën did not omit a single celebrity. Lindbergh landed in Paris. Lindbergh was the hero of Paris. Consequently, Lindbergh visited the Citroën plant. And Monsieur André Citroën's automobile called for the bashfully smiling aviator. He showed Lindbergh: the belt. He showed his workers: Lindbergh. The next day, the visit would be written up in all the papers. The Citroën brochure would state: "The Citroën Factory (boldfaced type) has become the symbol of French industry. The Atlantic hero Charles Lindbergh (likewise boldfaced type) has brought us greetings from American industry." In case people had not yet realized the true reason why the bold aviator had flown across the ocean, they now could guess: He had come to bring greetings to the Citroën plant! . . .

The Eiffel Tower is high. Above it, there is only heaven. Consequently, one ought to look to the sky. Soap salesmen write their names on lowly fences. Monsieur Citroën had to sign his name on the azure. He ordered airplanes. Modest associates of Lindbergh's had to sky-write Monsieur Citroën's name. Down below, the Parisians craned their necks and marveled. They had never read anything in the sky before, except starry hieroglyphs. But hieroglyphics is for Egyptologists or children. Monsieur Citroën signed his name in ordinary Latin letters. There was no escape from the pestering letters. They were down below and up above. They were ubiquitous. They buzzed. They glowed. They filled the countryside. They darkened the sun.

Monsieur Citroën quickly came back from the sky down to earth. The *Gazette Citroën* printed 15,000,000 copies. It ran encomiums to the automobile, conversations with the automobile, anecdotes about the automobile. It ran stories by deputies, poets, even opera singers. Of course, they all wrote about the same thing: the divine ten-horsepower phenomenon. Their mystical reflections were enframed in figures: "Torpedo—22,600."

Monsieur Citroën donated a magnificent car to the boy who got the highest marks on the baccalaureate examinations. Monsieur Citroën put up 150,000 signposts bearing his name on the roads of France. Monsieur Citroën sold 400,000 toy cars. Monsieur Citroën took part in all the auto shows: Morocco and Peru, Spain and Australia. Coste and Le Brie flew across the ocean. They arrived in Montevideo. What was the first thing they did? Why, they called upon the Citroën representative, of course. British legioneers came to Paris. Monsieur Citroën instantly sent them a whole squadron of automobiles. Citroën salesmen interviewed Monsieur Tardieu and Monsieur Decobra, Monsieur Sacha Guitry and Monsieur Pierre Mille. Every day, the papers were filled with sensational news: Citroën intends to light up Place de la Concorde. Citroën organizes a new expedition to Tibet. Citroën doubles production. Citroën. . . . Citroën. . . . Citroën. . . . Down below, there was Paris. Down below, there were deputies and writers; down below, there was the Louvre; down below, there was the tomb of Napoleon; down below, there was the blue dust of museums. Above all these things stood the Eiffel Tower. The Surrealist poets were in love with it, and they were about to award it a military medal. It was the proudest Parisian of all. It was taller than Notre Dame and more famous than Racine's *Phèdre*. Upon it, seven fateful letters blazed: C–I–T–R–O–Ë–N. Hurry, hurry, before it's too late! . . .

Monsieur Citroën loved to stagger people with figures. Numbers are always mysterious and charged with emotion. He dwelled on such facts as: Our factories occupy seventy hectares. Our machines have a total strength of 46,000 horsepower. By December 31, 1927, we had put a total of 319,074 cars on the market. We are now capable of producing a thousand cars a day.

Monsieur Citroën spoke about many things, many things, but not everything. His brochures, for instance, never mentioned that the net profits of the Citroën Works during the first six months of 1928 totalled 106,000,000 francs. The car-buyer wasn't interested. That was of interest only to stockholders. It was written about in the financial sections of respectable newspapers. However, there are figures that interest neither car-owners nor speculators, although they are just as mysterious and emotion-charged as data about hectares. One of the Citroën factories, the plant in Saint-Ouen, had registered 1,200 accidents within nine months.

Saint-Ouen had the punching workshops. They contained Monsieur

Citroën's pride and joy: Giant presses. Besides the presses, there were workers and a clock's second hand. Here is the report for a one-month period:

On September 7th, a worker had a finger torn off. On the 10th, a woman lost three fingers, a worker a hand, another woman three fingers. On the 11th, two fingers were torn off by the press, a hand was cut off by the bandsaw. On the 26th, one finger under the press. On October 5th, two fingers. The 6th was a big day: One worker, three fingers; another, four fingers; a third, his hand.

The figures in the brochures can be supplemented with others: In one of the Citroën factories, during a single month, thirty-three fingers were torn off. 1,200 cars, 18,000,000 net profit. 33 fingers.

There was no question that Monsieur Citroën took care of his employees. His workshops were a lot cleaner and brighter than other factories. But cars had to be low-priced. Monsieur Citroën had paid a lot of money for American machines. He would hire people one day and dismiss them the next: Bretons, Provençals, Arabs, Russians, women, adolescents. The giant presses banged away, and shreds of human flesh flew about everywhere.

A clock's second hand is a speedy hand. By nightfall, the worker understands very little. His head is filled with buzzing and blankness. He has lowered and lifted his hand eight hundred times with the accuracy of a press. This time, the hand wavered—and blood sullied the marvelous press. The hands were no longer obedient, they were confused, they trembled—and the saw brushed against one. It's very simple, and there's nothing you can say against it. Everybody needs a car. Thirty-three fingers—that's neither barbarous nor frivolous, it's merely low price-scales and a high mission that a self-willed destiny placed upon the shoulders of an ordinary human being named André Citroën.

5

In the old days, foreign and provincial tourists in Paris would hurry off to see the gargoyles of Notre Dame or the *Mona Lisa*. But today, the first thing they do is view the Citroën Works. Yesterday Mrs. Doran took her inquiring mind to the Louvre; tomorrow she's taking it to Versailles. But today? Today—Citroën. Even the Parisians go and see how cleverly that fine fellow Citroën manufactures his ten-horsepower wonders. Some of these visitors merely dream about owning one; respectfully they peer at any bolt. Others, on the contrary, examine the giant furnaces; they feel right at home; why, goodness, each of them has his very own Citroën, and each of them dashes off to the country on Sundays to breathe dust and gasoline.

There they go in Indian file: snobs in sports caps, solid citizens of independent means, with the ribbon of the Legion of Honor, plaster beauties, Englishwomen, old aunts from Auvergne, and ten or twelve anonymous derby-hats. In the foundry, where metal spurts as ruddy as the sun, where the workers, covered with oil and coaldust, bend over, straighten up, and bend over again, one of the derbies attentively says to his better half:

"Mother, do take off your boa, you'll catch a chill! . . ."

The hands of the visitors held a special Baedeker: "Plate no. 7. Particular attention should be paid to the four Sterling boilers. 32,000 pounds of steam the pair." The group is headed by a man wearing the Citroën emblem in his buttonhole. This man is the guide. He explains:

"Polishing of the metal with sand and compressed air by means of automatic sand-blasting. That is what produces the purity of the tone."

One of the owners of a Citroën smiles: Yes, yes, the purity of the tone! That Citroën is a sensible fellow, and he's also a true Frenchman. He realizes that a car has to be not just durable, but attractive as well.

"May I call your attention. . . . An interesting innovation. . . . Our chemical laboratory. . . . But please don't go too close! . . ."

The warning is superfluous: The old ladies have fled long since. Only the English lady with the inquiring mind snaps her lorgnette open. She has seen everything: fakirs, apaches, kangaroos. There's nothing she's afraid of.

In front of them, there's a man in a diving helmet. He has a rubber tube for air. He's surrounded by poisonous fumes. He works. He works like everyone here, at top speed, afraid to waste a second. But now he's being relieved. Ten minutes' rest. He takes off his helmet. He breathes hard. Ordinary air is a luxury for him. He's very pale. His face is wet. His palms are wet. He whistles slightly as he breathes. Then he coughs, gulps down some milk, and puts his helmet back on. The Englishwoman is gratified:

"How interesting! It's just like the Dog Caverns near Capri."

The happy car-owner is as thrilled as ever:

"Just think—the purity of the tone! . . ."

Around the dryland diver there is a deadly cloud. He doesn't think about Capri, or the purity of the tone, or his nearing death. He simply works.

"We still have so much to see. It's not worth hanging around here."

Arrows. Signs. A list of sights. The guide has a hard time outshouting the roar of the machines:

"The most powerful press in Europe, the Toledo. 1,400 tons. Run by two electric motors: one has 100 horsepower, the other. . . ."

The snob sighs:

"Here's the new aesthetics! The ideas of Corbusier-Sognier. . . . Can you seriously talk about a human being after that? . . . Just look at those teeth! The way they dig into the steel! It's more beautiful than any painting! . . ."

The gigantic stamper drops into the matrix. The visitors reverently ooh and aah.

"Did you hear? It weighs 150 tons! And what absolute accuracy!"

"That's a far cry from a worker's hand. It's accurate to the millimeter."

All at once, a commotion. The foreman yells. Workers come running. They leave their machines. A few minutes later, everything is back in order. But one of the workers is being hurried away. He staggers along with squinched eyes. He's lost his cap.

A derby asks:

"What happened?"

They're not allowed to talk to the workers. But the derby is so wrought up, he forgets all about sensible discipline. The worker is already running to his machine. On the way, he replies:

"Two fingers. . . . That's the press for you. . . ."

A young wife from the provinces is upset. She might even burst into tears. Her husband consoles her:

"It's still uncertain. . . . They can fix him up. Citroën has a really marvelous clinic."

The woman whispers:

"A good thing I didn't see the blood. . . ."

The Englishwoman, however, is unperturbed. She's seen everything: toreadors and sword-swallowers. She merely asks the guide:

"Which hand?"

The guide doesn't answer. The guide is thinking of some way to smooth it over. He mutters:

"It's not our fault! . . . We spend seven million a year on insurance. But they just refuse to realize they're dealing with machines!"

The tourists, however, aren't listening. They're already ecstatic about something else.

"They assemble an engine in twenty-five minutes. And just look how many parts there are! . . ."

The snob smiles:

"Yes, it's somewhat more complicated than a human being!"

But here's the last gate. The guide hands out printed matter. Don't forget, our easy installment plan! A deluxe convertible. An odometer. A clock. A speedometer. A fuel gauge. An oil-pressure gauge. Nitrocelluloid paint. Extra-thick carpeting. The windows can be lowered with one flick of the hand. And only 27,600 francs. 2,500 down. In view of the approaching holidays, you'll have to hurry.

One of the derbies smiles dreamily. He'll definitely buy. If not a convertible, then a Torpedo. He's already gotten a taste for it. He's seen everything. What accuracy and thoroughness! With a car like that, there's nothing to worry about. And the purity of the tone! . . .

The iron belt grinds along. The furances blast. The iron flows. A soft cloud surrounds the divers. The Toledo press works. The stamper drops down on the metal. 25,000 manpower and 46,000 horsepower fulfill their divine mission.

6

On the green cloth, the chips kept piling up and melting. Hours of flood, hours of ebb. How many workers were there at the Citroën plant? Recently there'd been 25,000; now there were 18,000; next, supposedly, there'd be 30,000. It all depends on the unknown customer.

Citroën paid a few sous more than other factories. All he had to do was hang out a sign—Workers Needed—and he'd be swamped. The busy season was over, Citroën was laying off. He never made cars for the future. After all, cars aren't stocks, they have to get cheaper.

Citroën hired anyone. Citroën demanded only one thing: Youth. Forty-seven? That wouldn't do. By forty-seven, a man's an old tire. He's got one foot in the grave, he can't live by the second hand. He feels like sitting down and calmly thinking: How did it all happen? . . . Monsieur André Citroën knew very well what age and fatigue are. He preferred the young. The Citroën factories were eternal youth, they were America, they were spring.

For eight years, André Vidal had been attaching rods to pistons. He knew the rods were manufactured in Clichy—his nephew worked there. But he didn't know what these rods were for, and he had never heard of a rectilinear retrograde motion. That was something the engineers knew. Vidal attached the rods. He got five francs fifty centimes an hour. Thousands of cars drove along roads throughout the world. The cars, all of them, naturally, had connecting rods, and these rods were attached by the hands of André Vidal. But after eight years there was a new foreman who didn't like Vidal. Was it his eyes? His voice? Or the way he coughed? Who knows? Human feelings are dark, even in the Citroën factories, where everything is precise and lucid.

Vidal was forty-four years old. When the work force was reduced, he was among those laid off. The rods were now attached by a young Italian. At first, Vidal cursed. He cursed everyone: the foreman, the Italian, and even Monsieur Citroën. Then he went home. He walked along, wondering what he would do now. He tried to work for a coalyard. But after a day they threw him out. He had worked at Citroën for eight years. He hadn't learned anything. He had merely forgotten how to carry sacks on his back. He had devoted his strength to some mysterious rods, and tens of thousands of cars raced at top speed.

Vidal knocked about Les Halles. He helped unload wagons and picked up frozen turnips. Then he went to the Champs Elysées. There he lingered by the beautiful automobiles. When the owners emerged from stores or cafés, Vidal held open the car door and doffed his hat. The car with the rods and pistons drove away. Sometimes Vidal would be handed a couple of sous. He would then soak bread in red wine and blissfully smack his lips. In the fall, he caught cold and subsequently died in the hospital. They buried him at municipal expense. He would rest in peace at the Ivry cemetery for five years. Then his bones, no pleasant sight, would be dug up, and someone else would be put in his place: a caster or a stamper.

Now it was spring, and even on Potter's Field the green sheath covering the earth was soft and lovely. Now it was spring—fresh-air prices were zooming up like stocks. Customers were pausing at display windows. They gazed at the cars. Citroën hung out a sacred sign. The entrance was mobbed: people dreaming about the kingdom of eternal youth. Vidal's place at the conveyor belt was vacant. Five years from now, his place in the Ivry cemetery would also be vacant.

7

The body was already mounted. The carpeting was laid and the ashtray inserted. The belt was still moving. A man lifted the nozzle of the gas pump. The response was a loud breathing. A car was born. It was the three-hundred-seventeenth car today. The gates opened. It rolled out into the spacious garage. Its new owner was already waiting. A minute from now, another car would roll out. That was definite and irrevocable.

The names of the customers were posted on a huge blackboard next to five-figure numbers: Monsieur Citroën understands the emotional effect of arithmetic. You're 68,917? Here's your car.

The meeting of a man with his new commander was as dry and laconic as can be. A checking of numbers. This one was a funeral-home representative. He was going to beat all his competitors and then get married. He would reach the deceased's house before anyone else. He would get married and be happy. This was a pair of newly-weds. They were setting up their life together. She was expecting; he had ordered a car. This one was a playboy, dreaming about suburban adventures: a pergola, a modiste, and gratis love among powdery lilacs. This one was the respectable owner of a drugstore. This one was an up-and-coming lawyer. All of them reverently gazed at the automobiles, which gleamed like an operating-room. Ahead of them lay kilometers, income, adventures; ahead of them lay a new life.

Every six minutes the gates swung open, and the next number on the board shivered dreamily. In the back, from where these shiny cars came rolling, there was the thunder of presses and the belt. The buyers sighed. They looked very calm, as though buying postcards or oranges. Only the flourish of the pen betrayed anxiety. Why, this was everything they'd been dreaming about for so long: ten-horsepower happiness on the installment plan! Their eyes squinted with yearning. Now they'd be touching the steering-wheel. They'd be losing themselves among tens of thousands of cars that were already dusty and weather-beaten.

They would never comprehend what they had really gotten. Proudly, they would show their friends the marvelous new thing they'd bought. They would forget these minutes, and if they happened to remember, they would smile: The trembling of a novice! . . . Tomorrow they would stop thinking altogether. But now, in this enormous shed filled with iron rumbling, they gloomily looked around. They were seeking refuge, as it were, with a living human being. But there were no people here. On the blackboard—a number. Behind the gates—the belt. They would have to resign themselves. The engines trembled, and this wasn't the place for simple human trembling.

8

Workers came from the country and died; appeasing oil oozed upon the marvelous presses; automobiles raced along the highways of Europe, those ancient roads of crusaders and charlatans. Monsieur André Citroën was just a tiny rod or piston. His name blazed on the Eiffel Tower and could be found in millions of minds. But he wasn't rich like Ford, or famous like Lindbergh, he wasn't all-mighty like the directors of the banking firm of Lazard Frères. He was devoting his life to a lofty ideal: he would give Europe speed, just as Buddha had given Asia peace of mind. But no monument will ever be raised to him in the squares of Paris. No one will ever compose heartfelt poetry about him. He will have to be content with the sales statistics.

Monsieur Citroën was a living human being. He had a moustache and passions. American presses shredded workers. The ten-horsepower automobiles ran down powerless pedestrians. A car is incompatible with moustaches and feelings.

On a scorching August day, when the heat was melting the bodies of casters, when the cars of tourists, bunching together like sheep, crushed one another, bleated desperately, and went berserk; on that agonizing day, the capital of the Citroën Company suddenly shot up from 100 million to 300 million. The Citroën shares were quoted at the directors of the banking firm of Lazard Frères. He was devoting blackboards, a prayer of gamblers, a noontime howl of the gang of brokers pouring into the streets of Paris, merging with the sirens of Citroën automobiles. On that day, Monsieur André Citroën, the autocrat of Clichy, Saint-Ouen, Javel, Guttenberg, Suresnes, Grenelles, and Levallois, disappeared. It wasn't an inadvertency of the Toledo press, it wasn't an automobile catastrophe. It was a complicated financial operation. Monsieur André Citroën was taken apart and put together again. He became Chairman of the Board of Directors. The stock-market gazettes tempted clients with "a widening of the financial base," and "beneficial control by one of the most powerful banks."

The man elected to be Vice-Chairman of the Board of Directors was Monsieur Philippe, the representative of the banking firm of Lazard Frères. Naturally Monsieur Philippe was only Vice-Chairman. But in back of Monsieur Philippe there was a tiny plate: Lazard Frères & Co. Lazard Frères was huge and ubiquitous. Was there anyone in the City who didn't know the "Lazard Brothers"? The Lazard bank is connected with the Bank of Indo-China, which is headed by Monsieur Octave Homberg, the rubber king. It is connected with the Royal Dutch, which is familiar with various smells: the smell of oil and the smell of the canaster in Sir Henry Deterding's pipe. For Pierre Chardain, Monsieur André Citroën is the Lord God. For the banking house of Lazard Frères, he merely runs one of their countless enterprises.

Monsieur Citroën expanded his business, but he had to restrict himself. He got to know that sublime self-limitation which Goethe prescribes for the true creator. He was now Chairman of the Board of Directors.

A 10-H.P. automobile lasts 60,000 miles. A worker lasts forty years. Monsieur André Citroën was unappeasable. The French market was almost sated. Monsieur Citroën shoved aside the map of France, *la belle France*, with 5,000 salesmen and 150,000 signposts. He picked up the map of Europe. It was all entwined with customs tariffs and diplomatic cobwebs. Naturally, he was an advocate of Pan-Europeanism. Oh, how he hated those vulgar borders! The motley colors of the map were an eyesore. He exclaimed:

"The American market has 100,000,000 buyers. Here in Europe there's a Chinese wall every two or three hundred kilometers. The national industry is endangered. It could choke to death. . . ."

The national industry is primarily he himself. And Monsieur Citroën breathed heavily. He loved fresh air and large markets. But conquering Europe wasn't in his power. He had to resort to military ruses, espionage, camouflage, slyness. He built assembly plants in London and Cologne, in Milan and Brussels. Warily, he made his way into Holland and Portugal, Spain and Denmark. He gained a firm foothold in the French colonies. He negotiated with the Polish government about building a huge factory. He organized a new expedition of his "caterpillars." This time he dreamt about the Middle East. He was certainly no enemy of the Soviet Union. He even began preaching. He gave lectures. He addressed congresses. He always spoke about the same thing: "We need new markets! . . ." He rushed about the departments of his beloved France, where salesmen and signposts dogged his every step. He rushed around like beasts of prey in the zoos of Leipzig or Rome, without cages, with an illusion of freedom: Jump if you like, but between you and the world there's a ditch that's very wide and very deep. Between you and the world—lies death.

The ministers of all European states, whether Fascist or Socialist, spoke with American bankers the way the princes of Suzdal had spoken with the Golden Horde. During these talks, they never remembered the thousand years of culture: Raphael or the Palace of Versailles or Faust. After all, they knew perfectly well that Harold Lloyd movies brought in more money than Faust, that the Palace of Versailles had absolutely no modern comforts, and that Mr. Morgan could buy up all the Raphaels in the world for a pittance.

Monsieur André Citroën was highly reverent of sacred things. In particularly solemn moments, he probably looked toward the West, although there were no markets there, although there was only water there, and beyond the water, Ford. He gazed toward the West, the way pious Jews gaze toward the East when praying. Monsieur Citroën's Zion, however, was Detroit, where there was one car for every two and one-third people.

In Detroit sat old man Ford. Monsieur Citroën's devout gazes could not reach him. Ford too was looking at a map. This map was much bigger than the one that unsettled Monsieur Citroën. Ford's map included both hemispheres. After all, Ford was also hunting for new markets, and for him Europe was what Portugal was for Monsieur Citroën. He had to conquer it. He measured the sales capacity of new colonies: England, 200,000 cars; Germany, 100,000; Russia, 100,000.

Monsieur André Citroën lowered his prices. The belt moved faster and faster. Jean Lebaque, the worker who produced joints, would soon die or go mad. Monsieur Citroën tried to laugh it off: You see, he was rationalizing production, hence, Citroënizing. A complicated verb! The action is even more complicated. He did what he could. But Ford was always ahead, his cars cost half as much. In France, Monsieur Citroën was protected by the same Chinese wall that he was constantly cursing. But how could he compete with Ford in Holland or Switzerland?

America now replied to Columbus's caravels with thousand-tonned steamers. Their holds were full of cars. Ford was even trying to penetrate Monsieur Citroën's sacred *départements* with their 5,000 salesmen and 150,000 signposts. Ford had already dropped the French price to 25,700 francs. Exactly the same price as a Citroën. But Ford's mind was still not at ease. He wanted to smash through the Great Wall of China. He built factories in France. He issued new stocks. These stocks were distributed by the Oustric Bank, the one that financed the Peugeot factories, just as the Lazard Bank financed the Citroën factories.

Monsieur André Citroën was surrounded by enemies. Peugeot had probably made an agreement with Ford! Peugeot manufactured either small five-H.P. cars or expensive, high-powered limousines. He never produced anything in between. He wasn't dismayed by Ford's campaign. Ford wasn't after him. Ford was after Citroën.

But Ford wasn't the whole of America. Even almighty Ford had enemies. They were right there in Detroit. The General Motors automobile trust, like Ford, wanted to cross the ocean. It took a different route, however. It had no intention of building factories in Europe. It didn't send engineers to the Old World, it sent diplomats and businessmen. It cleared the way with dollars: General Motors was headed by Mr. Pierpont Morgan. The trust had already come to terms with the German Opel works. The trust wanted to wipe out Ford. France was an excellent market, and General Motors lowered its Chevrolet prices in France.

Monsieur Citroën observed. Monsieur Citroën deliberated. He had already found out what kind of a bank that was Lazard Frères. New trials lay ahead of him. He could console himself with one thing: he wasn't alone. Mr. Morgan knew the price of everything: constitutions, independence, pride, chemistry, the League of Nations, and the thousand years of culture. Mr. Morgan could not only change ministers, he could redraw the map of Europe. The agreement between General Motors and the Citroën Company was, for him, a detail in a workday, a line in a memo-pad on his desk. For Monsieur André Citroën, it was a dreadful ordeal. It turned out that American presses can do more than crush the fingers of workers: they can stamp both iron and human life. From New York, you can't see the blazing letters on the Eiffel Tower: New York has so many towers and blazing lights of its own.

When Jean Lebaque's salary was reduced by one franc twenty centimes per hundred joints, he sighed, cursed, but he kept on working. He knew the belt wouldn't stop. Monsieur Citroën kept manufacturing automobiles. He was unable by now to think or rest. He devoted everything to giving people low-priced happiness. He didn't even hold on to his name. He had turned it into a common trademark. Now it belonged not just to him, but to all the company stockholders. He himself let the belt go on. He was shackled to it. Tomorrow the Ford factory would go up. Tomorrow he would have to lower prices again. The belt would spin even faster. This would mean so many more deaths. This would mean mutilation, despair, insanity for thirty thousand people. This would mean dismal sweat for Monsieur Citroën. He was no longer a gambler. He was merely a card. And at the green cloth, there were transatlantic players: Mr. Morgan and Mr. Ford.

Monsieur André Citroën worked. To Persia! To Bulgaria! To the Sahara! To the Pole! New salesmen! New signposts! This wasn't gambling. This was destiny. Faster! . . . After all, cars have to be cheaper.

Chapter Three
Tires

1

The Brazilian forests have many trees. Their names are known only to botanists. One of these trees, for instance, is called the hevea. It is a high, branchy tree with a light-gray, dappled bark. An ordinary tree. It might well have remained in the Brazilian forest among the other trees. For in Brazil, the people live like the forest—slow, wise, and obtuse. However, up north, in New York, the people are in a hurry to live. Perhaps they're afraid they'll die too late. In Paris, London, and Berlin, the people hurry everywhere. There are no branchy trees in these places. But there are lots of automobiles. Every day, there are more and more.

The modest tree with the dappled bark left the jungle. They all fell in love with it at once, the English, the Dutch, the French. Every shrewd Yankee dreams about it. It is raised in huge plantations. Its fate is the anxious concern of every bank in the world. It is discussed in diplomatic notes. Counting airplanes or estimating the fighting capacity of a new dreadnaught, ministers all think about this dappled tree. However, they don't know that this tree is dappled. They've never seen it. They're in a hurry to live and they need automobiles.

In Java and Ceylon, in Malaya and Indo-China, on quiet evenings, amid fever and suffering, among cents and piasters, among iron tears and iron dollars—the harmonious groves softly rustle. They rustle tenderly and meaningfully like Rubber Association stocks. They bring dividends to white folks and death to yellow folks. They rustle because underneath there is greed and poverty. They rustle in the evening because every morning naked coolies with hooked knives notch the tender, gray bark and open old wounds. The coolies and the trees understand one another. They bleed in the same way. But the coolie's blood doesn't cost anything and no one talks about it. On the other hand, the milk-white blood of the branchy tree is extremely valuable. It is quoted at all stock exchanges. It drives people out of their minds. For its sake, they are ready to shed tons of human blood. The trees know about this and they rustle in pity. The wounds in their bark will never heal.

Mr. Davis had a 2,500-acre plantation. Mr. Davis had 350,000 trees. Mr. Davis had 1,000 coolies. One coolie per 350 trees. The milky blood flowed into pails. Every tree gave over half a gallon a year. Mr. Davis collected almost 200,000 gallons of rubber a year. He had a beautiful villa. He had three limousines. He had a tennis court. He had a pet python and a thick book on how to mix cocktails. The python caught rats, like an ordinary kitten, and in his free time Mr. Davis prepared new and mysterious cocktails: South Pole or Queen Alexandra. Mr. Davis was bored. He had jungle fever. He had no one to play tennis with.

He had already been in Penang for fourteen years. When he had left London, no one there drank cocktails yet. He was young then and full of dreams. He looked at the sea and it struck him that Annie's eyes were astonishingly similar to the water of the Indian Ocean. Annie had also been young then. Once he had kissed her light-brown curls. Now Annie had cut her hair, her gray hair. Besides, he had forgotten what Annie looked like. Twice a year she wrote him long letters. She wrote about plays by George Bernard Shaw and concerts by Stravinsky. She wrote about stormy London and her wretched life. She asked Mr. Davis whether he was planning to return to England. Upon receiving a letter, Mr. Davis would stride through the long corridors of his house for a long time. He replied:

My dear friend,
You wouldn't recognize me. I've gone to seed, grown coarse. There's no decent society here. I've even stopped reading newspapers. I look

50

into the *Times* to check the rubber prices and throw it aside. What good are theaters or concerts to me now? I am an animal like my coolies. Sometimes a few of us planters get together, but we can't even start up a round of poker. It's too complicated. Jameson shows us his tricks again, Richard bores us to death with the same old jokes, and I myself, for the sake of diversion, mix cocktails. Then the conversation turns to the usual single topic:

"How do you cut? I cut in spirals, and every other day."

"That's not the right way! I cut in angles from above, and every day."

"You'll see, your trees won't last! . . ."

"Well, you started when you were six, you're a native."

And so on. There's a fight. Then they make up again. Dear, good Annie, would you recognize your Peter in the clumsy plantation owner? No! I give you my word! You wouldn't! And the years wear on. . . . Fourteen years. Can you imagine! I ought to go to London for at least a year. But what would become of the plantings? All my helpers are shiftless and ignorant. Trees are such delicate things. You have to treat them with kid gloves. I was once laid low with fever for two weeks—and two whole acres were ruined. I wouldn't dare dream of staying away for a long time. Just recently, I planted 750 new acres. The rooting-out and the plowing were so difficult! About fifty men died on me. Now I have to keep my eyes open. My little children will grow up in seven or eight years. That means that by 1933, my brain will be completely numb. 10,000 new trees! No, Annie, it's obvious I'll be buried here! My friends will have a drink and start arguing about whether I cut right or not. You're the only person who'll sigh for me. . . ."

Having written the letter, Mr. Davis didn't mix any new cocktails. He gulped down a huge glass of whiskey and, hoarse with sadness, he yelled for the dark-skinned Malayan girl, the twelve-year-old, who was as timid as a leaf of the hevea: "C'mere!" He called her Annie and he beat her, tenderly and maliciously. Then he went to bed with her. Then he fell asleep. In his dreams, he saw trees bleeding and bleeding white blood.

Mr. Davis wasn't the least bit greedy. He had bought a piano; but no one played it. He had bought pearls and sent them to Annie. Annie hid the pearls under the linen in her bureau, right next to the braids she had once cut off: Annie had a husband now. Mr. Davis didn't need money. But he eagerly followed the prices of rubber. He shouted:

"Not a cent less!"

He paid the coolies forty cents a day. A single cocktail was a lot costlier. He shouted:

"Not a cent more!"

He ate without gusto—it was hot, so hot! And he didn't care for any of the girls, Malayan, Indian, Chinese. They smelled of rotten bananas, dankness, fern. A decent woman should have the fragrance of linen and glycerine soap: that was Annie's fragrance. He swallowed bitter quinine. He would die in Penang. He was held here by the branchy trees, which poured out dollars. He beat the boy with a switch and tenderly stroked the light-gray bark. He kept buying more and more land. He rented more and more coolies. He was afraid to look in a mirror: The lord of thousands of acres was knowingly dead. He was as dead as his coolies. He was as dead as the trees that were thoroughly notched. But in Liverpool, rubber brought four shillings five pence, and people throughout the world were in a hurry to live. The dead Mr. Davis mixed cocktails. The python, which had overgorged itself on rats, fell asleep, asleep for many days, asleep for all time.

Coolies come from India and China. They are even brought from the Sunda Islands. Hundreds of thousands of coolies bend under the branchy trees. In Malay, Mr. Davis beat them. In Java, Minheer Van Croog. In Indo-China, Monsieur Gaston Balthasar, born in Carcasson, the son of a perfumer, and an admirer of Rostand.

The white curse in various langauges, but all of them hold a stick. What can you do! The coolies are shiftless and stupid, they prefer opium and sleep to dollars. The whites protect Culture, the Culture of Hellas and Rome. They also protect the rubber. The backs of the coolies are shredded like the bark of the hevea. If they die, new ones are brought to replace them. The agents recruit, the police recruit, hunger recruits.

When the branchy tree is seven years old, they start notching it. When a little Indian is seven years old, he is taken to the plantings. He earns ten cents a day. For this, he can buy a few small handfuls of rice—how much does a little Indian need, after all? He already has weak legs and he falls behind the others. He feels like catching a lizard or turning over a bug. Then the overseer, the strict *kangani*, draws a red stripe across the dark-skinned back.

Mr. Davis was told:

"A man ran away. The man was caught."

A coolie doesn't dare leave his work. In his office, Mr. Davis had papers and stamps; these were contracts. He had paid for the coolie's passage. He was their master for five years. A deserter lay before him. He said to the overseer:

"Ask him what he wants: prison or a lesson?"

Mr. Davis didn't know the Tamil language. The *kangani* interpreted.

"He begs bossman, no send him to police."

The deserter lay on the ground. He was stuck to the ground. Only his eyes, huge and moist like all the night of India, gaped at Mr. Davis's hooked fingers.

"He begs bossman, give lesson himself."

The hevea has to be notched carefully so the trunk won't be injured. Some notch it in spirals, some in a zigzag. But no one makes such a fuss about a coolie's back. Mr. Davis counted:

"Sixteen, seventeen, eighteen. . . ."

The coolie was as quiet as the earth. Where did he want to run? To his homeland, his starving family? Or merely into the jungle, to die? He wanted to get away from the branchy trees. The madman! Not even the almighty Mr. Davis can get away from them.

"Twenty-four, twenty-five. . . ."

The coolie would never run away again.

The managing offices of the rubber companies are located in Singapore. Specialists had drawn up a table: The minimum salary for plantation employees—200 Singapore dollars. That was enough to provide a single man with a modest living. Company employees, upon signing the contract, agreed not to marry for a specific number of years. Malayan or Chinese girls were cheap.

The newcomer cursed the Asian sky and the company's greed. He was a lanky, towheaded young man. He had no money and no luck. But he did have white skin. He received 200 dollars a month. The coolies worked from five in the morning. First they notched trees, then they collected sap. A coolie earned ten dollars a month. He could marry on that. He could have a dozen children. That was his own business, native business. The Europeans had brought him happiness: a contract with an X instead of a signature, ten dollars a month, and a kindhearted sermon with an ordinary stick.

The newcomer cursed rubber and the high cost of living. Just try getting along on 200 dollars! He was in a foul mood today.

"Who cut this tree? . . . *Kangani,* who's working here? Dock him ten cents! What a goddam country!

The newcomer remembered the lights of Piccadilly. Why had he come here? He'd been taken in. Gooey leaves. Gooey sap. Gooey gold. He wouldn't get away from here any more than the coolie. He would merely replace Mr. Davis when Mr. Davis really died.

In Indo-China, branchy trees and the backs of coolies also ooze. France, as we know, is not as heartless as England. France has for so long been the protectress of the oppressed, and when France was overrun by enemies, she brought the little Annamites to Marseilles to protect the protectress of the oppressed.

In France, in the city of Clermont-Ferrand, Monsieur Michelin had a magnificent factory. There he turned the milky blood into durable tires. Monsieur Michelin loved F. W. Taylor and rationalization. He loved America. Even more, he loved Indo-China.

Monsieur Michelin wasn't alone. Monsieur Octave Homberg also loved Indo-China. Monsieur Homberg was a writer. He had written several books about the colonial grandeur of France. Furthermore, he was head of the Rubber Company of Indo-China. He made money in the colonies. He wanted to spend it in France. He wasn't Mr. Davis with his python. He was a Frenchman and an ardent patriot. He was a bulwark of eighteen companies in Saigon: rubber, sugar, cotton, phosphate. But he dreamt about becoming a deputy from the Riviera, where the main industry was the green cloth of roulette. Let the coolies gather the precious sap! What could compare with the sky of France? Such were Monsieur Homberg's thoughts. Such were the thoughts of the stockholders of the Rubber Company of Indo-China.

And the coolies? Coolies don't think. Coolies die like saints— without an onerous thought. They die silently and agreeably. On the plantations of Phu-Rieg, which belonged to Monsieur Michelin & Co., one-third of the laborers died every year. On the plantations of Bodoy, 536 coolies out of 1,000 were left by the end of the year. The rest had died.

If a coolie didn't know how to die simply, the magnanimous colonialists came to his aid. There was something for the relief of the natives: *Régie d'opium* and *Régie d'alcoöl,* R.O. and R.A., the government monopolies on alcohol and opium. The Governor-General of Indo-China had recently dispatched a circular to his subordinates: "Allow me to send you a list of government stores which are to be opened in settlements still without alcohol and opium."

That governor was known in France as a fine connoisseur of the arts. He had a marvelous collection of modern paintings. Perhaps his library included a first edition of the *Paradis Artificiels*. Yet the governor wasn't just an aesthete, he was also a statesman. He knew, for instance, what a budget was. The coolie would spend his last piaster on opium. To the delight of Monsieur Michelin and Monsieur Homberg, steamers raced to France, freighted with white layers of rubber. The coolies had labored hard. They had labored hard and unselfishly. The money they received had long since gone to the directors of the R.O. and the R.A.

That's why coolies die with a smile. As they die, they have dreams as thrilling as the landscapes of Henri Rousseau, dreams that can bring tears to the eyes of Monsieur le Gouverneur-général.

2

Singapore was in an uproar. Liverpool was in an uproar. Mr. Davis forgot all about his cocktails. The coolies no longer ran away—the *kanganis* drove them away. They weren't needed anymore. They could die wherever they liked. The wounds on the heveas were closing up, were healing. In another month or two, the heveas would be the most ordinary trees again. But what would Mr. Davis do? He certainly wouldn't go back to that sentimental Annie! Besides, she had a jealous husband. . . .

The owners of rubber stocks besieged the banks. In London, on narrow Minching Lane, the rubber brokers were standing and moaning, just like Jews at the Wailing Wall in Jerusalem. The cabinet was holding secret meetings. The coolies were dying. The plantation owners were abandoning everything and hurrying back to Europe. It was a catastrophe!

What had happened? Could the Indians or Malayans have rebelled? Could this be an intrigue of Mr. Krassin's? No, the coolies were obediently dying under the branchy trees. Those who didn't die carried buckets of milky sap. But in Liverpool rubber was only nine pence. It was ruin. It was the end of rubber! Mr. Davis had miscalculated. He had planted far too many trees. Rubber was plunging. No one needed rubber even though Henry Ford was working tirelessly, even though millions of cars were snorting, growling, dashing, agonizing.

Mr. Churchill said to Sir John Stevenson:

"You must save rubber. . . . The power of the Empire depends on it. . . ."

Sir John Stevenson got down to work. His plan was soon ready:

"In order to save the plantations, we must artificially curtail the output. The further prices drop, the less rubber we shall put on the market. The price will then inevitably rise and restrictions will correspondingly slacken."

One of the M.P.'s sighed in distress:

"But that's Bolshevism! That's government interference with private commerce. That's a flouting of our principles. . . ."

"The Honorable Member of Parliament will have to choose between purity of principles and saving the plantations. The might of the Empire depends on it now. . . ."

The Honorable Member of Parliament, sighing for form's sake, did not vote for principles. The Stevenson Plan was approved. The production of rubber now became elastic, like rubber: it could both contract and expand. Subject to these movements, the coolies would die either *on* the plantations or *outside* the plantations. They would die because men are mortal.

Mr. Churchill congratulated Sir John Stevenson:

"Your name will go down in history. . . ."

And then, after a quick pause:

"—Rubber history. . . .

Mr. Churchill had a great sense of humor.

The rubber plantations belonged to Englishmen. But cars were made in America, and the Americans bought rubber from the English. There was a new law for Singapore: Divine wisdom. For Detroit, this law was foolish and unethical. It ought to be destroyed along with Darwin's theories and Soviet leaflets. Sir John Stevenson was a hypocrite and a criminal. He was quite worthy of Sir Henry Deterding.

Mr. Hoover angrily chewed a cigar. The cigar had gone out long ago, and Mr. Hoover was chewing wet, bitter tobacco.

"Government interference is, more than anything, immoral. That's why we're against monopolies. They want to paralyze our industry, but they won't succeed! . . ."

Mr. Hoover was no windbag. He knew what rubber was. Along with the cigar-butt, he spit out a torrent of names and numbers. He consulted with diplomats and botanists. He prepared for a long war.

And rubber? . . . Rubber went up. Mr. Davis started mixing cocktails again. Brokers on Minching Lane livened up; instead of groaning, they were brightly chirping:

"One shilling four pence!"

"One shilling six!"

The United States is a huge land of many facets. It contains cedars and bananas, Negroes and the Ku-Klux-Klan, oil and bison, Mr. Hoover and Charlie Chaplin. But the branchy tree simply cannot grow in these United States. The botanists reported:

"No member of this species of tree is capable of thriving outside the Equatorial Zone, i.e., the zone extending ten degrees north and south of the Equator. . . ."

Mr. Hoover sent away the botanists. He summoned admirals:

"We have to talk about Nicaragua. Also about the Philippine Islands. . . ."

They talked. But meanwhile rubber went up. At first, the buyers put on a brave front. They didn't want to overpay. They could wait it out. Today or tomorrow, the English would come to their senses. The collection of old rubber was announced in the United States. Long lines of trucks carrying dilapidated tires stretched in front of factories. But the rejuvenated rubber was flabby and impermanent. The gluttonous cars demanded more and more new tires. Now, influential men went to London to intercede.

Mr. Stuart Hotchkiss, Vice-President of the American Rubber Company, suggested to Churchill that all restrictions be removed:

"Freedom of trade is to our mutual interest. . . ."

Mr. Churchill smiled courteously.

"Let us not kowtow to the power of words. . . . I just cannot understand why English planters should be obliged to sell you rubber at a loss."

The Americans feasted their eyes on Mr. Churchill's necktie. Everyone knew that Mr. Churchill was a dandy. They also listened to a few charming puns. And they left empty-handed.

Mr. Churchill was a gambling man. He loved war and poker. In his life, he had been a Liberal and a Conservative, a writer and a painter, Lord High Admiral and Chancellor of the Exchequer. But he was only interested in gambling. He had failed to sink the German navy: an oversight. He had failed to wipe out the Russian Revolution: The opponent, as it turned out, had trumps in reserve. To make up for it, Mr. Churchill might now beat the Americans. The stakes were high, and Mr. Churchill was enthralled by the game. Instead of concessions, he responded to the American request with a new attack. He issued an edict for a ruthless battle against smuggling. Ships carrying rum and rubber crossed the Pacific. The rum was confiscated by the virtuous Yankees. And the rubber? The rubber, of course—by the English.

Mr. Hoover knew perfectly well that neither old tires nor smuggling would help. He addressed all the citizens of all the states of the Union: "We have to get our own rubber."

Rubber kept going up. American manufacturers panicked. They were ready to parrot all the tragic motions of the brokers on Minching Lane. The factories in Akron curtailed production. The unemployed shouted: "Bread!" American workers don't know how to starve quietly and stoically like coolies. They cursed and held suspicious meetings. A few companies announced that this year they would pay no dividends. The stock market was gloomy.

And so was Mr. Hoover. The United States government appealed to the government of Great Britain. Their tone was friendly. Their tone was heart to heart. They asked for an end to restrictions. What could they do? The rubber trees grow in Penang, and America needed rubber.

But Mr. Churchill was adamant. Even Mr. Hoover's unexpected tenderness failed to move that crotchety poet. You want to buy? Fine, we're willing to sell. But at *our* prices.

Mr. Churchill had promised Sir John Stevenson that his name would go down in history. However, in America, everyone spoke about the Churchill Plan, not the Stevenson Plan. England had to pay old debts to America. The cunning Mr. Churchill decided to sell rubber at three times the price in order to pay America with American dollars! One journalist explained that Churchill was rubbing out his gambling debts with a rubber eraser. The phrase caught on. Ah well, just like the Soviets! . . . Mr. Churchill, the founder of the *Fifty Club* and the inspirer of intervention, a snob and a worthy successor of Pitt, was called an "immoral Bolshevist" by the angry Americans. But for goodness' sakes, they needed rubber, and now that silly botany had to interfere! Equatorial Zone indeed! . . . Naturally, they had to take over the tiny Central American republics and start plantations there. But then they would have to wait eight years! . . . Yet no one in America would agree to wait even one minute, much less eight years! The stockholders were in a hurry to get dividends. Drivers were in a hurry to wear out their tires. And the unemployed were in a hurry to eat. Everyone was in a hurry. And everyone needed rubber.

Far from Akron, in Penang, lived Mr. Davis. Just recently, he had planted 500 more acres. He now received three shillings a pound. Still, he was very miserable. His python had up and died on him. He

58

was sick of cocktails. It was clear to him now that he would never see London again: Rubber was going up.

3

New York. The rubber exchange. The screen for posting the latest quotations from London. One shilling nine pence.

One of the customers whispered:

"Oh God, don't let it sink even a ha'-penny! . . ."

This was a buyer. Naturally he wanted to pay less. But Mr. Churchill's game was very cunning. If rubber went down to one shilling eight pence, a new restriction would be enforced. The Americans needed rubber. They cursed Churchill, but they tried to keep the prices up. One shilling nine pence.

"Thank God!"

London didn't even have to make an effort. New York was working for it. Mr. Churchill had won the round.

He would have been glad to end the game. But the game was only just starting. Mr. Churchill had a good head and the Malayan Peninsula. But who could say what the obstinate Mr. Hoover would think up next? . . .

It was not for nothing that he conferred with diplomats and botanists. He must have been up to something! That man had an iron forehead. He was a farmer's son and a bonafide Quaker. He drank only straight water. He hated imagination. Next to him, Mr. Churchill was a frivolous child. After all, Mr. Churchill drank port wine and wrote novels. But Mr. Hoover thought obtusely and tediously about his rubber.

Pharaoh once had a horrible dream: Seven lean cows ate up seven fat cows. Mr. Hoover drank only straight water. He wasn't Pharaoh. He was an engineer, a Quaker, an American. Yet he was haunted by Pharaoh's dream. It took the branchy tree seven years to grow. Then, and then only, could you notch the bark. When the rubber prices dropped, Mr. Davis planted no new acres. Now, to be sure, he was working his fingers to the bone. In seven or eight years, his yield would double. In seven. . . . But what about four years from now? People were in a hurry to live. A new car was born every minute. In four years, there'd be a rubber famine. Science had proven itself ungifted. It could invent artificial gin, much to Mr. Hoover's sorrow. But it couldn't invent artificial rubber. The United States was dependent on a frivolous gentleman. No! This simply couldn't go on! America had to have its own rubber!

A huge map of both hemispheres was spread out in front of Mr. Hoover. Several countries were outlined in red ink, countries where the finicky trees could be grown. The red ink wasn't allegorical. It made things more legible. But the inhabitants of the outlined countries could pray to the almighty God of all Quakers. It's customary to pray before dying. The businesslike American's red ink meant lots of things. It meant rubber, it meant blood.

Liberia? Grant a loan, buy land, send administrators. Don't stand on ceremony with Zulus. This poetic name was just right for them. Go on! The Philippines? There were a few difficulties here. Mainly, buying land and getting Chinese coolies. There were laws against it? So what! Suspend the laws. The United States had promised the Philippines independence? Fine. They had promised. But a lot had changed since then. God had simply created these islands for rubber. Mr. Shong said he had marvelous plantations there, and Mr. Shong was president of the Rubber Company. So buy land and get coolies. Go on! Brazil! Fortify our positions. Buy the press. Buy the ministers. Spare no expense! Stop up Argentina's mouth. Things were really getting interesting. . . . Guatemala? Finished? Very good! Nicaragua? . . . In a jiffy. . . .

Mr. Hoover had an iron forehead. He sat and he thought.

4

The hot, viscous night had the sickly sweet odor of bananas. In the North, bananas are a treat, but here they're just bread, the bread that's earned in the sweat of our brow, as the venerable fathers of all five hundred seminaries assure us. At night, however, there are no priests here, and no well-learned curses. Only darkness. It consists of a thousand tiny noises, the soughing of heavy branches, the whirring of bats, the hissing of boas.

"Who's there?"

One man asked another. At first, by mistake, the night answered, it answered with a nervous fit of leaves. Then once more:

"Who's there?"

Silence. One man couldn't understand the other. They even had different words for the night. One word was bright and broad, like a wheatfield. The other word, pitchblack and ardent, could scarcely be distinguished from the night itself. One man had a military cap with a badge; the other, a wide-brimmed felt hat. How could they possibly get together? . . . What could they talk about? The night? The bananas? The solitude?

No, they didn't converse. Silently they rolled in the grass and silently they strangled one another. The night, the whole night, with branches, birds, and even boas, was startled, and it scattered. The offensive beam of a searchlight tracked after it. The night was shredded, destroyed. Rifles and hand grenades applauded like fools in a circus? Boom!

The two men were gone. They had vanished with the night. The cap and the hat lay on the grass. Next to them, two heavy sacks stuffed with things that had just ceased being life: arms, blood, letters from Jane and Maria, cigarettes. It all cooled slowly, like the earth. Dew covered everything. Probably at the behest of Jane and Maria.

There was no cameraman here. Guess again! It was a real live hat! A real live death! And the crackling kept on and on. Thus, the morning would find twenty or two hundred bodies sprawling pathetically under the bananas, the ones that are bread. No one would gather them, though, and ungathered bananas are irksome and poignant like an unreaped field. As for Jane and Maria (twenty? two hundred?): Without those white pages full of funny flourishes, there is no human life, just as there is no night without sudden, acrid dew.

Some would be called *telegrams*. They would soar into the big cities, whistling en route: ". . .service number. . . . Sixteen words. . . . John. . . . Richard. . . . Edward. . . . At 11:55 PM. . . . On duty. . . ." Quickly they would turn into black dresses (rush orders can be sewn on any street) and laboriously calculated pensions.

The others, meanwhile, on mules, would creep up mountains, shouting in shame and fatigue, in order to attack a white settlement like a grenade: "Boom!" "Pablo. . . . Diego. . . . near the village of Morobina. . . ." Instead of a signature, a scrawl: "Fatherland and freedom." All this without cameramen, serious, grief-stricken, and all this in the same type of New York newspapers: "Our expeditionary corps was surrounded last night by one of the gangs of that bandit Sandino. The criminals were wiped out. Our losses were minor."

General Sandino was in the white settlement, amid mountains, amid grief, amid braying mules. He was writing an appeal: "To all the republics of Latin America. The Yankees want to swallow Nicaragua the way they have swallowed Panama, Cuba, Puerto Rico, Haiti, Santo Domingo. Brothers, remember Bolivar and San-Martin! We have been fighting for eight months. Our strength is exhausted! . . ."

He wrote and wrote. His words were solemn and grandiose. But his hand trembled with excitement. "Help us! Quickly!"

Beyond the mountains lurked Honduras and San Salvador. Mexico was gloomy and silent. It was no use his adding two more words next to the seal: "Fatherland and Liberty." Just two more grandiose words. . . .

Isn't there something sweeter than all words: Those long green pieces of paper fluttering south from Washington? What good are cartridges in bandoliers? They were already in the harbors, the brand-new torpedo-boats, as tidy as infirmaries. The United States is also a "fatherland." And liberty is at home there, it's even become a statue, paperweights, millions of postcards.

A letter from Nerova-Segovia: "Yesterday, a squad of bombers again shelled four villages. The Yankees dropped over one hundred bombs. They killed 72 people, including 18 women."

General Sandino sat and wrote: "Damn the killers of women! We are few, but we shall not give in. . . ." General Sandino had a wide-brimmed hat and he believed in spiritual nobility. He had three thousand guerrillas with him.

Mr. Hoover wasn't the least bit worried. He knew that to wipe out three thousand men, you only need a certain number of weeks, a certain number of dollars, a certain number of human lives. American soldiers love their country. Besides, they receive high pay. Consequently, they can die on occasion. Unfortunate? Of course. Mr. Hoover wasn't a monster. Mr. Hoover was a humanitarian. Hadn't he fed Viennese children and even the ogres on the Volga? He would gladly have spared that Sandino. He would have told him: "Go to Hollywood! You'll make a good extra."

Nicaragua, like any country, only dreamt about one thing: Prosperity. And that quarrelsome Sandino had gotten it into his head to talk about his country, about liberty, not about the statue, no, about silly liberty, perhaps about the liberty to live in white settlements and gather or even not gather bananas. Well, under the circumstances, this Sandino had to be wiped out.

A map was spread in front of Mr. Hoover. Nicaragua had been

outlined in red ink long ago. Mr. Hoover felt sorry not only for Jenny, the widow of an honest American soldier, but also for Maria, the widow of some Nicaraguan bandit. After all, the book on Mr. Hoover's desk said: "Thou shalt not kill." But it also spoke about the Promised Land. Without blood, that land had not yielded. The righteous Israelites had annihilated the heathens. Even the Lord God made exceptions. Eighteen women killed? How sad. But there are railroad catastrophes too. Cars hit women every day. We're bringing Nicaragua true prosperity, and besides, we've repeated this any number of times: We need our own rubber!

5

They romped and frisked on all the walls of all the towns in France, those three minions of the Republic. The tender, innocent little boy, who wasn't old enough to lie, praised that remarkable soap: Cadum. The wistful cow mooed night and day about milk chocolate. As for the third citizen, wearing huge goggles, he wasn't made of flesh, like all other human beings or even the cows of the Republic. Oh no. He was made of rubber tires. His name: Michelin Tires. He was resilient and light. Everyone needed him: No tires, no cars.

Monsieur André Michelin didn't have the slightest resemblance to his popular *doppelgänger*. He didn't have a ring-shaped paunch or a legendary smile. He had a full beard and a pince-nez. He didn't have air on the inside, just perfectly ordinary innards. He wasn't even a conjuror. He was a first-rate manufacturer. He imported Cochin-Chinese rubber. He bought rubber from the English. With the rubber, he turned out durable tires. In the hot, dreadful workshops, the rubber was tempered like steel over violent fire. The blood of the hevea, hitherto soft and pliant, became resilient. The tires would fear neither Carpathian rocks nor Siberian bumps.

Men with stopwatches walked through the Michelin factory: The factory was organized along American lines. True, Monsieur Michelin didn't shave off his beard. But that didn't prevent him from venerating America. He put out a magazine called *Prospérité*. Mr. Hoover became president of the United States because that word had been his platform: Prosperity. Monsieur Michelin gave his magazine gratis to anyone who was interested. He also gave away lots and lots of books: The moving life-story of F. W. Taylor, reports on the kindergartens attached to his factory, an apologia for peace between capital and labor. He wasn't just a fine manufacturer. Nor was he a gambling man like Monsieur Citroën. He was a great martyr of efficiency.

Out of the gearbox jumped a funny mannikin with tires in place of a tummy. He demanded: Faster! Make tires faster! Buy cars faster! Was it really worth dying slow if you could die fast, working yourself to death among men with stopwatches and model nurseries, if you could die on the long highway, bursting like a tire?

The Michelin workers weren't coolies. They were really rubber trees: You had to notch them sensibly. Monsieur Michelin set up nurseries. He paid bonuses for extra-large families. The more children a worker has, the faster he has to work. The stopwatch gauged new records.

Monsieur André Michelin published a magazine. Every day he thought of new steps towards perfection: gaining another minute, another forty seconds. His double merely smiled. His double had air inside, not blood. He rolled along the road. He laughed, and his laugh was extremely suspicious. Let people roll like him. They had blood inside? . . . So what! Let them roll! . . .

Here, nothing and no one ever stopped: not the cars, the workers, nor the rubber mannikin.

Perhaps Monsieur Michelin was sometimes overcome by fatigue. After all he didn't have air inside, he had thick blood. And then, he wasn't Mr. Hoover: his forehead was quite ordinary. However, there were one million cars in France. Every car devoured forty-five pounds of rubber a year. Hurry, you workers! You're not coolies. You've got kindergartens. You don't dare stop. You've got to work faster. Hunger is hunger anywhere: in Indo-China, in Auvergne. Death is death anywhere. The workers hurried. And the rubber mannikin won another minute for his life. The automobiles dashed, and the mannikin dashed. He had huge goggles. He had an unbearable smile. He was hollow on the inside. He was a new Death, without an amateurish scythe, without a ludicrous, old-fashioned shroud, he was all rings, all tires, he dashed and sped—50, 100, 200 miles an hour, always on the lookout for people whose time had come. He was here, there, everywhere, all over happy-go-lucky France.

6

Mr. Hoover contemplated the map. The red ink had long since dried. So had the blood. Mr. Hoover should have been happy: He was now president of the most powerful republic in the world. All the citizens dreamt of shaking his big, capable hand. The Germans called him a humanitarian: they remembered the rancid bacon of the American Relief Agency. Negroes called him "Lincoln": He had beaten the Democrat Smith. The Ku-Klux-Klan called him "a great guy": He was a Quaker by birth and by heritage. Girls and women called him "good Herbert": After all, he was in favor of complete temperance. Smugglers called him "a sensible guy": During his administration, whiskey doubled in price. All Americans venerated Mr. Hoover. Only anarchists and incorrigible alcoholics were against him. Mr. Hoover should have been very happy.

But an iron forehead imposes high responsibilities. Mr. Hoover sat and thought. Nicaragua was subdued. Brazil was tamed. In the Philippines, things were progressing. In Sumatra, Americans had bought enormous plantations. And now the botanists had made some concessions: they had widened that accursed zone. It turned out that Mexico wasn't so bad! . . . In ten years, America would have enough rubber. But who could tell—by then someone might invent artificial rubber. Someone might think up new means of locomotion. For America, ten years was a century. For Mr. Hoover, ten years was old age and memoirs. The rubber famine would begin in three years. The Stevenson Plan had been cancelled—it was no longer useful. Rubber stood on its own two feet. Mr. Churchill had outsmarted Mr. Hoover. He had saved the plantations in Malaya. And Mr. Hoover was furious. His iron forehead was rippled with wrinkles. He had to wait, even though he dare not wait, even though waiting would be the death of America. He wanted to forget about rubber, unwind, relish a glass of straight water, gaze at the blue sky, that one diversion of all Quakers. But rubber thoughts are viscous and persistent. He drank water—and the water smelled like scorched rubber. He gazed at the sky—and the sky was as white as the milky sap. He went to sleep—and he dreamt Pharaoh's dream again. Mr. Hoover whispered something in his sleep, the whisper was bitter and eternal like the rustle of the leafy trees.

Mr. Churchill had more imagination. It was not for nothing that he had fought with the Boers and depicted tragic landscapes. But Mr.

Churchill wasn't so cheerful either, though he had won the round, though Mr. Davis called him the "saviour of rubber." The Yankees took the matter in hand. They would soon have their own plantations. The Dutch had to yield to Great Britain in everything. Why else did these phlegmatic pygmies have their lucrative colonies? Holland was an unofficial "dominion." As far as petroleum went, the Dutch upheld the interests of Great Britain. But when it came to rubber, they let them down. The planters in Sumatra did not accept the Stevenson Plan. They took advantage of the price war to penetrate the American market. To make matters worse, they had sold the Americans huge plantations. Mr. Churchill was not a merchant. He didn't give a damn about dividends. But he was at the card table. Every card was an event. The Dutch had spoiled his game. Some Keynesians would scoff at his economic knowledge again. The beaten card would be seized upon by the Liberals. He couldn't stand being laughed at, and people did nothing but laugh their heads off at him, at his military adventures, his novels, his plan for naval warfare, even his neckties. Now they would jeer at his rubber policies. He had to win! Within three years, the prices would double. Three years. . . . And in seven? The game had only begun and yet he had to throw down his cards, he had to say it was time to head home, morning was coming. He had to play, to play for the rest of this life, to play even though he was faced with certain defeat. Those bloody cards! It was so much better to write novels. . . . But no, he was obliged to think about rubber. Just what is rubber anyway? An eraser in the hand of Churchill the artist? A mackintosh worn by Churchill the globe-trotter? An enema bag, galoshes, soles? Nonsense! Rubber was automobiles, it was trucks, it was trenches, it was victory. And *we* have the rubber! . . .

But what about tomorrow? What about Sumatra, Indo-China, Brazil, the Philippines? Mr. Churchill yawned convulsively. How pale he was! How tired he was! That's the kind of face you see on a Baccarat fanatic in the morning, when he's got a revolver in his pocket or simply Veronal tablets. To sleep! . . . But the game went on. Rubber sailed across the ocean, more and more of it. It was here, it was there—everyone had it. Are there really such things as landscapes and port wines? The world is made of rubber. Astonished, Mr. Churchill felt his vest. Why of all the—! Only now did he notice that he had a rubber heart! It didn't matter whom he went with, the Right, the Left; it didn't matter whom he fought. He didn't love anyone and he didn't believe in anything. Something in his chest first expanded, then contracted. Mr. Churchill's family doctor, from force of habit, still called it the "heart."

During the day, Mr. Davis had been informed that a coolie had tried to steal a pound of rubber. Mr. Davis ordered him to be thrashed—thirty stout blows. In the evening, Mr. Davis played poker with a friend. Now it was night and he was asleep. He slept there, uncomfortable and deformed, a big hairy man. It was hot, the cover had slipped off, he slept alone in the long empty house. Even the python had died. Mr. Davis had repulsive dreams: His Annie no longer smelled of glycerine soap. She smelled awful. What was that smell? . . . Even the Malayan girls smelled better. The hairy man kept rolling around in his sleep. He was unable to free himself of that obtrusive smell.

"Annie, my old friend. Forgive a rude planter his impertinence. Annie, what's that you smell of? . . ."

Annie remained silent. She only trembled with embarrassment. Perhaps she wanted to blush but couldn't. She was all white, terribly white. What a vile smell! Only the milky sap of the rubber tree smells like that when it's turning sour in the pails. But that wasn't sap, that was Annie. Barely managing to stifle his disgust, Mr. Davis made up his mind to kiss Annie's hand. She had a husband? Well, Mr. Davis had a burning heart. Mr. Davis took Annie's hand. Her hand recoiled. The hairy naked man let out a piercing shriek. All around him: the burning night, the Asian sky, sleeping coolies, and hundreds of thousands of branchy trees. Annie's hand was elastic and cold. It wasn't human flesh! . . .

"Annie, what's your hand made of?"

Annie was silent. The coolies and the rubber trees were silent.

The coolie who had received thirty stout blows couldn't sleep. He coughed, and a red clot fell upon the earth, so familiar with the white blood of heveas. Earlier, the coolie hadn't notched trees, he had drawn the planters around in rickshas. He couldn't talk now, he could only gasp. He was very ill. No, not ill. He was dying. He dragged himself to the temple. There he saw God. God was made of bronze, God was calm and inscrutable. The fat Buddha smiled exactly like the rubber mannikin on the fences of France. But Buddha wasn't in a hurry. Unstirring, he sat in the cool temple. He sat for a year, an age, an eternity. Something was written underneath Buddha: "Some come to me along roads of heroism, some along roads of sacrifice, and some along roads of weariness, and all come to me along these roads." The coolie couldn't read, but he was very weary. For ten years he had pulled people in the ricksha, and for four years he had notched trees. He lay on the earth before God, and

God promised him only one thing, the one thing that even fat bronze gods can promise: generous rest.

All around, the branchy trees were rustling. They oozed and rustled. They too were weary, like Hoover, like Churchill, like Mr. Davis, like the coolies, like the rubber mannikin, like all people and all automobiles. They begged: "Rest! Rest!" And with empty bronze eyes, the fat Buddha gazed into the night, which knows no future, no past; with empty eyes into the empty night.

Chapter Four
A Poetic Digression

1

It was a clear autumn. Paris was living its normal life. The priests spoke to their female parishioners about eternity, they listened and doused themselves with perfume: "Vient le jour." The bookstores displayed the latest sensations: *Your Body Belongs to YOU, You'll Become a Courtesan,* and *The Adulterer's End.* Theater posters heralded the newest productions: Théâtre Gymnase—*La Joie de l'Amour:* Théâtre Folies Dramatiques—*Groom at Maxim's.* The Surrealist poets swore to wipe out civilization, and toward this end they wrote down their dreams. One poet had dreamt about a huge coconut, another about his concierge. Art-lovers visited the newest 600 exhibitions. They were enthralled, if not by the pictures, then by the multidigited prices: At the latest auction, Picasso had gone as high as 45,000, and Modigliani had zoomed beyond 100,000. A clothing store, celebrating its first anniversary, offered discounts on its wares. Housewives said you could get a knitted jacket there for 27 francs and 95 centimes. In high political spheres, they only talked about important matters: At the Nice congress of the radical party, Monsieur Hériot had beaten Monsieur Caillot. In the course of a single day, the police registered sixteen auto collisions, two fires, and four suicides: these figures weren't above average. Every man in the street was preoccupied with his own worries, not with Monsieur Caillot's defeat or even *The Adulterer's End:* the *"terme,"* i.e., rent-day, was seventy-two hours away. The stock exchange registered an increase in oil and utilities. The Rumanian loans were fluctuating, and Tunisian phosphate dropped one point. In other words, all was well in this best of all possible cities.

All at once, a minor disturbance. Among the posters for *La Joie de l'Amour,* among Cadum soap and dog taxes, exclamation points began flashing. Certain people were writing about blood. But actually, it was a matter of oil. The English supported the Arabs. Unhappily, oil deposits had been unearthed in the Rif. Exclamations were powerless. The word STRIKE burst like a bomb on walls. However, no bomb exploded. It was the last feeble roll of postwar thunder, a souvenir of 1919, when Place de l'Opéra had quaked and when presumably immobile investments had burnt out on thin electric wires.

That had been six years ago. Now Paris had Monsieur Herriot's victory, the *terme*, and *Your Body Belongs to YOU.* Paris had had no revolution at all. But today Paris had a minor disturbance. The streets were suddenly deserted and transparent, like a forest clearing in autumn. Herds of cars stubbornly cowered in garages. Worried people, as usual, ran along the boulevards. They thought about stocks, which were going up by the hour. On the Champs-Elysées, plaster beauties were walking their perennial melancholy and their dwarfish Scotch Terriers. Policemen smiled calmly. Shop windows glittered. Stocks rose. Dogs yelped. But for one minute, the emptiness of the streets aroused a slight anxiety: it was like a memento mori. The stillness of the suburbs reached Place de la Concorde, Place de l'Étoile, and the plaster heart of Paris. The city, which had gone through four revolutions and over four hundred uprisings—the city smiled. It smiled with a justifiable irony, and perhaps an unjustifiable melancholy.

On some boulevards in Paris there are chestnut trees; on some, plane trees; on others, lindens. Rue de la Paix is famous for jewelers and tailors. The Champs-Elysées for car dealers and perfume boutiques. Montparnasse for artists. Passy for quiet. Place de la Bourse for the howling of brokers. And Saint-Germain for old-fashioned villas.

In the suburbs of Paris, there are smokestacks instead of trees. The streets are bleak here, like a rainy dawn. The tiny stores sell margarine, buttons, and Marseilles soap. The tavern organ whines.

Scraps of posters on the fences: today, a new sensation: *Kiss of Death*. The red light of a police station. A disheveled kitten. In the middle of the street, an ugly child with a huge head urinates. A woman beats a mattress, she beats it furiously, vexedly, as if the mattress were her own bad destiny. Thin, skewbald hair flutters in the wind. Dust from the mattress mingles with all the heavy, sluggish dust that is the sky here Rue de la République or Rue de Jean-Jaurés, long, empty—house-numbers, scraps of posters, soap, margarine. Life itself seems long and empty on the windy November morning under the wail of the factory sirens.

In between the puny, crestfallen houses, there are huge factory buildings. In the morning, they soak in people; in the evening, they dump them out. A man leaves three hundred cast screws here and a bit of his body heat. He walks out with a fistful of coins. He can buy half a pound of margarine, even toss a few coins on the tin bar of a tavern, so that they'll clink dolefully, so that the hurdy-gurdy will moan in reply, so that the calvados will make the unbearably long street twist and tangle, that same Rue de la République or Rue de Jean Jaurès.

Suresnes is a suburb of Paris. It has the Citroën and Talbot auto factories, an arsenal, a steelyard. It also has, of course, a Rue de Jean Juarès, and on it, a co-op store with Marseilles soap. Here in Suresnes, they manufacture forty-horsepower engines, and, groaning with fatigue, the workers go to bed at nine, falling into a sleep as thick as tar. Here, they vote Communist, cry their eyes out watching *Kiss of Death,* and dream about a mirrored wardrobe. In the summer, cars whiz down the long streets: Parisians dashing to the ocean to breathe salt and iodine. Yearning for rocks and Gothic churches. Suresnes isn't even worth stopping in. Suresnes has a stench of soot, machine oil, gasoline, and when the cars go past the auto factory, the drivers turn their faces away.

Today the dawn hurried for nothing, the sirens howled for nothing, the gates opened their maw for nothing. Today wasn't Sunday and it wasn't the end of the world. The black scrolls on the calendar demanded: Go! The machines were indignant:

"Today is Monday. You're crazy! . . ."

"Fire them! Catch the instigators! Call the police!"

"C'mon! You're not kids! You're obliged to work. Otherwise we can't fill our orders. After all, you've got families, you have to eat. . . ."

"What is this? Mass hypnosis? Laziness? Bribery?"

"Smash them! Melt them down! Recast them! So that they won't be men, they'll be signals without pauses. Without mirrored wardrobes. 800 revolutions a second! . . ."

The houses were silent. All of Rue de la République was silent, just like Rue de Jean-Jaurès or Rue Carnot. Only the wind tore at the poster shreds: *Kiss of Death.*

In Paris, on Place de la Concorde, a young Surrealist, squinting ironically, said to his not so young admiratrix:

"If I'm not mistaken, in literary theory this is known as a 'poetic digression.' "

2

Now they were marching down the long streets. They stopped at certain gates and made a racket. They laughed and cursed and coughed, a dreary revelry. Maliciously and tenderly, they gazed at the entrance the way a deserter gazes at his ship.

Rue Carnot. Concrete. Bolted gates. It was the factory of the Radio Technology Corporation. The gates were shut. The empty courtyard was visible through the lattice. Some women were still working in the shops, too stubborn or too timid. The crowd yelled:

"Drop your work! Shame on you! . . . Scabs! . . ."

There were shadows at the windows. Some were embarrassed, some irate. But it was hard to guess what they were thinking, these shadows: the director's shadow, the mechanic's shadow, the switchboard-operator's shadow.

The shouting in the streets became louder and harsher.

"Cowards! Traitors!"

The factory director, Monsieur Demelet, was somewhat at a loss. He was only twenty-nine and not at all accustomed to poetic digressions. Besides, he had an exceedingly courteous profile. True, the doors were solid. They would yell a while and then leave. . . . Only, a factory isn't just a business or dividends. It is a holy place. People work hard here. They create beautiful things. What did exclamation points on fences have to do with that? . . . Let the loafers scream at meetings. Honest workers want to work. No one has the right to stir them up. That is sacrilege!

There they were, at the very gates! What could he do now? . . . Monsieur Demelet hesitated.

One of the engineers, Léon Lafosse, came to his aid. He was older than his boss and he had seen quite a bit in his time. Earlier he had worked at the Renault car plant. He was a draftsman by profession, but he didn't do any drafting at the factory: he kept order, punished, dismissed. He was a support, a true support. Just look at him: A Hercules! He loved showing off his size: Imagine, six feet tall! Broad shoulders, a huge round head, a round face, round eyes, round American glasses. If he didn't think much, then at least all his thoughts were very useful to the Radio Technology Corporation. And he was no upper-class softie. He came from a working-class background. That was why he sincerely despised workers: A talented man has no trouble working his way up. His speech was ungainly, but he chose strong words. And strong were his drinks: The tavern-keepers in Suresnes knew that Monsieur Lafosse drank vermouth only from large glasses, never diluting it with water.

Lafosse was indignant. How could these loudmouths dare infringe upon the holiest of holies: working hours, time, bonuses, the sacredness of management, his round American glasses? . . .

"I'll teach them, Monsieur Demelet. . . ."

Lafosse strode over to the hydrant in the courtyard. The old watchman helped him. The watchman as usual was drunk. Engineers were at the windows. One of them shrugged: What for? . . . It had all happened so fast! They couldn't even collect themselves. What business of theirs was politics? They worked. Radio was important to everyone. Why were those people against them? . . . They had only just been ordinary engineers, now they were soldiers in a besieged stronghold. Nervously they felt their pants pockets: Was the revolver still there? One man checked to see if it was loaded. Another gloomily turned away. He had been in the war. He didn't want to fight anymore. Do you hear: He didn't want to fight! . . .

But no one heard anything. The switchboard-operator dropped her headphones and shut her eyes. In the workshops, women were working at the tables. They may have been trembling, but how could anyone tell amid the iron shudders of the machines? The machines kept going, indifferent to the roar of the crowd and the pallor of the young engineer. The orders had to be filled on schedule. Today wasn't Sunday. 800 revolutions a second.

The director's shadow jumped about convulsively: Oh God, that clodhopper would destroy him! . . . Lafosse had miscalculated. The water had merely fed the fire. Now the strikers were in earnest. Shoulders piled against the lattice. A windowpane screeched tragically. A lump of plaster fell into Lafosse's face, and Hercules groaned. This wasn't like docking women! There were lots of them! They had rocks! Why had he started this business in the first place? He remembered that seven years ago workers had thrown a foreman into the Seine. That happened at Renault. Hide? But what would the director say?

Lafosse had a gun in his pocket. He ran to get another one, a military revolver. He was a draftsman. He had a family. He loved vermouth. He was anything but a soldier. But he couldn't stop now. He strode over to the watchman's booth. It was a good observation post.

The doors were apparently yielding. He couldn't delay any longer. That one there. . . . Lafosse aimed, but his hand shook. Missed! Rocks flew through the window. He fired again. This time, drowning out the roar of the crowd, a lone scream resounded. A woman's scream.

3

André Sabatier's father had been a metalworker. His mother worked in a factory. When André was fourteen, he also went to work in a plant. Sabatier was not Lafosse, he remained a worker. The Sabatier family had a custom: the men worked at the arsenal, the women at the Radio Technology Corporation.

Ministers bombastically spoke about the high moral standards of the French worker. Poets, trying to keep abreast of their times, eulogized the beauty of conveyor belts or the lyricism of molten steel. *L'Humanité* rhapsodized about Chinese generals or a new speech of Voroshilov's. But here, year after year, the wind tore at the poster shreds and the sirens wailed in the morning. André burned his mouth with coffee and dived into the gluttonous gates. Years wore by. There were no fires, no revolution, no catastrophes.

Paris was dancing the foxtrot and avidly reading *La Garçonne*. When André was twenty, he met Jeanne. It was simple and solid like the streets of Suresnes. André was drafted, Jeanne went to work in the factory. She was the wife of a Sabatier, so she worked at the Radio Technology Corporation. Then a child was born. André was in the service. Then André came back, fondled his son, and went to the factory.

In the evenings, André read. He read about courageous explorers, Louise Michel, and the Russian Revolution. The neighboring co-op store carried Marseilles soap. On the First of May, the workers went to meetings with celluloid sweetbrier in their buttonholes. They walked and sang. On May 2, the sirens derisively wailed again.

That was André Sabatier's life for twenty-four years. Only his neighbors and his comrades at work knew him. He was quiet and bashful. Then came October 12. A slight hitch occurred in the life of Suresnes.

André's sister worked at the factory of the Radio Technology Corporation. Today she went on strike. Together with the others, she shouted at the gates:

"C'mon out!"

André was at home. His sister was out. Where could she possibly be? Policemen were in the street. André went to see if something had happened. He didn't return for a long time: Even he was carried away. He stood at the gates yelling at the scabs:

"Cowards!"

Now André's mother became very worried and went to the factory: They had sent out a lot of policemen, and anything could happen! . . .

Lafosse. A jet of water. Curses. André ran up to the lattice:

"Traitors!"

Someone behind him said:

"Let's go back! . . . It's enough! . . ."

But how could they go back? André pushed against the gate to make it yield. A shot. Behind him, someone screamed:

"It's an ambush! Gangsters! Killers! . . ."

For an instant, the crowd recoiled. Hands hunted: bottle fragments, stones, bricks. André didn't go back from the lattice. His eyes, usually meek, now became dry and hard. He wouldn't go away. Not for anything.

"Killers! . . ."

Another shot. This time Lafosse didn't miss. André fell back. He fell silently. His mother screamed. She was right next to him, she had seen everything: blood, brains, his short agony.

"Help! For God's sake!"

But no one could stop. Lafosse fired again. Rocks flew again. And the drunken watchman was still pouring water on André's body.

Shadows floated behind the windows.

"Police! Soldiers!"

Who were they afraid of? The dead worker? The women? Or perhaps the long streets. . . .

"Hundreds of policemen! Faster! . . ."

Lafosse crawled into the cellar on all fours. Of course he was six feet tall and had huge fists. . . . But there so many of them. Not thirty, but thirty thousand, millions. They would throw themselves on Lafosse. He tried to console himself: no one had seen him. He would say it was someone else. The hell with it, the hell with his promotion! He had to save his own skin.

Lafosse ran into the toilet. There he dumped the cartridges. He hadn't shot! His word of honor, he hadn't! His gun wasn't loaded. That was what he said to the pipes and the darkness. He lay in the cellar, hiding his head in his arms. It was here that the director found him.

"You can come out now."

Lafosse peered around suspiciously.

"But, but. . . ."

"I tell you, you can come out. Everything's over. The police are here."

Only Lafosse wouldn't leave. There were shadows before him, thousands of shadows and one shadow: Of course, Lafosse was devoted to the Radio Technology Corporation. But Lafosse, still and all, was a human being. He stammered:

"There? . . ."

Monsieur Demelet understood. He replied hurriedly:

"One. . . . Badly, it seems. . . ."

There were three women at André's body: his mother, his wife, his sister. They wept. Everyone had forgotten them by now: the director, Lafosse, the streets of Suresnes, the authors of the exclamation points. They are not part of history. They wept ordinary female tears.

Sergeant Ballerat interrogated Monsieur Demelet. The director replied:

"I didn't see anything. I was out getting the police. The matter's clear, anyway. The strikers were firing, and by accident they hit one of their own men."

Lafosse likewise hadn't seen anything. He had merely tried to calm the mob. For that, he had suffered cruelly. Lafosse pointed to his forehead. Just look at that wound! With great difficulty, the sergeant managed to make out a tiny scratch.

On Rue de Jean-Jaurès, a policemen said with all the wisdom of his age and profession:

"One man down. . . . You know the old saying: If you want to make an omelette, *mon ami,* you have to break eggs. . . ."

André Sabatier now lay on his bed. Comrades came by, gloomily crushing their caps. Next door, a three-year-old boy was whimpering. His name was André, too. And he too would probably become a worker.

4

The director, and after him the employees, testified: Sabatier was killed by the strikers. The same thing was reported in the newspapers.

The Radio Technology Corporation was the French branch of a gigantic trust. The stock market knew precisely what the Marconi Group was. And not just the stock market. So did ministers, deputies, and journalists.

Sergeant Ballerat, however, was a simple police sergeant. It was his job to conduct an investigation. It was no special trouble for him to determine that the shots had come from the watchman's booth, that Sabatier had been standing at the lattice, facing the courtyard, that the bullet had entered his left temple, and hence, that Sabatier was not killed by the strikers.

Monsieur Demelet went to Police Commissioner Lambert. With utmost delicacy, he asked:

"If by some chance the culprit were to give himself up, could he, in your opinion, rely on his name not being made public right away? . . ."

France has a code of laws, and Monsieur Demelet must have heard about it. But Monsieur Demelet was director of the Radio Technology Corporation, and he smiled courteously. The Commissioner was caught off-guard. He wasn't used to diplomatic negotiations. Perhaps Monsieur le Directeur wished to supply some leads for finding the killer? . . . The Commissioner was a very simple man. Monsieur Demelet couldn't get anywhere with him.

Lafosse had to confess. He couldn't be arrested like some common killer. If he turned himself in, the papers would write about self-defense. Luckily, it had come to light that Sabatier was a Communist! They could hire a first-class lawyer. . . .

Monsieur Demelet discussed something for a long time with Lafosse, and Lafosse suddenly felt sorry. He yearned for justice. He was driven to the police station by Monsieur Demelet. But first Lafosse went home to say goodbye to his wife and son. He also had a little boy. The boy was going to become an engineer, if not a director. A round head. Round eyes. Round glasses.

Lafosse went in the marvelous car belonging to Monsieur le Directeur. Before him lay long streets. On one of them: a coffin, an unknown woman, a strange child. Lafosse felt sad. Lafosse, still and all, was a human being.

Few people had known about Sabatier when he was alive. When he died, he became a hero. He lay in his coffin and hurried through the suburbs. Some people crossed themselves, some clenched their fists. He was everywhere: in taverns, editorial rooms, workshops. With no further ado, he walked into co-op stores and the Chamber of Deputies. When he got underway, he was followed by 100,000 people. Cloths fluttered, asters withered, and the disorganized singing recalled the wail of sirens. There were reporters and sailors here, cars and wreaths, Morocco and wet sand, and all the long avenues of the Paris suburbs. André Sabatier dived into the earth the way he used to dive into the gates of the factory.

Several days elapsed. The papers ran stories about new murders. The exclamation points shriveled and dropped with the last leaves. The rainy weather began. People forgot all about Sabatier. He once again became modest and unknown as during his lifetime: a photograph on a dresser and the sparse tears of Jeanne.

People spoke about Lafosse as "that poor guy." Some were astonished: How long is he going to stay in jail? . . . Lafosse wasn't incarcerated for long: six days. A car picked him up at the prison gates. He quickly slammed the door. He was as tall and stately as ever, but his cheeks no longer smiled, his round eyes didn't shine, and even his glasses didn't sit right. Let people forget all about Sabatier. Lafosse remembered him very well.

He moved to another part of town. He changed his name. Léon Lafosse vanished. Now it was Monsieur Leblanc drinking vermouth. How bitter that vermouth was! . . . Had the taste changed? Or had Lafosse's palate changed along with his name? · . . It was as if he had never left that dark cellar. He had once had a life. Now he had fear. On the street, he was afraid of other people; at home, of the stillness. So he told the police he was afraid of vengeance-seekers. Who could say? Perhaps he only feared remembering? . . .

The factory of the Radio Technology Corporation worked as before. The stocks were quoted on the market. Monsieur Demelet gave orders. Lafosse's successor penalized the women workers. But Lafosse lay in the cellar. What had he done? He had defended private property and the right to work, the very highest things, the most sacred. They're taught at school and they're what a dying man whispers to his attorney. Was it Lafosse's fault that not all people were happy? He was just a minor employee. He earned fifty francs a day, a little more than a worker. Well yes, it was true, he *had* run to the hydrant first. But that was part of his job: Hosing people if need be, just as he hosed quicklime. He had fired. Otherwise, *he* would have been killed. They had once shot Germans, hadn't they? . . . And those Germans had had families too. Why then all those whispers about some child? His round lips twisted in agony on his round face. Lafosse kept justifying himself, on and on, to the night, to the streets, to the unknown woman. Then the night set in, and Monsieur Leblanc gulped down the bitter vermouth.

The machines roared. The Marconi Group stocks kept going up.

5

Fifteen months passed. In Paris, everything changed: ministers, clothes, dances. Nobody talked about Monsieur Caillaux anymore. The politicians were busy electing the Senate speaker. The Prince of Wales had fallen from his horse. The Théâtre Mathurin was showing *The Innocent Sinner*. The Bon Marché department store announced its grandiose winter white sale. It was a gray, foggy January. Well-to-do Parisians were hurrying south. The franc was on its feet again, and all French francs were blessing Monsieur Poincaré. Café denizens were arguing about fakirs: Were they mediums or simply swindlers? . . .

Then, unexpectedly, André Sabatier resurfaced. Attorneys preposterously flapped the sleeves of their robes. The prosecutor adjusted his chain. A carafe contained water, tepid and yellowish like the judicial conscience. Round eyeglasses emerged from a side door. They shone embarrassedly. Lafosse had become Lafosse again. He forgot all about the long nights. Monsieur Demelet saw only an industrious employee.

The presiding judge asked:

"Tell me, do you regret what happened?"

With total zeal, Lafosse replied:

"I sincerely do."

He was telling the truth. Of course he regretted it! He was anything but satisfied with his job. What kind of fun was it hosing people like quicklime? . . . He only got fifty francs a day. He had shot in an emergency. It wasn't a shooting-gallery at a county fair. But he had had no choice. Otherwise, Sabatier would be on trial here today for the murder of Engineer Lafosse.

Monsieur Demelet was steadfast and magnanimous. He testified: The gates were broken through, Sabatier was inside, Lafosse's life was in danger. After that, who could dare to say that the Radio Technology Corporation did not look after its employees?

The employees supported the director. True, Engineer Raquet's testimony contradicted certain things in Monsieur Demelet's testimony. But Engineer Raquet was discharged right after that. Mlle. Cotten, the telephone operator, had been sitting at the window. She testified under oath that the gates had not been opened.

"Are you now employed at the factory of the Radio Technology Corporation?"

"No. I was dismissed."

Monsieur Demelet was dressed exquisitely. He replied exquisitely to the questions. He had driven to the police. When the shot was fired, he had been in his car in front of the gates. He had seen everything with his own eyes.

Madame Maidrot lived across from the factory. She was intimidated by the robes of the lawyers and the chain of the district attorney. She answered very softly, but she did answer:

"I heard noise, and I ran out into the street. There was no car there. People were yelling at the gates. And the gates were closed. Then a shot was fired and a man fell. . . . No. he wasn't inside. . . . He fell on the street, right at the gates. . . ."

The presiding judge once again asked Monsieur Demelet:

"Do you abide by your testimony?"

"Yes, I abide by it."

"And you, Madame?"

"Yes, I do. . . ."

They stood against one another: the exquisitely dressed director and the Suresnes housewife, one of those who beat their mattresses in the morning. They had two truths. . . . The jurors had two truths. Two, not one.

Then Lafosse's lawyer playfully asked Madame Maidrot:

"Tell me, Madame, are you not a sympathizer? . . ."

At first she didn't realize what he meant, but then she understood, and she answered simply:

"No indeed. My goodness! I don't sympathize at all with the Communist Party."

Monsieur Demelet was the director of a huge business. He did not wince before difficulties, he persisted:

"I drove to the police. I went to Commissioner Lambert."

Commissioner Lambert was unusually tactless. He still didn't realize what the Radio Technology Corporation was. He said:

"Monsieur Demelet didn't come to me. I found out what happened from a police officer."

The attorney made a face. You can't ask a police commissioner if he's a sympathizer. Rather vexed, the attorney said:

"The commissioner is simply afraid. . . ."

The spectators looked at one another surprised: What could the Commissioner be afraid of? The dead worker? A revolt? The prosecutor? . . . Only Lafosse wasn't surprised. He knew how long even the shortest June nights can be.

Experts brought in a painstakingly drawn plan. The "death area" was shaded in. Sabatier was killed right here. . . . The jurors sighed. Yes, of course, right here. . . . But can one sit in judgment over Frenchmen for killing Germans? . . .

Above the door stood a marble Themis. Her eyes were blindfolded. She held scales, good, large scales, as in the co-op store on Rue de Jean-Jaurès.

The presiding judge was still searching for the truth—one truth for everyone. His eyes were tired. He reminded the defendant:

"You killed an innocent man. Sabatier wasn't even an agitator. He had only come to look for his sister. . . ."

But can you sit in judgment over an aviator for bombing a kindergarten? The sleeves of the attorneys fluttered. There were shouts on both sides: It's war! Everyone forgot about the painstakingly shaded plan.

"We all know the schemes of the Third Internationale! . . ."

"The hand of Moscow!"

"Bourgeoisie and social compromisers. . . ."

The round glasses were extinguished. They were outside the argument. They were aloof. The lawyers flaunted their acumen. They offered emotions and quotations. They drank the warm water and ominously wheezed.

The jurors hid their yawns. It was getting late: almost midnight. They had gobbled down their lunch, they hadn't even had time to enjoy a good smoke. They were sick of political arguments. As though they didn't know who to vote for! Before Monsieur Poincaré the franc had dropped, now it was stable. What was there to talk about? Morocco, oil, Mossul, Mussolini, Stalin, Moscow. . . . A quarter to twelve.

Lafosse's lawyer was an expensive lawyer. He could read the jurors' minds. He said:

"If Sabatier had gone to work that day, he wouldn't have been shot."

That was simple and understandable to everyone. Shaking off their somnolence, the jurors straightened up with an air of importance and then retired for deliberation.

No one could breathe in the courtroom. The policemen pressed the curious mob back from the doors. A young woman with a child sat on a bench. She was there as a reminder that André Sabatier was not a myth, not a poster on walls, that he had really lived, and that he had died at twenty-four. She turned away from the idle gazes. The boy had fallen asleep in her arms. Opposite her was Lafosse. He had carefully listened to everything. He had answered all the questions of the presiding judge respectfully and briefly, as though the judge were the director of the Radio Technology Corporation. After all, Lafosse was just a minor employee of a universally venerated firm.

The jury did not deliberate for long. War is war. Nine jurors said unanimously:

"He's innocent. It was self-defense."

And they added even more simply, in a familiar tone, as when you play cards in a café:

"We have to defend ourselves too. . . ."

Three jurors tried to argue:

"The experts. . . . The gates. . . . He came for his sister. . . ."

But they were three. War is war. The foreman read:

"With our consciences before God and before man. . . . No. . . . No. . . . No. . . ."

"Lafosse, you are free."

Lafosse bowed politely and instantly became Leblanc again. They let him out through a back exit. A car awaited him there. Again an agonizing life began for him; long nights, rustles, stares of passers-by, and the puzzling bitterness of vermouth.

Jeanne Sabatier left. The judges and the policemen left. Only the yellow, senile goddess remained in the courtroom. Her eyes were blindfolded. Too bad. She had been unable to see Monsieur Demelet's magnificent clothes!

Suresnes. Long streets. It would be foolish to stroll on them. People go to work on them in the morning, and go home to sleep in the evening. Carloads of tourists drive over them. The people who make cars stand at the workbenches. Man can die. The machine cannot stop. This is not a novel. This is a stock-market bulletin and this is a political history. There is no room here for poetic digressions.

Chapter Five

Gasoline

1

A highway. A long string of cars. Inside the cars, of course, there were people. That man was driving because he was a doctor. That one because he was after a girl. That one was selling lightbulbs. And that one had decided to kill a jeweler. All of them were driving because they owned a car. They weren't driving, the cars were driving, and the cars were driving because they were cars.

Suddenly, a car halted amid suburban bleakness, amid chippings, mangy kittens, and pesky kids, under a harsh, whitish sun. There were posts and pumps all around. The car wanted to gulp something. There were various signs on the posts: letters, tongues of flame, jagged lightning. The price was noted in chalk: 12.70 or 12.80. A driver, with a gun in his pocket or with sample lightbulbs, absentmindedly glanced at the lightning and the flame. He simply needed gas. He didn't think about what lay ahead of him: war, communal graves, trophies of victory. He paid 12.70 or 12.80. He thought about lightbulbs or a jeweler. He stepped on the gas. Grinning, the car whizzed off. Only the car knew where or why.

It can be depicted as follows:
Heather and a yearning moon—the floodlamp of suspicious

movie-takes, in which the extras eat sandwiches with heroic slowness. Naturally, Scotland. Naturally, a castle. Naturally, a loch. And naturally, on this night, a lone eccentric roams along the shore, trying to pinpoint the water, the stars, and the mocking eyes of some Mary or Kate. Here is his airy, agitated shadow. He's no spring chicken: Gray moustache, a dark, sun-burned skin; in his eyes, a harsh fire flares up every so often, as black as the night is black in different climes. Perhaps he's not in love. Perhaps he's merely alarmed by the moon and the dampness, the unexpected crossing of shadows, the unexpected gleaming of water, the enigmatic melody of his steps; perhaps he's merely alarmed by the trite presence of—not Mary, not Kate, but death, that obligatory supernumerary, death, without whom there is no loch, no castle, not even the shortest human night. This man is sad and homely. He wears a threadbare coat. His monocle is scratched and his watch barely holds on an old strap. Perhaps he's just a poor devil of a dreamer, madly in love with antiquities, and dragging himself here to feast his eyes on mossy rocks, to imagine himself a Jacobite, ready to die a cruel and agonizing death for the freedom of Scotland. Perhaps he's a hapless poet, wasting his time every Saturday by sending all the editors in the United Kingdom his ballads that are as pale and yearning as the moon.

At the gates of the castle: another shadow. No loch here, no flame in the eyes, no romanticism. The moon is here too, it helps to discern the shiny mackintosh, the gold clasp of the fountain pen, even the resolutely pressed lips. Oh, that man is hard and persistent! But the gates won't open. He was here this morning, he was here during the day. He's here again. Who? Mary? . . . Who knows! . . . The doorkeeper is as arrogant as King James, and it's no use slipping him King James, and it's no use slipping him a crackling calling card and crackling banknotes. The gates won't open.

Then the moon falls, the green moon, into the green water. Dying, it once again imbues the white mist. Now, the shadow, which sighed on the shore, which has a severe fire and a scratched monocle, runs into another shadow amid willows and silence. Someone could write a ballad about that. The rustle of the shadows is unbearable. Even the unfeeling night has to shudder. That's apparent in the swishing of the leaves, the plashing of the water, and in the narrow, staring windows, which suddenly light up. The new shadow (is it death?) bows with a creak, or more precisely: it only bends its dry metallic neck:

"Mr. Teagle is waiting for you in the smoking room. . . ."

The shadow at the gates knows nothing. The shadow at the gate, sensitive to the cold, huddles in its overcoat, which is wide like an old-fashioned cloak.

Mr. Teagle carefully lit his Havana. Meanwhile the host filled his pipe with strong, cheap tobacco. It's easier to change your faith, your friends, your convictions, or your country than to change your tobacco. Once, the host had been very poor. It had been hard for him to pay ten cents for four ounces of tobacco. He got used to this heavy, thick smoke, to this aroma of sailor taverns and crude, daredevil youth. Yes indeed, he never betrayed his tobacco!

Mr. Teagle carefully blew out a stream of costly smoke. He spoke carefully:

"Regarding the possibility of a separate agreement with Moscow. . . ."

A few bits of bad tobacco tumbled on the rug. The host's hand just barely twitched. He smiled. He was facing a new battle. Hence, a new victory. After all, Lord John Fisher, the creator of Great Britain's navy, had said to him: "You are a Napoleon in courage and a Cromwell in depth." Mr. Teagle could smoke a Havana and talk about a separate agreement; Napoleon, otherwise known as Cromwell, was calm. He was surrounded by the gray smoke of victory.

"That's senseless, ergo, immoral. . . ."

He knew that victory would be his. Whereas Mr. Teagle and the separate agreement—they were merely fog, a whitish fog, like the color of the loch, like the invented gait of the obligatory supernumerary who roamed the lanes of the park and whom poets and, under suitable circumstances, non-poets called Death. What nonsense! You say "Death"? But that's senseless, ergo, immoral.

Who was he? An admiral? A field marshal? A minister of foreign affairs? No, he was just a businessman. To be sure, King George had knighted him. But he didn't care about titles. He only cared about his business. He was simply a businessman. He dealt in petroleum. He was head of Royal Dutch. His name was Henry Wilhelm August Deterding. With him were his guests: Here was the unexpected shadow from the loch, Sir John Cadman, director of Anglo-Persian, an ally of the host's. And here was Mr. Teagle, president of Standard Oil of New Jersey, who so carefully smoked a Havana, afraid to drop an ash, afraid to drop a word; he was a competitor, if you like, a tenderly loved enemy. Beyond the narrow windows were the moon and the heather. Three gentlemen, smiling delicately and enigmatically, had a long talk about the foul-smelling liquid.

The ancient Persians didn't have a stock exchange, but they did foresense the lofty significance of those pieces of paper now known as, say, Anglo-Persian: They idolized oil. Greasy, dirty priests smiled enigmatically by the wells, and the eternal fire did not go out. Even the stench of petroleum was the sweetest smell in the nostrils of pilgrims.

Sir John Cadman also smiled enigmatically. During the war, he solemnly proclaimed: "We will anoint you with the oil of victory." Notwithstanding his title of honorary chairman of the Oil Commission, he permitted himself a delightful pun: *oil* refers to both salve and petroleum. When brave Tommies were dying in the swamps of Flanders, Sir John performed the sublime rite of final unction.

Now he was a Sir. Earlier he had been just a plain Mr. He had once been a child. He hadn't thought about the divine existence of oil. He had used a kerosene lamp, kindheartedly, even familiarly, and it had smoked dreamily, covering his childhood with poignant soot. Novels by Dickens, a nice home, golden, honeyed happiness! . . . The ancient Persians slept peacefully on the pages of high-school textbooks, and little John still didn't dream of his priestly destination.

Now Sir John was filled with religious ardor. He knew whom people worshipped. Seven years ago in Lisbon, the bishops of the Roman-Catholic One Apostolic and Militant Church, the successors of the selfless and the martyred, celebrated absolutely magnificent masses. They begged the Almighty to raise the stocks of Anglo-Persian. Incense, of course, smells nicer than petroleum, but incense is merely fragrant resin. The bishops of the city of Lisbon had to repeat the ancient prayers of the dirty Persian priests.

"And remember Venezuela. . . ."

Mr. Teagle tried to scare his foe. He forgot that this wasn't an ordinary businessman who dealt in oil as others deal in soap or apples. This was Cromwell and Napoleon. Sir Henry Deterding might be afraid of dampness and silence. But he wasn't afraid of Americans.

2

Mr. Teagle wasn't above boasting from time to time.

"I myself was a worker in the fields. When I finished college (I was just taking my last exams), I suddenly got a wire from my Dad: 'Come immediately.' I thought something had happened at home. I packed fast. Hopped an express. I walked into Dad's office, and he pointed to a worker's blouse: "Put it on and get to work! . . ." Well, I didn't argue. I made twenty cents an hour, like a simple worker. But I did learn my business right on the spot. . . ."

How Henry Deterding must have smirked at this edifying picture! Mr. Teagle's biography was straight out of a Protestant primer. The prudent papa guarding his first-born against the seven deadly sins, all spawned, as we know, by indolence. Oil had gotten a hereditary aristocracy! Mr. Teagle's father was the owner of the Schofield-Shemmer and Teagle oilfields, and his maternal grandfather was the first partner of the great Rockefeller.

Henry Deterding never went to college and no one had bothered with his education. He had left the tiny Netherlands for Java, in quest of fortune. A modest clerk in a Batavian bank, he received sixty florins a month—less than young Teagle on the paternal oilfields and the paternal feedbag. The clerk, however, did not lose heart. He believed in Fortune—he only *seemed* modest.

When he was thirty, he encountered Fortune. It didn't happen in an old castle, and Fortune was nothing like the traditional Dame. The name was quite prosaic: Mynheer Kessler. Mynheer Kessler was the director of the young but solid enterprise Royal Dutch. The modest clerk caught his attention. Bank ledgers, the scratching of quills, a cheap tie. . . . Mynheer Kessler was not just capable of finding oil deposits. With a historic sigh, he said: "That young Dutchman has a great future ahead of him." The clerk stopped being a clerk. He busied himself with oil. Five years later he replaced Mynheer Kessler: He became director of Royal Dutch. Within a year, he united Royal Dutch with Shell. He penetrated Mexico and Rumania, Venezuela and Canada. In the small Batavian bank, the accounts of the customers were still kept according to the entries of the ex-clerk. But perspicacious stock-market speculators were talking about a new oil-king.

All his life, Napoleon yearned for his big green patch on the map. Upon becoming head of Royal Dutch, Deterding mounted an offensive into Russia. In 1903, he was the first to get to the Caucasus. Right before the war, he exported hundreds of thousands of tons from Russia.

On a nasty day, that was damp and windy, the bass guns of the *Aurora* gloomily boomed: "Enough!" No one in Russia thought about Henry Deterding. People were thinking about peace on earth and four ounces of rationed bread. Deterding read a radiogram: "To all, to all, to all. . . . Today workers, soldiers, and peasants. . . . The rest is illegible." He was shrewd and grasped the meaning of the diffident dots. That day his pipe must have gone out frequently. Deterding nervously kept striking matches.

Now his pipe was smoking. Good-naturedly, he looked at Mr. Teagle. Mr. Teagle was smiling carefully.

"Ten years ago Russia meant revolution. Now it means— oil. . . ."

For Mr. Teagle, Russia was a country with huge, though ill-equipped, oilfields. For Sir Henry, it was an enigmatic patch and his own biography, twenty-five years of struggle, an illegible radiogram, Krassin's metallic eyes, Georgians, machine guns, Standard Oil, the courteous, slightly sarcastic Rakovsky, Genoa. The Hague, negotiations, ruptures, concessions, ultimatums, and after all that, silence, huge and incomprehensible, like the patch on the map.

The Americans were selling oil. But who else needed oil if not the Americans? They were selling now. Within ten years, they would have to buy. Russia had 150,000,000 souls. Now the peasants were demanding kerosene for lamps. Tomorrow they would be demanding gasoline for tractors. Sir Henry extracted oil where there were no people whatsoever. It was sensible, hence, moral.

"But what about the excess? . . . What about Venezuela? . . . What about the independents? . . ."

The unknown shadow was still freezing at the castle gates. The shadow had a magnificent Waterman fountain pen. It had excellent recommendations and a thick notebook. It wasn't a shadow, you see, it was a special correspondent to the *Times*. It was so anxious to speak with the three gentlemen! But the gates of the castle were locked tight.

The world has to be organized. Chaos is criminal. Chaos is whitish fog and the presence of that obligatory supernumerary. But the world should not be organized by politicians, soldiers, or diplomats. He, Henry Deterding, had been given a high mission. He would give sense to human life, hence morality. If you don't work, you don't eat. Yes, he was also a Socialist, but his Socialism wasn't a childish pipedream, it was a real thing, it was an oil empire.

The dream that cruelly haunted Tamburlaine, Caesar, Napoleon was still alive. It gave Deterding hot, sleepless nights. The poor Corsican believed in the bravery of adolescents. Woodrow Wilson, amid the voluptuous anxieties of a belated newlywed, grandly dictated the draft for the covenant of the League of Nations. Sir Henry kept sending gratified glances at the lacquered globe. He had the right to turn it a bit: Mexico, Curaçao, Glasgow, Rumania, Gibraltar, Albania, Port-Said, Suez, Ceylon, Batavia; there it was, truly, "the Empire on which the sun never sets!"

Yes, but what about the green patch that crawled over two continents? . . . The world has to be organized. He had tried everything. He forgot all about the radiogram and the pipe that kept going out every minute. He couldn't very well yield the green patch to the Americans, could he? In the year 1922, he bought 200,000 tons of Soviet petroleum. He said: "No decent person ought to buy Soviet petroleum. This oil is stolen." Meanwhile, he conversed amiably with Krassin, and Krassin's eyes shone cunningly, and Sir Henry purchased stolen oil. At the same time, he bought up the shares of the former owners of the oilfields. These shares cost next to nothing after the angry bass booming of the *Aurora*, and it was easier to come to terms with these stockholders than with the real owners of the petroleum. Deterding bought oil and sold oil. He bought the voided shares, and all the newspapers in the world carried the announcement: "Careful, don't buy stolen oil!" Thus spoke the ex-owners of the ex-shares. Thus spoke the president of the new company of former but legal owners, Sir Henry Deterding. He told interviewers: "The Russian petroleum belongs to its former owners, hence it belongs to me." He said to the Soviet sellers: "You can sell *me* this petroleum, but exclusively to *me*, and at an appropriate discount. . . ." He did everything he could, for the world has to be organized.

3

Some are named pounds sterling, others dollars, still others, poetically, as though they were tulip fields, are called florins. They are all equally tiresome. Deterding didn't even have time to get a new watchband. He smoked bad tobacco. He did love sports, however. The society section in the petroleum newspaper ran a photo: "Sir Henry and Lady Deterding ice-skating in Saint-Moritz." The Royal Dutch stockholders could delight in the strength of their sixty-year-old protector. Sir Henry even gave a speech in Amsterdam on the benefits of physical culture. But do you really need millions for skating? In the winter, the canals in Delft and Dodrecht freeze up, and little Dutch boys, who don't even know what stocks are, merrily cut across the ice, which is as blue as delftware.

What did Deterding need money for? Prometheus' country was as warm as could be. He dreamt about fire, not a stove. There was another ruler, the ex-bulwark of Anglo-Persia, Sir Basil Zaharoff. His fortune was estimated at millions of English pounds. He was eighty years old and all alone. John D. Rockefeller accumulated money for years. Then he began giving it away, with all the diligence of a Quaker and a householder. He distributed almost all of it. It was sad, like the verses of *Ecclesiastes*. It was exact, like the swaying of waves. Sir Henry, however, did not labor for money. He wanted to organize the world.

He believed in the immortality of the spirit. He also dealt in oil. He just couldn't give the green patch up to the Americans. When Standard Oil wanted to strike a bargain with the Soviets, Deterding wired pious Rockefeller, who was already scraping at the door to Paradise. What? . . . Rockefeller wanted to give money to those notorious atheists, who persecuted the Christian church? . . . Deterding himself didn't fear hell. He was ready to pay money even to those miscreants and recidivists. He only asked for one thing: To pay cheap.

He threatened the Russians and he led them into temptation. The green patch remained an enigma. Now Sir Henry lost patience. He had thick, bristly eyebrows. He had an ardent heart. The brows thickened. The pipe gloomily puffed and panted. Sir Henry Deterding declared war on the green enigma.

Krassin once said to Deterding: "The past doesn't count. We have to start all over again." His eyes shone cunningly. Sir Henry admired their brightness. He himself hated the old. The old was the whitish fog at the loch. The old is death. More than once he had destroyed everything around him. He betrayed everything, except the cheap tobacco. The stocks of the ex-owners were not dogma for him. They were simply a good ploy. He was all set to start all over again. Let them burn the scarecrow of capitalism on Red Square. As long as they remembered that the oil belonged to him, Henry Deterding, and not because there were heaps of worthless papers in his safe, no, but because he alone was capable of creating an oil empire and hence giving mankind an orderly morality.

On the ghostly North Sea, a gigantic dreadnought smokes gloomily. It rules five continents. Palm trees grow for it, diamonds glitter in the earth for it, groves of rubber trees bleed for it, Rabindranath Tagore writes poetry praising the wisdom of India for it. This dreadnought is known as Great Britain. Its guns were ready to salute the scratched monocle. Of course, Henry Wilhelm August was a foreigner. But the freedom-loving British only peruse the passports of penniless immigrants. On the captain's bridge, next to Basil Zaharoff's Greek profile, one could see Deterding's Dutch pipe.

Sir Henry declared war on one sixth of the world. Sir Henry had a wonderful army. A few years earlier, a London court had tried a case involving his subordinate company Astra-Romana.

They were cross-examining the former head of Great Britain's counter-espionage service, Mr. MacDogon:

"You received four thousand pounds a year. Yet you are in no way a specialist in petroleum. Can you explain to us the exact nature of your duties?"

Mr. MacDogon sighed sarcastically.

"Excuse me, but my functions would be extremely difficult to define."

Sir Henry spoke of Lloyd George as "my friend." That didn't prevent him from being on good terms with Chamberlain. He disdained petty politics, after all—elections, changes of cabinet, highfalutin words and highfalutin wigs. He declared war against an unruly power. The Dreadnought was marvelously equipped. Its smoke was black and ominous.

On a lovely day in May, police brigades surrounded an unassuming house on Moorgate Street. The cipher-clerk of the Soviet trade delegation, a man named Khudyakov, looked into the sportly fist of a police officer. Khudyakov may well have wanted to ask the unbidden guest for the renowned "warrant," but his English was poor, and besides, the sportsman had a club. Khudyakov wordlessly fell to the floor. The policeman returned to his superior with a tiding of victory.

Sir Henry said: "He who acts, wins."

Two weeks later, Chamberlain signed a warlike note. Sir Henry was going to take the green power by starving it out. He already saw a grand coalition. Only, not a word about oil! Talk about the blood of the people shot down, the desecration of the Church, freedom of speech, talk in verses if you like, talk and talk, eloquently and sincerely! The commander-in-chief remained invisible. His name was ineffable, like the name of YAVEH. In some unknown room, he was smoking the cheap tobacco of the common man.

Napoleon headed east to create a single oil empire.

4

A spacious office. Green cloth. The cloying smell of tobacco and honey. The president of North Caucasian Oil Fields was speaking with confidence and emphasis. This was the divisional general being informed about the plan of attack.

"The most essential event of this past year was the removal of the Russian embassy. It is to be hoped that France will follow the example of Great Britain. Sir Henry Deterding will exert all possible pressure on the French government. . . ."

The gentlemen heaved sighs of relief: "Ah, if Sir Henry! . . ." Enraptured, they whispered to one another:

"He said that by the end of a year the Kremlin's power will collapse. . . ."

"He" of course was Sir Henry. Sir Henry was quick-tempered and imprudent. He liked to pontificate. He would brook no contradiction. Any flag whatsoever could flutter on the Caucasus, but the Caucasian oil must belong to him.

The secretary ordered a stateroom: Sir Henry was going to Paris.

Paris was laughing, drinking aperitifs, reading about the races in Deauville and the new Citroën cars. It wasn't waiting for Deterding at all. Sentimental couples kissed under the plane trees. Enthusiasts demanded freedom for Sacco and Vanzetti. In popular dance-halls, accordions were playing devil-may-care Javas. Deputies were fishing and angling for votes. Paris as always smelled of face-powder and gasoline. It didn't know that gas is petroleum, that the cabin had already been ordered, that the blue smoke over Gare St. Lazare was Sir Henry's road to a burning Moscow.

Georges Clemenceau was finishing his rather vainglorious life with aphorisms about the vanity of all glory. He wrote about Demosthenes. Furthermore, he liked observing his Scottish Terrier. The dog didn't care for dry bread, but the instant Clemenceau strewed crumbs for sparrows, the dog would gobble them down. Clemenceau noted: "So human, n'est-ce pas?"

Naïve people called Clemenceau a cynic. Sir Henry Deterding smiled. After all, Clemenceau fed on ministerial crises and normal human melancholy. He believed in the charms of Mata-Hari, the roll of drums, the mystique of blood, and oratorical perfection, He could still recognize iron or coal. But what about oil? . . . During the Conference of Versailles he was warned: The English are trying to trick us. They want to get their hands on all the petroleum. Jokers claim that Clemenceau the Terrible replied with a scornful grin: "Well, we've still got electricity!"

A year later, another Frenchman, Monsieur Millerand, proudly declared: "The Mossul petroleum is ours and we demand a free hand." This time, Sir Henry smirked: They would have a free hand. Free and empty. After that, quite a number of French soldiers remained in Syria. They shot Arabs. The bullets were English.

But as for oil, the French didn't have a drop. On the other hand, some people purchased Royal Dutch shares. When the price of oil went up, the securities went up. This was bad for industry, it meant recession and unemployment, yet classical happiness for hundreds of investors.

The French had no oil but lots of cars. They bought Royal Dutch or Standard Oil petroleum. Tankers sailed across the Black Sea. Still, Sir Henry waged war with the green patch. Sir Henry Deterding knew very well what human life is made of. He knew what high politics are. He also knew what foul-smelling oil is.

Diplomats are enigmatic and interesting people, not unlike mediums or Chicago mobsters. Monsieur Cambon, the quondam French ambassador in Berlin, graciously indulged the curiosity of the uninitiated. He put out a book entitled: *The Diplomat*. He explained in detail how a model diplomat is to smile, and how people are to smile at him.

The uninitiated are legion. Besides Monsieur Cambon's book, they read ordinary Parisian newspapers: *Le Matin* or *Echo de Paris*. These newspapers wrote about a certain diplomat: "Gangster . . . butcher . . . killer . . . spy. . . ."

Monsieur Cambon is one of the Immortals of the Academy. Could he really have invented all the smiles he describes? . . . Besides, the "gangster" wasn't simply a diplomat, he was the ambassador of an obstinate power, which didn't want to give Sir Henry any oilfields. Although Monsieur Cambon, apart from belonging to the Academy, was the head of the French branch of Standard Oil, he must have forgotten all about petroleum while chatting about diplomatic etiquette.

In Paris you talked with real diplomats in accordance with Monsieur Cambon's manual. Here, for instance, was the next guest, Monsieur Bratianu, the prime minister of Rumania. Needless to say, he smiled and the French smiled at him: After all, Monsieur Bratianu was no Rakovsky.

There were three brothers, and all of them were Bratianus. They loved English stocks, Rumanian oil, railroad dividends, and French loans. They even loved the more-than-modest lei. It's hard to say what the life of this enterprising family would have been in another country. But the Rumanians like high art, and the Brothers Bratianu ruled the Rumanians gloriously.

The head Bratianu sighed to the Paris reporters:

"Rakovsky? . . . I regret only one thing. That I didn't hang him in time. . . ."

Paris, all blue and langorous, sipped orange-drinks. Sir Henry, for Paris, was one of the rich strangers that toss away thousands of francs merely to see Napoleon's tomb or the Venus de Milo. Apparently, some of these simpletons actually weep in front of the armless statue! Did Monsieur Deterding also weep? . . . Who can define the whiteness of marble and the sensitivity of the human heart?

Paris did not think about oil. Only one dreamer, sitting on a café terrace under huge stars, amid the odor of gilly-flowers and limousines, was whispering:

"Just look at what it says here! . . . The nominal capital of Royal Dutch is six hundred million florins. Add Shell. That's five hundred million florins. Add Batavia. Three hundred million. Add. . . ."

His friend sighed. At the figures? At the word "florins"? What a pretty word!

Paris did not think about oil. For a minute, it was troubled by the intrigues of the Eastern barbarians. In a small tavern on Boulevard Saint-Marcel, which bears the long but wise name *Tout Va Bien*, the owner of a gravestone workshop and the youngest accountant of the Banque de Paris were drinking Picon-Curaçao. On the table, next to the greasy pack of cards, lay the evening paper, hot off the press.

"Did you read about New York? . . . Biggest heat-wave ever. Three people have already died of sunstroke."

"Well, it's still better than a cold wave. Do you remember the summer of 1917? It was eleven degrees below freezing, Centigrade. That's a far cry from New York. Every day somebody fell down dead on the street."

The gravestone man sighed, though he was on the best of terms with death.

"And what do you say to our suckers? Windbags! The English are a lot smarter. Imagine keeping a German spy at your side! He can steal all the plans."

"Of course! Then he tortured thousands of decent people. He cracked the safes himself. He nationalized women for his own use."

"If we had a real and strong government, they would have packed him off to Siberia long ago."

"Siberia's harmless now. . . . Oof! It's hot! . . ."

"Yeah, just like New York. . . . C'mon, *mon ami*, let's play a round of cards. . . . What luck! Nothing but trumps. . . ."

In the stillest part of Paris, where titled old ladies live, and priests, and footmen, and also envoys of the great powers, where instead of cafés there are churches and policemen—in this old-age home, which the discourteous sansculottes ventilated only once, there stands a venerable mansion. It is quiet and proper like all its neighbors; the gates are locked tight; the courtyard is strewn with red sand. Inside this venerable mansion, in a spacious office, amid old Gobelins enframing the beard of Karl Marx, amid official folders and cigars that seem vaguely like stage-props, sat a lone man. He was leafing through the same newspaper read by the philosophers on Boulevard Saint-Marcel. "Thug . . . sadist . . . cheater. . . ." He grinned. Then he became hard and dark again, sinking into the shadow of the office, the grayness of houses and days.

His face, clean-shaven, slightly puffy, enlivened by the hint of a smirk, was the face of an indulgent priest or a desperate actor. In his eyes, the naïve enthusiasm of the Bulgarian *chetnik* was frequently replaced by the despondence of a man who knows a lot, who has roamed the world over, who has seen both Sir Henry and the nineteenth-century Ukraine.

Yes, the ambassador of the green patch, Christian Rakovsky, had seen Sir Henry. Fate had brought them together. Not on a romantic barricade of the previous century, but in the sumptuous salon of the Hotel Claridge. They were surrounded not by rebels or gendarmes but by attentive footmen, and they spoke not about the world revolution but about oil.

Henry Deterding was the son of a small nation and he was the son of rather modest parents. He might well have remained a commonplace clerk. Rakovsky's life-story appealed to him and surprised him. This Bulgarian from Rumania might have also remained a teacher somewhere in Varna. He became the envoy of a world power. Why had he tied his life to some idiotic revolution? . . . Sir Henry didn't despise the revolution, he just sneered at it. Organize, gentlemen, do not destroy! Couldn't that same Rakovsky have become the viceroy of Oil-Rumania? Instead, the green patch and a smirk. After a faultless luncheon in the Claridge, Sir Henry felt a slight bitterness.

In the gray silence of his office, Rakovsky read the evening tabloid. He could see Deterding's eyebrows, those thick, bristly eyebrows. Rakovsky had known English tanks and he had known hunger. He knew what war is.

Night gathered in the office. At the gates, the policemen dozed drearily. The district of devout spies and hereditary gout listened to the peal of bells, a peal from heaven, a peal as sweet as the bleating of celestial lambs.

A car braked at the tall building on Kuznyetsky. The car was proper and so was its passenger. Monsieur Herberte smiled in accordance with Monsieur Cambon's book. He was a true diplomat. He spoke about his instructions from Paris. He spoke about the dignity of the *République* and public opinion. He spoke loftily and delicately. It was like poems by Victor Hugo. Monsieur Herberte did not speak about oil.

Sir Henry Deterding could go back to London. Inside the venerable mansion, they were already deciphering a telegram: Concessions indispensable.

Reporters crowded at the locked gates. They spoke about one thing only: When was he leaving? . . . The policemen held their tongue. They knew nothing. They weren't even people, they were blue shadows in blue Paris. They only had kepis and numbers. The reporters anxiously cackled: "Quand? Quand?" The windowpanes of the venerable mansion glittered melancholy. Sir Henry had won another battle.

In the spacious office, there were open suitcases, files turned inside out, and the gold of the fireplace, in which written notes were glowing. It was like a battlefield, and a few letters on the floor were still groaning. Amid the gala disorder—still the same lone, weary man. If his eyes were still burning, that came from sleepless nights. He was long since accustomed to other people's treachery, the comfort of exile, when a man carries with him only the dubious warmth of hasty handshakes, a few names, a change of linen, and his own sad irreconcilability.

His grandfather was a *chetnik,* a rebel, and the word "prison" in the Rakovsky family sounded roughly like the word "summer cottage" in other families. His mother was solemnly excommunicated from the Church. Little Christian was offered paradise on the crooked side of the saber. Once he dropped into a church, and it occurred to him that he might seduce the peasants from the pulpit with the sublime commandments of the Gospel of Communism.

Whenever he was asked what he was, Bulgarian or Rumanian, he replied, tongue in cheek: "I'm not Homer. Two countries are fighting for the honor of not counting me as their native son."

He studied medicine at Geneva. He also studied with the Russian emigrés, Axelrod, Plekhanov. He mastered the hard science of efficient revolution. Then he exchanged his Geneva professors for Berlin professors and Axelrod for Liebknecht. However, he was quickly expelled from Germany. His doctorate was granted him by the Faculty at Montpelier. He was in Bulgaria again, and in Rumania. In the revolutionary circles of ten countries, in those kindhearted and ascetic monasteries of the turn of the century, one could more and more frequently hear the name Rakovsky. Internationalism was no abstract dogma for him. He changed countries easily, and he quoted Marx in any dialect. There he was in Saint Petersburg. But northern romanticism was of brief duration. Rakovsky was expelled from Russia. There was still France, "the cradle of the revolution," "the land of freedom," the bashful but ardent love of all those rebels of diverse tribes, still vacillating at the threshold of a new and incomprehensible century. Here was the languor that the French call the "douceur de la vie"; the limpidity of the sky, the roundness of the hills, the clarity of words and feelings surrounded Rakovsky for an hour or a year. He was a physician in the tiny hamlet of Beaulieu-sur-Seine. Before him, the Loire flowed quietly. Long, long ago, Joachim du Bellay had said that the Loire is far lovelier than the turbulent Tiber. At the cornerstone ceremony for a new bridge, Rakovsky gave a brilliant speech. He spoke about the nobility of revolution and all the virtues of the republic. He was ready to become a Frenchman, perhaps a deputy. He was ready to love the revolution of 1793 and the simple human happiness of 1903. But the paradise of Beaulieu-sur-Seine was not the paradise on the crooked side of the saber. His request for naturalization flew into the fireplace; the bridge would be finished after the nice doctor's departure and the local Gambettas were rid of a dangerous rival.

Rumania was full of agitation. So Rakovsky went to Rumania. There he instantly became a leader. Peasants and workers said: "Our doctor!" He was arrested. Expelled? But of course! However, the police were troubled by one circumstance. No matter how you turned it, Rakovsky was a Rumanian subject. Then the resourceful ministers declared him a foreigner. There were demonstrations on the streets of Bucharest. Policemen pushed back the crowd. One lad was especially vociferous. They took him to the police station. "Name?"—"Panaït Istrati." Not yet thinking about the splendor of French literature, the adolescent sullenly bristled: "The devils! They're expelling our doctor! . . ."

Rakovsky was expelled. Rakovsky returned. He was expelled again. This game went on for some time. Constantinople. The Young Turks didn't lose any time. Arrest, all the picturesqueness of Turkish prisons, and then a vulgar expulsion. In Switzerland, Rakovsky met Lenin. Rakovsky's grandfather and father believed in Russia. That was sentimentality, and also self-defense. Now Christian Rakovsky's face, the face of an orthodox Marxist, turned to the East. He loved Balzac's novels, he loved the cafés of the Latin Quarter, he loved French *pathos* and French *frivolité*. But he only believed in the Russian revolution.

He was back in Rumania. War. He was back in Rumania, hence back in jail. This time he would most likely be shot. Then the long-awaited Russian revolution came to the rescue. The word didn't reach the Rumanian front that quickly. But a man with some literacy read a gazette from the capital, and all his countrymen from Perm or Pensa smiled. They cursed Captain Petrov for the rotten cabbage; they yelled: "Time to go home!" In their joy, they opened the gates of the Rumanian prison. One of them merrily shouted to Rakovsky: "C'mon out, Comrade!"

Then? Then ten years of work, as hot, dark, and asthmatic as seething lava: Makhno, the CHEKA, the Denikin army, jerkins, famine, armored cars, victories, the New Economic Policy, diplomatic tuxes, factional arguments, crisis upon crisis, nightly meetings, hoarseness, palpitations, then—then no more biography of Christian Rakovsky, but the history of the great revolution, about which his grandson would give eloquent speeches at the cornerstone ceremony for a new bridge across the Khoper or the Sukhona.

The portmanteaux were tied up. The ashes in the fireplace were cold. Everything appeared to be ready. . . . The reporters told one another:

"His secretary ordered two tickets on the North Express."

"That means tomorrow? . . ."

"Yes, tomorrow at three. . . ."

They left. Only the policemen remained at the venerable mansion. The whole quarter of splendid tartuffes was asleep.

With a smirk, Rakovsky counted: The eighth time . . . the eighth or the ninth? . . .

The Gobelins might bristle in vexation, but Marx smirked. Marx, it seemed, was satisfied. Instead of diplomatic etiquette, he finally saw the classical smirk of a rebel.

Early morning. In the courtyard, a car was discreetly huffing and puffing. Along came Istrati. He wanted to leave with Rakovsky. He had no interest in negotiations about debts, the Baku oilfields, or Deterding's anger. But now this commonplace automobile contained the soul of the revolution. Istrati loved fame like Turkish delight. But Istrati was a hobo and he asked:

"Me too! . . ."

The curtains in the car were drawn. Thus the policemen couldn't tell who had driven out of the embassy so early in the morning.

The autumn sky was pure and lofty. It was the sky of France. It was the sky of the paradise lost which hadn't come true in Beaulieu-sur-Loire. What color was the sky above the true paradise, the one that little Christian had been given on the crooked side of the saber? Or didn't that paradise exist? The engine purred. The needle bent towards 60, 70, 80. The car raced toward the German border. The reporters would waste their time searching the North Express. The man they wrote so much about had whisked away as suddenly as the wind.

All at once, the car halted:

"We need gas!"

The yellow little house proudly sported: *Shell*. It was Sir Henry escorting Rakovsky.

5

The Chamber of Deputies. The lackey with the massive chain around his neck solemnly proclaimed:

"Monsieur le Président."

Monsieur Buisson entered the chamber. He was a Socialist and a noble person. Freedom of conscience was far more comprehensible to him than fuel. Slightly bewildered, the swallow-tailed dickey peered into the room. The Empire easychairs stood torpid. The deputies were as noisy as schoolboys, and Monsieur Buisson good-naturedly banged his ruler. A dull lesson! They'd be talking about oil today. . . .

A number of seats were empty. Elections were in the offing, and the smartest deputies were at their posts—IN THE FAR-FLUNG DEPTHS OF PROVINCES. There they bombastically shook hands with veterinarians and notaries, paid compliments to tavern-keepers and attorneys, promised one man a job in a tobacco store, one man a pension, one man universal equality, and one man the after-life. There, pounding a table in a smoke-filled tavern, they swore to uphold the interests of industrialists, the independently wealthy, the workers, the interests of all and sundry, build a new bridge, lay a marvelous highway, lower rents, outwit the Americans, and save fifty-eight-year-old Marianne yet another time.

The deputies listened with only half an ear. Who could be interested in oil anyway? . . . Some wrote letters to constituents: Durand wanted to place his nephew in Algiers, and Dupont was outraged at his competitors' intrigues. They all had to be answered. Other deputies in sheer boredom were carving their initials in their seats. Even the bench on which the government sat was mottled with monograms like a schooldesk. Whispers. Laughter. The rustle of newsprint. From time to time, the banging of the presidential ruler: Quiet!

"Cracking is no good with oil that contains sulphur. . . ."

Yawns. The rumble of voices. The swishing of paper. The president's bell. The chamber livened up when one of the speakers said:

"Instead of the 'cherchez la femme' of old vaudeville ditties, we now can say 'cherchez le pétrole.' "

Another deputy instantly retorted:

"Don't compare oil to a woman! A woman is a goddess!"

Mirth, and a remark from a misanthrope:

"Not only that, but she doesn't catch fire. . . ."

The issue of the inflammability of beauties was far more comprehensible and far more pleasant than the unknown "cracking."

The speeches went on and on. Now the Socialist Charles Baron had the floor. He was a Southerner, he had a gray mane and a classical roar. Naturally he was full of bombast. He loved to say:

"My grandfather was in the Convention, and my grandfather told Marat. . . ."

He considered the Declaration of the Rights of Man sacrosanct. He spoke about oil as eloquently as his grandfather had spoken about the precepts of Jean-Jacques.

However, the Chamber of 1928 was not the Convention and Citoyen Baron had savoir-faire:

"Sir Henry Deterding has gone further; he even attempted to exert influence on the French government. I must express my admiration for our government and Monsieur Poincaré. . . ."

Monsieur Poincaré was dry and adamant. Monsieur Poincaré quickly interrupted the inspired Southerner:

"No one has attempted to exert influence on me."

The pens of the stenographers scratched. The lackeys with chains congealed. A light silvery dust settled on the face of Clio, the darkest of all the muses.

The oil-import law was passed. The minutes contained an alphabetical list of the deputies who voted "Aye" or "Nay," abstained or were on leave. Next came the words: "The following deputies could not take part in the vote: Messrs. Cachin, Doriot, Duclos, Marty, Vaillant-Couturier." That was expressed pleasantly, abstractly, and yet quite accurately. The above-mentioned deputies could not take part in the vote because they happened to be in La Santé prison.

6

Henry Deterding had won the battle. But he hadn't wiped the green patch off the map. In Baku, they continued pumping up oil, and despite its destination, despite morality, this oil did not flow into the Royal Dutch or Shell tanks. Deterding prepared for a new offensive. At the same time he negotiated. He proposed a peaceful settlement. What was there to do? The more he won, the more he lost. He had looked for oil everywhere. It turned out that there was too much oil. Prices started plummeting. Car-owners were overjoyed. Sir Henry frowned: Morality was in danger! Those Eastern fumblers were selling oil for a lot less than the world price. In Venezuela, new deposits were being unearthed daily. The "independents" were practically giving it away. Sir Henry nervously glanced at the stock market report. The white pages are like the shadow at the loch.

Then his old enemy pounced upon him. Standard Oil dropped the price in India by twenty dollars a ton. That was a stab in the back. Royal Dutch dividends shrank. Deterding negotiated for a loan in America. He wanted eighty million dollars. But Standard Oil wasn't asleep, and the American bankers procrastinated.

His dream was a single empire, but humanity wasn't ripe for that. Oh well, so let there be three empires. That was better than chaos. Sir Henry was obstinate, but he knew when to give in. He invited his ally Anglo-Persian and his foe Standard Oil to a conference. They were going to carve up the world.

The guests drove up to the ancient castle of Achnacarry: Sir John Cadman and Mr. Teagle. The moon stood over the castle. Next to the castle lay the loch. The three gentlemen had long talks with one another. The gates were locked tight. The secretaries and stenographers were dispatched to a villa eight miles from the castle. This was no place for spies.

They were quite different from one another, these three oil emperors. Sir John Cadman was a scholar. He had peacefully lectured on political economy. Then all at once, just as Newton had lit upon the law of gravitation, Cadman understood the law of ruling the world. From then on, he knew only one word: oil. He taught the government of Great Britain how to fight America. A modest professor at the University of Birmingham, he became head of Anglo-Persian and Sir John. Here he was a calculator. Mr. Teagle was a force, a hereditary force, the great power of Rockefeller. And Deterding? Deterding was merely a will, a will that had to conquer everyone.

Carefully smoking his Havana, Mr. Teagle said:

"Fine, we'll cut up the markets; we'll crush the independents. But what about Russia? . . ."

Sir Henry smirked:

"We can easily come to terms with them."

He would take the green patch. He would take it with concessions, friendliness, no matter what! He would not give it to that careful gentleman.

The shadow froze and froze at the gates of the castle. Finally the gates opened. The special correspondent from the *Times* was magnanimously received by Mr. Teagle.

"Can you tell us the reason for your coming to Achnacarry Castle?"

The journalist held his breath. He was about to get the most sensational interview. He, an unknown reporter, would become editor-in-chief tomorrow.

Carefully smiling, Mr. Teagle said:

"I and Sir John Cadman were the guests of Sir Henry and Lady Deterding."

"But the purpose? Excuse me, Mr. Teagle, what was your purpose. . . ."

"Fine, I'll tell you. Our main purpose was to go fishing and hunt grouse. There are many grouse all around the castle, and we were delighted to indulge in this rare sport."

"But . . . but . . ."

The journalist was tongue-tied. He was dispirited. The grouse started growing. They became mythological griffins. The journalist was pale. He dropped his wonderful fountain pen. Mr. Teagle, still carefully smiling, said:

"However, I won't hide the fact that in free moments we did speak about oil. We determined that there is too much oil available and that the extraction of oil ought to be restricted for the sake of the consumers themselves. Do you understand me? For the sake of the consumers themselves."

Half an hour later the journalist was on the phone:

"Hello? Are you there? Yes, yes. First: grouse. Ordinary grouse. Birds. Then—it's simple. . . . Don't you understand? . . . Why, they've carved up the world. Wait, do you understand me? It's for the sake of the consumers themselves. . . ."

On the steps of all stock exchanges, London and Paris, New York and Amsterdam: a storm. Boaters and derbies flew by. Canes loomed like croziers. The howling of thousands of throats fused into a single rumble from a colossal megaphone:

"Royal Dutch: yesterday—36,000; today—41,000."

Sir Henry calmly looked askance at the stock report. The time would come when the three empires would merge into one!

War is an illusion, war is a need, war is for poets, war is the time of the stench of cheap tobacco, when the eyebrows beetle, and the heart throbs: Attack! War is the dream of an oil empire. Gone were the basses of the *Aurora,* the machinations of the Americans, Rakovsky's smirk. Chamberlain's pen scratching, the French talking about national honor, the Dutch quoting from Scripture, and Sir Henry issuing new orders every hour.

Now the peace had been signed. The green patch had given in. The Americans had given in. And Sir Henry had given in. But what had the basses of the *Aurora* boomed? Why was Sir Henry forming an ominous coalition? Peace is boring and ancient; it's older than war. Peace was sixty florins a month and the frayed sleeves of the young clerk. Even the strong tobacco tasted insipid. It was a weekday for Sir Henry.

Foolish people thought this weekday was a holiday. Everyone congratulated Deterding. He had won. He had haggled out a reduction of five percent from the Soviets. He said this money would go to the ex-owners; he, Sir Henry, was protecting the rights of impoverished emigrés. Could that really be a victory? He had given in, but by giving in he had won. He had won the green patch. These lunatics would never knock down prices again. The independents were wiped out. The lacquered globe turned obediently. Sir Henry gazed lovingly at the familiar patch. That blue unicorn—that was the Caspian Sea. The oil was flowing. . . . However, they had to be reminded: The tanks must be kept in good working order. So that the oil wouldn't evaporate. . . . It was *his* oil! . . . Five percent. . . . Needless to say, a victory! Sir Henry had an oil empire. Sir Henry had a son as successor to the throne. Along with everything else, Sir Henry believed in immortality.

Deterding was back in his homeland, Holland. Actually, his homeland was much vaster. The Dutch poet Van Eeden said: "The merchant's homeland is the entire earth." Deterding must have liked that verse. He was at home everywhere: In London and Batavia, in the Hague and in Baku. But it goes without saying: He loved his tiny Holland. Here everyone was proud of him, just as peasants are proud of a local boy who becomes a brigadier or a notary. And thus the poet Doornebos wrote an epic poem about Deterding. He called Sir Henry, "The stony pillar of the Netherlands." Sir Henry requited love with love. He sent poor students to the colonies to seek their fortune. He donated priceless paintings to museums. He owned a delightful villa in the Hague. He had another house in the Hague, visible from far away, all red and haughty. The administration of the empire. The façade, instead of heraldic lions or griffins, had one solemn word: "Batavia." Every year, no matter where he was, Sir Henry hurried to the Hague on a specific day for the ball in honor of his Queen. He was an English lord. He could of course become president of Venezuela or shah of Persia. But he hated titles. He was merely a loyal subject of Wilhelmina, by the grace of God Queen of the Netherlands.

Could it all have been a joke? Sir Henry did enjoy joking. Could everyone here, from Queen Wilhelmina to the newsboy delivering the *Telegraph*, merely have been a loyal subject of Henry Wilhelm August Deterding?

Quiet Delft had a celebration today. The *Polytechnicum* was awarding Sir Henry an honorary doctorate. Now Sir Henry wasn't Sir John Cadman. He hadn't dried out his mind with science. But he *was* the "stony pillar of the Netherlands," and that same poet Doornebos swore that Sir Henry was a confidant of Minerva. The professors blinked enthusiastically. They were such great admirers of that goddess. The rector wore the traditional mortarboard and chain. The rector spoke flowingly:

"The pride of the Netherlands. . . . The entire world venerates him. . . . And we are honored to. . . ."

The huge auditorium was jammed. The loyal subjects, up in the gallery, held their breath. Prince Henryk was moved. Prince Henryk wasn't a king, he was just the husband of a queen; and he wasn't the oil emperor, he had a modest civilian list. Prince Henryk fully understood who was in front of him. His hands were folded devoutly. The new doctor, meanwhile, listened to the speeches with a slight smile. Yes, yes, of course, Minerva! . . .

The quiet streets, along the obligatory canals, were crowded with pitiful mortals, who hadn't been admitted to the celebration. They cheered Sir Henry. They cheered Dr. Deterding. They cheered the emperor of oil.

And then? . . . Then the people dispersed. From the narrow canals, night came creeping. Here the news reports end. They are supplemented by the author's imagination. Dr. Deterding now conversed with the night. The conversation was awkward, laborious, dark. It was a lot easier talking to Mr. Teagle or even Rakovsky. The night wouldn't give in, but the doctor was obstinate and quick-tempered.

Just where had he seen that street? . . . Ah, yes. In an old painting. He had bought the painting in London, at an auction. He had donated it to an Amsterdam museum. Let it hang there. Streets shouldn't talk. The night should hold its tongue. The rector of the *Polytechnicum* had ended his welcoming speech long since. Behind white curtains the Dutch were drinking coffee and reading, some the

Bible, others the stock reports. They read: "Royal Dutch—the ten commandments—honor—work in the sweat—Shell—in God's image—dividends—shalt not covet—gasoline prices have gone up again—for the sake of consumers themselves—put your soul. . . ."

Thus spoke the newspapers and Scriptures. Thus spoke Dr. Deterding. The night, however, the tiresome, intractable night, spoke otherwise. You couldn't even outshout it. After all, it conversed in silence. The doctor hurried along the obligatory canals, along the narrow, almost invisible, the merely conjectured streets.

Delft is not multilingual Rotterdam. Delft is filled with Dutchmen and Dutchwomen, modest and loyal subjects of Queen Wilhelmina. Where did these shadows come from? . . .

"Sir, we are your subjects."

"Of the Netherlands?"

"No, of oil."

"We are destroyed. We got rich. We no longer exist. We died. In trenches. We're Mexican. We were for Obregon. And we—we were against him, We were for you. For oil. We're from Albania. We slaughtered the others. And we're from the Riff. There's oil there too. From Mossul. Clemenceau didn't understand. You did. You, Sir. We're French soldiers. We're Georgians. We shouted: 'Sakartvela!' We didn't realize it meant oil. They shot us. At dawn. We're Poles. We're Venezuelans. We're brokers. We're generals. We're children. . . ."

"Stop. Get to the point! What do you want? Stocks? Higher prices? Peace?"

"Sir, we're dead."

"So you want death?"

"Dr. Deterding, you've forgotten. What about immortality? . . ."

"Now I understand. You want immortality?"

"Your Majesty, take pity. We don't want immortality. We don't want anything. We don't exist."

Sir Henry peered around. Still the same night, a streetlamp and a shadow. Just one shadow.

"You there. . . . Excuse me, are you from Venezuela too?"

The shadow was silent. Then Sir Henry remembered: the castle, the loch, the moon. Mr. Teagle was waiting for him in the smoking parlor. And the shadow had hurried along the paths.

"You, sir, are—death."

The shadow was silent. The shadow had an amazing resemblance to Sir Henry, to Henry Wilhelm August.

The canals were filled with dark water, miry water. Perhaps it wasn't water, but oil. Oil everywhere. Extraction of oil had to be curtailed immediately, urgently. Stop up the wells. Announce that there's no more oil. Anywhere. Otherwise it will always keep on like that. Today—Venezuela. Tomorrow—Colombia or the Urals. The prices plunge. The empire collapses. Why had he lived? What would he reply to the Judge? What would he reply to these shadows from all the Venezuelas?

But wait! Oil is the energy of the world. Everyone needs oil. For the sake of the consumers. Steamers, cars, planes. Whirl! Faster! Why were they sitting behind the curtains? They were compelled to hurry! House, fly up! Bridge, cast off! And throw away the Bible! I'll read it for you. Later. Some time. After death. I order you: Dash! 100, 200, 300 miles an hour! . . .

What if they get tired? If they beg: "Why so fast? Why? Where to? To death? . . . After all, it's easier for a man to stop than for oil. Oil flows. They'll sell it for pennies. They'll use Royal Dutch stock certificates to light fireplaces. There's so much oil! That was oil in the canals. Or else, not oil. Blood. It was all the same! There was too much blood. And everyone would get tired. Like him. He was tired, so tired. He reeled. The shadow reeled too.

"Sir, I'll stop with you."

"Sir Henry, you're mistaken. I've come for the others. I've come for the Albanians. Fill your pipe and remember: The empire is waiting. I haven't come for you. After all, you, Sir Henry, are immortal."

Chapter Six

The Stock Exchange

"Citroën—1841. . . ."

It was the Acropolis and St. Peter's Cathedral. Here they honor the one God, with the ineffable name, and here they worship three thousand saints. Their names, ringing and enigmatic, fill the high vaults; they overflow into the square, spread through the narrow streets of Paris; they inundate banking offices, with their ripples of bookkeeping, sorrow of clerks, and cigar-butts on glass counters; they ooze everywhere: newspaper offices, ministerial cabinets, boudoirs of kept women, where powder and pearls are strewn on the carpet; airily they soar up the Eiffel Tower to turn into waves of divine ether, which envelops a farm in Normandy and the deck of an ocean liner and a Citroën automobile in the sands of the Sahara. Grand names, a sweat as spicy and heavy as musk, viscous blood, stuffy dreams, memory, salutary despair: Royal Dutch, Rio Tinto, Thomson Houston, Canadian Pacific, Malopolska, Santa Fe. No, these are not copper, not oil, not the coarse flesh of the universe. Those are the names of saints, the fluctuations of numbers and waves, the devout shudder of mankind.

Somewhere far away, anonymous people die cheerlessly without even realizing that here, in this temple with its indispensable columns, every day from twelve noon to two PM, the faithful ardently pray for them.

Rumania. Black earth. No tree, no blade of grass. Only oil derricks, blazing heat, stench. Sir Henry's loyal subjects were toiling among pipes and tanks. They were sullen, dirty, and permeated with the smell of oil.

Here, however, there was only a tender name:

"Astra-Romana! Selling eighty at 376!"

In Penang, as usual, the rubber trees were bleeding. The milky juice smelled as it went sour. Mr. Davis tossed and turned on damp sheets, felled by an attack of fever. The coolies whirled and dropped like mosquitoes.

"Buying Malacca at 311!"

In Capetown, blacks were hunting for diamonds. Johannesburg—295. In the port of Salonika, they were loading leaves of tender tobacco: 1,117. In Indo-China: phosphate: 310. Sentimental Anglo-Saxons dashed off to Europe with their better halves: Sleeping-cars—674. Swedish matches—2,895. Is there anyone who doesn't need matches? . . . Doctors prescribed mineral waters for their liver patients: Vichy—2,645. Liver patients guzzled liqueurs on the sly: Cusenier—2,850. In Galicia, the pickaxes of miners banged away: Dombrova—1,948. A pair of radiant newlyweds walked into a hotel. Six huge bellboys dragged the long trunks which were pasted over with stickers as gaudy as a globe. Hotel Continental—665. In Geneva, they condemned gas warfare, but there were still fertilizers, there was still human nature. Nitrate—323. Tourists strode into a Montparnasse café to see how the great artists live. The tourists drank beer, of course, and looked around for not-too-expensive girls. Rontonde—189.

The worshipers in the grand temple saw no oil, no girls, no zinc. They didn't even see the pretty green certificates, on which all kinds of things were printed: rubber trees, derricks, naked Negroes, smokestacks, wheat-fields. The certificates lay in the darkness of fireproof safes. The people here merely handed one another numbers, sounds, airiest ether.

Their ears were keen: they listened to what the earth said. The moment a fire broke out in Transylvania or a new Mexican general emerged, the columns of figures began to tremble. At the Norwegian elections, the Conservatives were wiped out! New silver deposits were discovered. The figures shook. The voice shook: "Buying, buying, buying! . . ."

Rubber exports from the English colonies dropped in May from 49,800 tons to 43,960, and Ford reopened his factories. Padang stocks went up.

The revolution in China was abating. Imports were possible. . . . A barrier en route: Captain, you'll have to shell out 800 pounds! . . . This current year—6,084 ships. Suez took a leap upwards: 1,264. Buying!

New York registered a surplus of sugar. 145,000 tons too much. Sugar stockholders dolefully sighed: Point-à-pitre took a tumble— 2,685.

A new means of reproduction was invented: Neogravure. It was for the good of humanity, to be sure. But *Publication périodique* stocks plunged: 635.

Elections were due in South Africa within two weeks. General Smuts? . . . Or General Herzog? . . . Their chances were equal. Goldfield and Brakpan goldmine stocks kept rising and falling. General Smuts? . . . General Herzog? . . .

But now everything was forgotten: the victorious Rio Tinto copper, the sugar disease, and the South African generals; even that scandal about Colomb-Oil was forgotten: it had had neither oil, nor money, nor people to get even with and arrest. Now everything was forgotten. Now there was only the name of Citroën under the vaults:

"Citroën—1,840!"

"1,845! Buying!"

"1,860!"

As always, at the Clichy, Levallois, and Javel factories, the iron belt was screeching. Pierre Chardain was installing shackle-plates. The typists were clattering. The buyers were fidgeting in the garage. Monsieur André Citroën was preparing a report about customs restrictions: The automobile industry was being strangled! . . . The Toledo press was stamping metal and oil. There, it was Tuesday, a weekday, a workday.

But here, there was howling, enthusiasm, despair, catastrophe: Citroën! Buy Citroën! Only Citroën! Faster! You can see—1,865! It's unbelievable! Recoup! Get rich! Save yourselves! Faster! 1,880!

In cramped phone-booths, sweaty brokers, were yelping:

"Hello! Citroën. 60, 65, 70, 65, 70, 80."

There, amid cigar-butts on the counter and the ripples of ledgers, the director of a tiny bank wouldn't let go of the phone receiver. He was silent. He was listening: 65, 70. . . . Then he mopped his forehead with his sleeve and screeched:

111

"It's a syndicate. . . . Michot, hello! Buy! Up to 90. . . ."

The gamblers crowded at the counter. Powder peeled from the women's faces: It was hot. The men stuck their cigar-butts into inkwells. They hastily scrawled down orders. Hands trembled and letters leaped—the seven sacred letters: CITROËN.

A young, young clerk darted up and away. He had stomach cramps, you see, but he dashed into the café next door. There he did not drink coffee. He called up his uncle, a retired janitor of the Lycée Michelet:

"You can buy ten shares of Citroën. They're totally safe. I saw Collot's orders. That means there's no risk. . . . But you have to act fast! . . ."

Newsboys scurried about with gray smeary papers.The papers of course had lots of pages and lots of news. In Grenoble, for instance, a teenager had stabbed an old woman. The king of Spain had conversed very coolly with Primo de Rivera. Experts were resting. In Slovakia, gypsies were being tried for cannibalism. But all these things flashed by. Real life began further on: The stock exchange registered a sharp increase in Citroën. Informed circles maintained that this bullish flurry was linked to the attempt of a huge American trust to concentrate all the Citroën shares in its hands. Headline: AMERICAN DANGER. Subhead: General Motors marches on Europe. Notice: Rumor has it Citroën is negotiating with General Motors. A telegram from Moscow via Riga: This time it wasn't a famine or an uprising in Georgia. Citroën was organizing an expedition to Turkestan, Citroën was preparing to come to terms with the Soviets. Industry section: with a view toward widening its exports, Citroën would soon increase production to 1,000 cars a day. Sports page: Supposedly, Citroën would soon be putting out a new model with all the features of the earlier ones, but at an even lower price. Stock market news: 1,960. 1,975.

The belt screeched. The presses thundered. In Javel and in Levallois. . . .

Chelone, the broker, went skipping down narrow Rue Vivienne. He didn't see anything. He was full of lofty self-oblivion. He had a ginger moustache and the eyes of a Bacchante. He knocked down some old lady. He didn't even have time to say: "Pardon me!" Like a bird he fluttered up the steps of the temple. He screamed. He screamed the ancient "Evoë!":

"85! Buying! . . ."

In the tiny street flanking the Stock Exchange you'll find a plain-looking but noteworthy restaurant named The Golden Duck. Here the stockjobbers have their brunch. They laud the pheasant pâté and Mexican Eagle, they have a bite of Shell with mayonnaise, they wash down the fall of the electrical syndicate with Pommard '21. From to time, panting brokers rush into the restaurant. The brunchers look at their notebooks and—their mouths full—they murmur: "Go as far as 425. . . ." The brokers hurry away. They, too, hope to make something on this *Brakpan*. The time will come when they too will brunch here, issuing momentous instructions between sips of brut champagne: Stop, buy, no higher than 70.

The porter of course knows all the patrons. He doesn't mind playing the market a bit himself. Handing Monsieur Leblois his topcoat, he respectfully but knowledgeably asks:

"What do you think, Monsieur Leblois, is copper going to rise?"

Monsieur Leblois, coppery-red with turkey and Pommard, briskly cackles:

"Like dough, mon ami! No doubt about it. . . ."

The porter knows who drinks plain bordeaux and who drinks Lafitte '78, who speculates in small potatoes and who forms large syndicates. Monsieur Aubert invariably tips him one franc. You couldn't have a ball on that, but Monsieur Aubert pulls the really big deals. It was he who recently caused the *Kali* stock to sink. He spread a rumor that new potash deposits had been found in Persia and near the Dead Sea, and thus he depressed the quotes by eight points. The porter sacredly believes in Monsieur Aubert's power and he sends rapturous glances at the small table in the corner: Monsieur Aubert sucks on his asparagus and gazes indifferently into the distance. It's hard to tell whether he's cheerful or sad, or what he's speculating on, a slump or a boom, or what he's preoccupied with, copper or coal.

At all the tables, all they're talking about is Citroën. After hearing the brokers pant, the patrons stain the tablecloths with wine as dark as oxblood. That man there, for instance, sold eighty shares of Citroën two hours ago. Can he just calmly munch on his artichoke leaves? . . . Only Monsieur Aubert is unruffled. He doesn't care about Citroën. Might he be busy thinking about Salonika? . . . Who knows! Melancholy, he sucks his asparagus. Now a young man with a notebook approaches his table. He shows something to Monsieur Aubert. He, not missing a bite, mumbles:

"Fine. Keep on."

The porter, puffing away a speck of dust from the bowler, whispers:

"What do you think about Citroën, Monsieur Aubert?"

Monsieur Aubert shrugs:

"I *don't* think about it. Have them bring my car!"

Monsieur Aubert sits down in his car. It's not a Citroën. No, Monsieur Aubert has earned enough on both copper and potash to afford a Buick. He drives along, indolently swaying. He doesn't peer out the window at the other cars. He doesn't read the stock report.

Calmly he presses a buzzer. The copper plate on the door says: *Editorial Office of the Financier of the Republic*. Monsieur Aubert nods hello. The editor whispers in a stammer:

"Well, what is it? What? . . ."

The editor is wearing a sweater. His moustache jumps comically. He looks like a brood-hen. First of all, Monsieur Aubert takes a cigarette, taps it against his cigarette-case, lights it. Then he sits down on a worn oil-cloth chair, and, lazily drawling, he says:

"Okay. Latest rate: 80. And now, get to work. The best thing would be to take a bite of the consortiums. . . ."

Wiping an old pen on his sweater, the editor painstakingly traces out big letters full of sumptuous flourishes: "We have been informed about Citroën's negotiations with General Motors and even with the Opel and Fiat works. A rise in prices is thus fully justified and we can only recommend to our. . . ."

The old pen scratches. The editor breathes loudly: He's obviously all worked up.

2

Monsieur Aubert read Marcel Proust. He lived among Siamese cats, Van Gogh landscapes, and ancient globes, all alone, with his foppish and unclean manservant Louis. No one would have guessed that this was the home of a stockjobber. Annual reports, price bulletins, newspaper clippings were jumbled with Surrealist poetry, snapshots of Marseilles dives, and silvery cigar-ashes.

Monsieur Aubert hadn't always dealt with phosphate and copper. Once he had been a writer, and even a Socialist. He had wanted to follow in Émile Zola's footsteps and fight for justice. He had despised luxury and Anatole France's *The Red Lily*, the life-story of

Monsieur Millerand, and the jackalish howling at the Stock Exchange. He was young and uncompromising. He lived in a tiny room on Rue Monge and rode the trolley second-class.

Years passed. Paul Aubert's novel *The Tale of a Foundling*, published with the savings of his old aunt, sold a total of fourteen copies. No one wrote a single line about it. The book wasn't even bad. But in Paris, dozens of new novels come out every day, and critics have only two hands and one stomach. Aubert was offended: not just by the critics but also by humanity.

He wrote provocative articles for a left-wing paper. He called for a revolution: only a revolution could air out Europe! . . . But instead of a revolution, the municipal elections came along, and the Socialist Party noisily celebrated a victory: In Blois, it had received sixty-eight votes. Monsieur Aubert fell into a deep depression. But then he met Lucienne. Lucienne was an ordinary blue-eyed typist. After delicately ascertaining her new beau's income, she had supper with him just once in a cheap tavern, played a little at being hard to get, sighed a little—she did have blue eyes after all—and then imperturbably married an insurance agent. Paul told a friend of his, a medical student, that he had an old blind dog and that he needed strychnine for it.

He could have died. The Golden Duck would never have gotten to know this so solid patron! . . . He didn't die. Perhaps the weather was too good, the sun too triumphant, on that September morning. Perhaps our misanthrope feared stomach cramps. He walked the streets all day long, then he went to sleep, and waking up in the morning, he somewhat wearily stretched. There was nothing you could do. You had to live. Justice was rubbish, there would be no revolution. Lucienne, yes, and all the others, they could be gotten easily. All you had to have was money. So, friend Paul, we'll make ourselves some money! . . .

In his heart of hearts, however, Aubert didn't get rid of his weakness for literature. He became a minor contributor to one of the stock-market gazettes. But, while inditing an apotheosis of a fishy bank, Hutkins & Co., or even glorifying the stocks of a fantasy, Guatemala Mines, he often repeated Chamfort's favorite saying: "In each man's life there comes the moment when his heart must either burst or turn to stone." He hid the phial in the closet; hence, he had to palm off those certificates for nonexistent mines on naïve hicks. The choice was made!

Two years went by. The journalist Paul Aubert became Monsieur Aubert, a regular at The Golden Duck, a frequent guest at the best homes in Paris. Oil stocks came to his rescue. He gambled on a boom and he won. His pale, melancholy face was transformed into a barometer, and every day hundreds of people tried to guess whether his spirits were high or low. . . .

Once, he ran into Lucienne. He suggested a drive through the Bois de Boulogne. Lucienne stole a glance at the Buick and smiled abashedly: Her husband only dreamt about a small Citroën. Aubert could have had her. He didn't. Was it embarrassment or a revival of feeling, or merely laziness? . . . Courteously he helped her out of the car and, noticing consternation in her blue eyes, he smiled:

"You see, Lucienne, I'm very busy now. I don't write novels any more; I'm in a much cruder business: I play the stock market. In other words, my heart has turned to stone. . . ."

Monsieur Aubert didn't select Citroën by chance. He considered everything: the animation on the car market, the natural growth of the certificates, the rumors about negotiations with America, the agreement with Poland, and, last but not least, the imminent annual meeting. The preliminary work had already been done for him by Monsieur Citroën. All that was left was to close the deal. The stocks were at 1,560. It would be easy to hike them to 2,200. A skillful sale wouldn't cost him more than 100 apiece. In this way, he could earn 500 on each. The operation required liquid funds. One and a half million. So we'll form a small syndicate. Monsieur Poulaille, Monsieur Cressillon, editor of the *Financier of the Republic*, and finally he, Aubert. 500,000 for the press. After buying the first round, Monsieur Poulaille got a loan on the stocks. Get the quote up to 2,000. Don't overdo it. Each partner was guaranteed 600-700 thousand clear.

The syndicate was launched in a *chambre séparée* of the Normandie restaurant and consecrated with something truly worthy of the event: Mouton-Rothschild 1893.

One morning, much to his surprise, Monsieur André Citroën read in all the well-informed newspapers that he had beaten out his competitors and that the future belonged to him. He was astounded but not offended. After all, he knew the difference between a joke and an ordinary stock syndicate. On the whole, he didn't have anything against an upswing. If only these unknown benefactors knew when to quit! . . . If they went too far, there might be a sharp drop, and Monsieur Citroën's credit would be tellingly impugned. The important thing was to have sense enough to walk away from the green cloth in time! Monsieur Citroën sighed. He fully realized that there was no leaving. "Buying! . . ." Monsieur Citroën picked up the receiver:

"How much?"

He was fascinated by the way they gambled. Now he wasn't chairman of the board of directors, no, he was just a player. His heart hammered. An unintelligible noise came from the receiver, like a roaring from a seashell: it was the roar of time. Finally: 75! Monsieur Citroën smirked: Those people were lucky! . . . Another nine. . . .

Paris has three thousand newspapers and magazines devoted to the stock market: *The Economic Survey, Pro and Con, The Small Financier, Money, The Stock Exchange Courier, Tendency, Little Quotations, French Bank, The Frenchman's Portfolio, The Financial Voice, Capital, The Stock Market and the Republic, Argus, A Propos, Up and Down.*

The syndicate formed by Monsieur Aubert allocated only 500,000 for the press. Ah well, they would have to restrict themselves to a chosen few. The campaign began with the syndicate stockholder *The Financier of the Republic.* It was immediately supported by thirty-six newspapers. The rest kept silent. They kept silent because all men are optimists, especially the editors of stock-market periodicals. They hope to earn on their courteous silence.

Hello! Hello! Mr. Sloan, president of General Motors, arrived in Paris. Mr. Sloan's trip was intimately linked to the future of the Citroën works.

Incidentally, General Motors was a lot stronger and busier than Ford. General Motors had put out 1,842,443 cars in 1928, which added up to forty-two percent of the total American production.

The Citroën works underwent another radical renovation. They were ready for increased production. The coming season promised to be especially brilliant. The curve of orders rose sharply. Fifty-two percent of all Parisian cars were Citroëns. In Madrid, the taxis were Citroëns. In Japan, a Citroën branch was opened.

The financial side of the André Citroën enterprise was fully deserving of trust. Citroën, as we all know, was backed by the powerful Lazard Frères bank.

The preceding year had brought dividends of 24.85. This year an increase in both the turnover and the dividends could be expected.

The newspapers wrote significantly and poetically. They cited national interests and the triumph of efficiency.

The uncle of the brash clerk, the ex-janitor, couldn't resist. He had a tiny pension. There wasn't enough money for a glass of rum or a pinch of minty snuff. He decided to earn a little extra. Everybody was making a fortune on those stocks. Was he worse than others? He bought ten shares of Citroën. He no longer slept at night. Standing by the lamp, he reread the stock bulletin for the hundredth time. Citroën was growing, but the old man was confused by the puzzling words: "Generally there is a wait-and-see tendency, due to a postponement in any decision by experts, and due to the coming elections in England." The old man heaved a loud and mournful sigh: Good Lord! What did England have to do with it! Why, the Citroën works weren't in London. They were right here, on Quai de Javel. . . . What would happen tomorrow with those experts? Only one hundred more per share, and then he could sell. Without stocks, you can have peace of mind! . . .

Mr. Aubert was as unruffled as ever. He read Paul Valéry before going to sleep. Then he drank a glass of Vichy, wound his watch, and sank into a dense, fervent sleep. He dreamt about brokers, paperweights, Lucienne's low-cut dress, and gaudy, clamorous parrots. All these visions were fleeting and disconnected. Night came. He didn't dream anymore. But then, unexpectedly, a huge, abusive sun emerged. It was copper. It shone like a frying-pan. Monsieur Aubert couldn't open his eyes. It was really very simple. He had forgotten to switch off the lamp! . . . Now he could sleep in peace. But the last dream had made him grimace. The sun had been copper. . . . Today, at the stock exchange, no one had wanted to hear anything about Citroën. They were all mad for *Anaconda* or *Dodge*. Damn that copper sun! It had risen at the wrong time. . . .

In New York, copper prices rose sharply. Yesterday: eighteen cents! Copper stocks went up. Through wires, amid bucolic swallows, amid sluggish, drowsy, gigantic fish, in the sky, under water, the delirious numbers zoomed along: Nevada—46. And instantly, the Paris brokers launched into a heartrending wail:

"Rio Tinto—6,700! Buying!"

"6,800!"

Try as he might, Monsieur Aubert couldn't fall asleep. He could hear the buzzing of the wires and the scraping of chalk. It was copper. It was rising loudly. Citroën was squeezed down. Citroën was shunted aside. That wasn't Monsieur Aubert's fault. He had done everything in his power. He couldn't foresee the copper sun. What if the whole deal collapsed? Monsieur Aubert drank some Vichy and lumbered about in his bed.

He could of course start selling tomorrow. The stocks would sink down to 720-780. He'd be left with a narrow profit. No! Impossible! . . . Better to lose it all! . . .

Many years had elapsed since the day when the disillusioned Monsieur Aubert had decided to exchange the glory of Émile Zola for an account-current in one of the curb market banks. He had made millions and he had squandered them. He had convinced himself that money could buy anything: Lucienne, a Buick, Surrealist verse, respectful bows, friendly embraces, anything except, possibly, happiness. It was simple, like an old melodrama. There was no such thing as happiness. There was only: gambling. Nothing else could make that stone heart pound faster. Monsieur Aubert had speculated in Citroën. He had to win. Copper was a blow, but not death. The syndicate could easily wait a few days. The fever would abate. Monsieur Aubert would gain his objective. Gain it without fail. Without fail. . . .

Monsieur Aubert fell asleep.

In the morning, Louis, with a deferential and brazen smile, scented and with black fingernails, brought a few letters and the newspapers. Monsieur Aubert instantly flung open the paper. Here was the most important thing: copper. Hmm! In London—76 pounds a ton. Disgusting! . . . Rain, bad weather. . . . Absentmindedly, he leafed through the gazette. What was wrong with those experts? . . . Suddenly, he sat up straight. His usual calm vanished. Monsieur Aubert's fingers ripped maliciously through the soft newsprint. He read: "The growth of the Citroën stocks is obviously of a speculative nature, and we feel obliged to warn prospective buyers. . . ." Louis stood there with the bathrobe ready. Monsieur Aubert screamed:

"My suit! And snappy! . . ."

He was filled with despair, rage, energy. An unknown enemy confronted him. That was better than the copper! . . . The matter was clear: Someone was selling short. The whole thing could end in an ordinary catastrophe.

Coffee? The hell with it! The car! Faster! . . . There was only one thing to do: Wipe the other guy out or die.

Paul Valéry's poems tumbled to the floor.

3

The Paris stock exchange is grand and beautiful! Without it, no locomotives would churn up smoke in the Argentine prairies, no gas would burn in the workingman's kitchen, no diamonds would sparkle on the flesh of the wives of usurers, there would be no Rumanian liberals, no trolleys in Lisbon, no cars, no progress, no culture.

The clerk Jean René, as it happened, never thought about the grandeur of the world about him. Obediently he entered titles of certificates, names of clients, and figures in huge ledgers. Some of these names got rich, others got poor. They had cars, children, guns, servants, tears. For Jean René, they were only names. He thought about his wife who had pleurisy and for whom the doctor had prescribed a nourishing diet. The doctor had merely spoken those two words as if Jean René weren't a modest clerk at Raymond Barré & Co. but one of those grand names, as if he were Monsieur Cressillon, opposite whose name was written: "3,000 Citroën, at the current rate." Where would René get that "nourishing diet"? The clerk's hand trembled? He had nearly smudged Monsieur Mattieux's eighth order: 425 Rio Tinto.

Yesterday, on the Paris Stock Exchange, 2,980,008 securities were traded for the total sum of 1,621,864,425 francs. One billion six hundred million. Jean René received 750 francs a month, 25 francs a day. The owners of the Raymond Barré & Co. banking house had earned over four million during the previous year. The bank was part of many syndicates. It had brought about the decline in Norwegian nitrogen, thereby making a million in two weeks. Monsieur Raymond Barré had bought a villa near Nice. He had rheumatism, and he liked hot weather. Monsieur Barré did not raise the clerk's salary. Who could tell what tomorrow had in store? . . . Suppose some financial operation ruined him? He had to be thrifty! The villa in Nice was capital, and the salaries paid to employees were a loss of money. Besides, some banks paid only 600 a month. He wasn't running a charity. . . .

Some of René's co-workers lived in clover. They had cars, went to the Moulin Rouge, and bought expensive ties. They got the same 750 francs a month. But they didn't dully copy out names and figures like René. No indeed. They pondered why that Monsieur Barré was selling Norwegian nitrogen, why Monsieur Cressillon had given instructions to buy Citroën. They knew the influence and importance of each client. Inconspicuously scraping their rusty pens, they entered the sanctuary. They began playing the market. They made deals with small speculators, they sold tips for a few hundred francs. Casually, they thrust their monthly pay into their vest pockets. Cigarette-money! But René was honest and stupid. He only knew his duty: to wipe his pen on a rag, tilt his head, and painstakingly copy out the name of the person, then the name of the stock, then the figure, and all these things in a lovely chiseled hand, without mistakes. Whenever anyone spoke to him about a tip, he shrugged in bewilderment. He wasn't a speculator, after all, he was just an ordinary clerk.

This is how it happened: First, the doctor spoke about a nourishing diet. Then Louise stopped eating, she even refused chicken broth. She was running a high fever. The doctor came and phlegmatically waved his stethoscope. He prescribed medicine. The fever went down, and Louise went back to work. She sewed hats in a shop on Rue Pépinière. But she kept coughing and complained that she had no strength left. At night, she shivered feverishly. René sent her back to the doctor. Louise came home with a long prescription and eyes red with weeping. The doctor had told her she had tuberculosis and she absolutely had to go to a sanatorium in the south.

Jean René murmured to one of the small clients:

"I know about a sure thing. *Lisbon* has to go up. Buy some shares and give me one quarter of your profit. I've never done anything like this before, but my wife's very sick. . . ."

René didn't know very much about stock-market mentality, even though he had been employed at Raymond Barré & Co. for eleven years. His advice to the client was rash. Monsieur Coledeau had indeed ordered a large number of Lisbon shares, and it went without saying that Monsieur Coledeau was an important client. But René failed to understand the cunning ploy. Monsieur Coledeau was in a consortium that speculated on a drop in *Lisbon*. The purchase was just a decoy. Within a few days, Lisbon started plunging headlong. The client made a terrible scene. He banged the knob of his cane on the glass counter. He screamed at René: "You dirty thief!" Monsieur Barré took René aside:

"You are damaging the reputation of our bank. If this ever happens again, I shall have no choice but to dismiss you instantly."

A few weeks went by. It was time for ice-packs and oxygen. Louise died early one morning. She lay with an open mouth, like a fish. She had suffocated. She had no air. Air was somewhere far away, perhaps in Nice. . . .

Now, in the venerable banking firm of Raymond Barré & Co., there occurred the incredible incident which all the clerks in the quarter talked about for a long, long time. Jean René, as always, sat there tilting his head and writing. But before him, he could see Louise's open mouth. He got everything mixed up: Monsieur Cressillon had ordered a purchase of Citroën. René made the entry in the "sell" column. Even worse, he stuck Monsieur Cressillon's order in his pocket together with his handkerchief. He prevented Monsieur Cressillon from buying 3,200 shares. He possibly delayed the growth of the securities by one day. Unwittingly, he had interfered in the life of the sanctuary.

Monsieur Cressillon shouted:

"That clerk's been bribed. He must have gotten a few francs. . . . I would never have dreamt, Monsieur Barré, that your bank could employ spies from different syndicates! . . . I've lost 11,000. It's a good thing I noticed in time."

Monsieur Cressillon told Monsieur Aubert about the unpleasant incident. But Monsieur Aubert didn't even smile.

"What's wrong, Monsieur Aubert? What are you so worried about? . . . I think this copper fever will taper off—if not today, then tomorrow. And what about that clerk! . . . Ha ha! How do you like the whole story? . . ."

"I don't like stock-market jokes. As for the copper, you're certainly right. But there are a few complications: Just look at what's written here. . . . That's either Fochard or the Banque Delonnais. . . ."

They conversed in The Golden Duck. Monsieur Aubert was no longer secretive. He even advised the porter to buy Citroën. He reinforced it with his own authority.

A broker came up. Monsieur Aubert checked through the figures. Wiping his lips, he said to the waiter:

"You may have a duck in your sign, but you don't know beans about preparing duck à la Rouennaise. Take it away! . . ."

Then he calmly said to Monsieur Cressillon:

"The campaign has begun. Citroën has gone down sixty. . . ."

At that moment, Jean René was humbly walking behind the hearse. He didn't weep. But from time to time he drearily blew his nose. A small wreath of beads lay on the coffin. At home, a double bed was left. That was all. Naturally, René had been fired from the Raymond Barré & Co. bank. Louise was dead. He would come home alone. Without the coffin. What would happen now? . . . The thoughts in René's head were tangled like unkempt hair. This was no life, it was a living death. Should he resign himself? . . . Church. . . . Confession. . . . Heaven. . . . Meeting Louise. . . . Or join the Communist Party and yell on the streets, in a hoarse, bitter voice: "Enemies, enemies, enemies!"? . . . Or else: Take a gun and break into Monsieur Cressillon's apartment at night? There were securities there, diamonds, money. . . . Then—just eat and sleep. Sleep a lot so as not to remember anything. So as not to remember Louise. Forget altogether. . . . Altogether. . . .

The watchman, lazily yawning, opened the gates of the cemetery.

"Right, left, and then left again. Row sixteen. . . ."

René blew his nose. He was burying his wife, after all. However, no one was interested. He wasn't even a clerk. He was now outside of the stock market and outside of life. The best thing would be to die. There was still lots of room on row sixteen.

4

Monsieur Aubert didn't find our immediately who his enemies were. The Banque Delonnais was mixed up in the affair, but it was Monsieur Sandou who had formed the syndicate, even though people were saying that Monsieur Sandou wasn't even in Paris, he had gone on a holiday in Biarritz about two weeks ago. Monsieur Sandou was working secretly. He spent the whole day on the telephone. He had paid the press more than Monsieur Aubert, and the newspapers that had been courteously silent began talking.

"The financial backing of the André Citroën Company is not reliable. One must bear in mind the recent difficulties besetting Monsieur Citroën. It is dangerous investing capital in an enterprise so frequently subject to the whims of one individual."

"Specialists aver that in regard to durability, Citroën cars leave much to be desired, whereas the little Renaults and Peugeots withstand the most difficult ordeals."

"In connection with the animation of Citroën securities on the stock market, may we remind our readers of a gossip column concerning the casino at Deauville. A Parisian manufacturer by the name of A. . . . C. . . . once lost twelve million there in the course of a single night."

"It is rumored that Ford has reached an agreement with the Peugeot works."

"We have been informed that Ford has begun construction of his factory in France. He plans to lower the price of his automobiles while raising the salaries of his workers. This is, without question, an extremely interesting experiment."

"The French automotive industry is now faced with the ominous question of market saturation and overproduction. The difficulties afflicting one of the largest factories in Paris would seem to indicate that a crisis is imminent."

Monsieur Sandou glanced through the newspapers carelessly and indifferently. He knew how much he had paid each one and what each one would write. He himself didn't believe in Ford or in a crisis. He had started the game after being dealt good cards. His main trump was Monsieur Fillot's illness. Monsieur Fillot had cancer of the liver. A committee of doctors had given him about two more weeks. Besides cancer of the liver, Monsieur Fillot had 90,000 Citroën shares and a blockhead of a son, who could hardly wait for his father to die so that he could invest the inheritance in a racing stable. He knew nothing about securities and cared for only one thing: racing. After Monsieur Fillot's death, his son would immediately dump all the securities. First of all, he would sell the Citroën stocks to cover the inheritance taxes. Monsieur Sandou knew all this for certain. He didn't read Paul Valéry and he didn't think about aphorisms by Chamfort. He only concentrated on his business. He had henchmen everywhere. Soon 90,000 shares would be dumped on the market. Everything had to be prepared: the press, minor fluctuations, sales of small parcels. Then Monsieur Fillot's stocks would be the *coup de grâce*.

The campaign got off to a good start. The quote began to drop. Monsieur Aubert gave the newspapers 200,000 extra. But Monsieur Sandou disposed of much more capital. The opportune moment for the rise had been missed thanks to that ill-starred copper. Citroën fell twenty points, then recouped ten, but instead of a sharp rise Monsieur Aubert saw only minor fits and starts, up and down. Monsieur Sandou, together with the Banque Delonnais, threw a few more thousand securities on the market. Citroën dropped to eighty. Monsieur Cressillon started grumbling: That Aubert had inveigled him into an unprofitable deal! . . . He could have sent money to America at high interest! A lot safer, and a lot more lucrative. . . .

The editor of the *Democratic Stock Market* unexpectedly demanded an unheard-of sum from Monsieur Aubert: 50,000. And upon not receiving it, he switched his course and began writing about a "speculative gamble."

Monsieur Aubert tried to float a loan on his shares at one of the major banks, but the bank refused. Even here he could feel the omnipresence of Monsieur Sandou.

The syndicate's capital ran dry. The purchases stopped. The shares began to melt like sugar in hot tea. The belt screeched as much as ever. Impatient buyers crowded at the gates as much as ever. Brand-new cars honked provocatively as much as ever. Monsieur André Citroën tried to figure out how he could conquer the Eastern markets. None of his factories had burned down. But Monsieur Aubert stopped reading Marcel Proust. He even stopped brunching at The Golden Duck. He had lost his appetite and he was tormented by fierce migraines. Whenever he ran into people, he still made an effort to smile, but the brokers, looking at his malicious, tormented face, said:

"Did you see Aubert? . . . There's a bearish market coming up. . . ."

The ex-janitor suffered a night of horrible dreams, in which he already saw himself, cap in hand, at the entrance to a café, begging for alms. He sold his ten shares. At a loss of 1,360 francs. What could he do? He would go without snuff and drink rum only on Sundays!

Suddenly, the whole stock market quaked. Something had gone wrong with the experts. They didn't agree. They couldn't agree. A long crisis lay ahead. A panic broke out in New York. Another panic in Paris. Everyone dumped tens of thousands of shares on the market. Money! Just money! There was a pitiful howling around the temple:

"Selling! Selling! Selling!"

Citroën, weakened by Monsieur Sandou's campaign, had given in. Numbers flickered before Monsieur Aubert's eyes. But he couldn't count. He no longer thought of anything. He had been wrong to consider himself an experienced financier. He was just a frustrated writer with a mediocre imagination and weak nerves.

In the evening, Monsieur Aubert summoned Louis:

"You can go to the movies or the theater tonight. I don't need you anymore."

Louis respectfully thanked Monsieur Aubert. In the kitchen, however, he grinned nastily: "Things are going bad for us! . . . He lost heavily on the market, and he can't see anyone. . . . He lost because he's a moron." Now if Louis had money, he'd earn a million right away. You shouldn't read poetry, you have to use your brains! . . .

Louis didn't go to the movies or the theater, he went to a dance hall. There he danced all evening with two seamstresses, who snuggled up against his shirt enthusiastically. One of them even said:

"You smell of the latest perfumes, don't you. . . ."

Louis smiled condescendingly:

"A special blend made to my order. It's a lot more modern than Guerlain. . . ."

Louis could have gone off with one of them, the cheerful and pretty brunette. But that would have taken money: twenty francs for a bottle of bubbly so that the girl wouldn't play hard to get, thirty francs for a hotel room, taxi, tips—in short, he couldn't get away with less than a hundred francs. Louis cursed Monsieur Aubert: A creep like that had luck! What was a hundred francs to him? . . . And Louis had to deny himself the important things in life. He owned only two ties, both striped, and now dotted ties were in fashion. . . . When would he finally come into money? . . .

Despite his successes, Louis returned home in a sullen mood. Removing his shoes, he softly walked into the dining room to get a bottle of port wine from the buffet. He glanced through the crack in the door: Was Monsieur Aubert working? What he saw at first took him aback: Monsieur Aubert was lying on the carpet by the desk. Could he have been that drunk? . . .

Louis carefully walked into the study and servilely began asking Monsieur Aubert:

"Would you like me to undress you? . . . Perhaps you would like a glass of Vichy? . . ."

Monsieur Aubert didn't answer. With the same humble smile, Louis peered around the room: Where were the bottles? . . . He saw a tiny phial on the desk and an unfinished letter. Curiosity was Louis's cardinal sin. Squinting, he began to read: "No one is to blame for my death. Whatever remains after the liquidation of my obligations is to go to a cat hospital. For the information of Monsieur le Commissaire de Police, I may add that Chamfort did not foresee the third possibility: The heart can turn to stone and then it can still burst."

Louis didn't stop to ponder the meaning of those last few words. He ran into his room and put on shoes. Being unshod struck him as suspicious. Despite the note and the signature, who could tell what those dicks might think? Then he went back to the study. He stared at Monsieur Aubert with both interest and contempt: Those dribbling lips! . . . He couldn't deny himself a small pleasure. With the tip of his shoe he nonchalantly nudged Monsieur Aubert's head. He enviously eyed the dotted necktie: Damn it! Damn everything! . . . For cats! . . . The lousy bastard! . . . Sighing, he hurried off to the local police station.

5

"Experts took up their work again last night. A compromise was finally reached. Needless to say, the stock market registered this happy occurrence with a sharp rise in all quotes. . . ."

Monsieur Aubert, of course, did not live to see victory. He hadn't had the money or the nerves. Monsieur Cressillon turned out to be much happier: He managed to cover all his expenditures and make a profit. Citroën stocks went up to 120. And Monsieur Cressillon smiled as he relished his trout at The Golden Duck: They were reconciled. Hahaha! . . . But Monsieur Sandou didn't feel like laughing. The latest events had smoked him out of his alleged Biarritz like a beast from its lair. Everything was against him here: The overall trend of the market, the press, which ran the new information from Monsieur Citroën, and finally, nature itself: It turned out that instead of cancer Monsieur Fillot had a harmless tumor. The doctors, you see, had made a mistake! Those murderers! Monsieur Fillot was mending; within a month or two he could go back to work.

Citroëns were hale and hearty. Citroëns were continuing their upward swing, which had been interrupted for a while. Monsieur Citroën's factories hadn't burned down after all, the orders hadn't dwindled. Pierre Chardain, as always, was fastening shackle-plates, and Lazard Frères were still all-powerful and unshakable. What did they care about cheap witticisms by the editor of the *Democratic Stock Market*? The editor only had a rusty pen and four children, but the Lazard Frères had capital and truth.

Monsieur Sandou had lost the game. He had sold short 120,000 shares at the lowest possible price. Now he had to deliver them. He had to pay the high quote. The journalists had devoured his personal capital. His wife was waiting at home. She had on an evening dress. She was beautiful and youthful. True, her youth was not inexpensive. But all of Monsieur Sandou's friends enviously kept saying: "Just look at Madame Sandou! She never gets any older!" Madame Sandou smiled vividly: Tonight was the premiere at the Ballets Russes. Everyone was going to be there. They had a box. Everyone would look at her marvelous dress. She asked Monsieur Sandou:

"Aren't you tired, darling?"

She still flirted with her husband even though they had been married for fourteen years. Monsieur Sandou didn't answer. She looked at him, and all at once the smile vanished from her face.

"What happened? . . . The market? . . ."

Monsieur Sandou kept silent. Silently, he strode into his study and locked the door behind him. Madame Sandou stood at the door and begged:

"Tell me what happened. . . . Pierre, darling, open the door! Open it for just one minute! I'll go right away! I'm so upset! . . ."

But Monsieur Sandou was silent. She pressed her ear against the chink. She listened. It seemed to her that he was opening a closet. She fell to her knees.

"Pierre, I beg you! . . ."

Now her face lost all the cream, powder, white, lipstick. Now no one would say that Madame Sandou was youthful. Time had done its work. She was forty-three, after all. She was crying. She screamed. She stood up. . . . Oh God, what was he doing? . . .

An elderly, hideous woman in a ball gown, with powdered, excessively white arms, a face convulsed and dirty from black tears, whining like a puppy at the wide door of the lordly study.

"Citroën—1960. Buying! Buying!"

Brokers are yelling, chalk is scratching, and the pens of clerks are grinding in offices. People go broke and hit the jackpot. Those who left the game are long forgotten. There are no people here, after all. There are only names and numbers, the lofty and tender names of three thousand securities. Royal Dutch, Rio Tinto, Malakka—oil, copper, rubber; names and numbers; numbers swarm, whirl, buzz, like locusts. Numbers decide everything here.

There are no people at the stock exchange. In fact, there are no people anywhere. Citroën is stocks, it's lightbulbs on the Eiffel Tower, it's the iron belt, presses, acids, Michelin tires, Deterding gasoline, it's the dust and howling on the straight highway, the trembling of needles and dials, the heartbeat of engines, but there are no people anywhere—people are just a fabrication.

Chapter Seven

Roads

1

Cars don't have a homeland. Like oil stocks or like classic love, they can easily cross borders. Italian Fiats clamber up the cliffs of Norway. Ever-worried specialists in Renault taxis jolt around the bumpy streets of Moscow. Ford is ubiquitous, he's in Australia, he's also in Japan. American Chevrolet trucks carry Sumatran tobacco and Palestine oranges. A Spanish banker owns a German Mercedes. 10-H.P. Citroëns in display windows in Piccadilly or Berlin cause dreamy passers-by to halt.

The automobile has come to show even the slowest minds that the earth is truly round, that the heart is just a poetic relic, that a human being contains two standard gauges: one indicates miles, the other minutes.

Karl Lang was a taxi-driver. He worked for the Berlinia company. He made ten marks or, on a good day, fifteen. He drove a decent 10-H.P. car, and at the taxi-stand he chewed big, stale sandwiches.

There are lots of taxi-drivers in the world, more and more of them every day. They have replaced not only coachmen but also the ancient Eumenides. Ford, Citroën, Opel keep putting new cars on the market. Their wheeze is an unquenchable demand. Rubber trees bleed. Oil gushes from underground. Man threw away his pitchfork or his smoothing plane. He became a driver.

Karl's father had been a fisherman. He caught herring. He knew when the fish were coming. He knew when a storm was brewing. He knew the tints of the water and he knew about death. He had blue nets with small meshes and he had a big family, but he was happy.

Karl understood that the sea lay behind him. Karl looked ahead and he sat down behind the wheel.

He drove passengers and chewed sandwiches. The engine consisted of hundreds of parts. The city consisted of hundreds of streets. Karl was a part of the engine and a part of the city. He stepped on the gas. He turned the wheel. He thrust the blood-red hand-signal into the night. Right, left, and right again. Shadows whisked across the street. They were funny and pitiful like herrings. Only cars existed in the city. They dashed, they passed one another, they got sick, they squabbled with brazen horns. The meter ticked significantly. It kept count of the turns of the wheels and Karl's sandwiches.

Karl's father had thought about lots of things: the wind, the girls in the houses of Sankt-Pauli, the cantankerousness of Schultz the tavern-keeper, Kaiser Wilhelm, his own death. He was able to think a lot: after all, he was a fisherman.

Karl thought about nothing. In back, a fare. In front, a cunning web of streets and traffic-lights. If he thought about the girl he had seen last night at the dance-hall, or even his sandwich, he might smash frail ribs and shiny fenders. When he halted at an intersection of two streets, two long streets of the huge network, two lines that no one needed, he was so tired that he began to doze off. He didn't even try to think. A man's thoughts are longer than streets and there's no point even starting. A shadow will come up, mumble the name of some street equally long and useless, mumble a number, and once again traffic-lights will flicker, and door-plates and addresses, and shadows scurrying across the asphalt, and the indefatigable meter.

Karl Lang often heard the word: "Faster!" He didn't know who was hurrying him, the people or the taxi. Why were those restless shadows hurrying? And who hurried them—other shadows or merely the throbbing of the engine. Karl didn't think about it. He was just an ordinary taxi-driver, and there are so many of them, so many taxi-drivers, they all step on the gas, thrust out blood-red hand-signals and keep silent. The horns speak for them.

In the morning, a man with a portfolio sat in Karl's taxi. "Faster!'' He had overslept. His alarm clock was a quarter of an hour slow. He had dreamt about bowling and about his dead uncle's lilac-colored suspenders. Now the director would say with a cough: "Again?" He had come late last week too. His cufflink had rolled under the dresser. And the director was such a stickler for tidiness! . . . He jumped into the taxi. Two marks. It would wreck his whole budget. That would mean no movies for two weeks. No matter! Just faster! . . . Driving past a clocktower, he trembled convulsively. Or perhaps it wasn't him, perhaps it was the motor. Karl knew only one thing: Kochstrasse 32a.

Then he took another fare to another street and another office. Then someone pushed a suitcase into the car. The passenger shouted: Potsdam Station! Faster! . . . : He kept snatching his watch from his pocket. The hand was, naturally, turning. And the passenger was all huddled up even though it was a hot day. He was huddled up, but his forehead was sweaty. The train was leaving in twelve minutes. It wasn't his fault. He had been talking to Weinberg about extending the note, and Weinberg wouldn't do it. If he missed the train, that milksop Wolf would change his mind. He would buy the cement in town, from Harmann. That would be the end of him. Weinberg wouldn't wait any longer. There'd be a subpoena and poverty. Magdeburg was his last chance. The train was leaving in five minutes. A line of cars blocked the road. They were all in a rush. None would back up. The passenger clutched warm coins. He was afraid to see the clock on the station which stared, bitter and inflamed, like Weinberg's eyes. Now he vanished in the crowd. Karl hadn't seen him. Karl's hand clutched coins.

Then a fat, heat-prostrated man cried: "To the stock exchange!" The fat man had his share of worries. He had just found out about Hoover's speech today. He didn't give a damn about war debts. But now his securities had dropped ten points. He had to sell them before it was too late. The telephone was useless; the operator had apathetically answered: "All lines are busy." How could a telephone operator understand what the stock market is? Not even that cabby knew! . . . Had Löwenstein already found out about that damn speech? . . . If Löwenstein dropped his packet then that was that, he could paper his walls with his certificates. . . . Why were they stopping? An ambulance? The hell with it! He was injured too. He too needed first aid. A day from now he'd be a common beggar. Faster! . . . The sweat rolled down the man's body. It was rendered fat. His collar was slovenly. His eyes, as dull and greenish as an oyster, were desperate. He counted out coins, and then he dropped them, his fingers were trembling. Then he suddenly laughed, stridently and stupidly: "Hahaha, too late, my word of honor, too late! . . ."

Karl stood at the corner and chewed a sandwich. A woman reached for the handle. She was so nervous that she couldn't get the door open and she wailed. Twenty to five. He wouldn't wait, he'd leave. It wasn't her fault. Rudi had held up dinner. And he wouldn't understand. Of course he'd leave. He had probably left already. Gone to that awful vaudeville woman. She had sent her picture. Hideous. *She* was much more interesting. And smarter. And better read. Yes, but she was late. The woman tugged at the strap: Faster! Her lips, unbearably red, stretched out into a turn signal. Five to five. . . . Oh God! . . .

Then Karl drove a man to the eye hospital. Then he drove an old lady with packages. Then he drove a couple to a dinner party. Everyone rushed. Everyone panted and looked at their watches. No one looked at Karl and Karl didn't notice his fares.

At night, he drove a drunk. The drunk was mumbling blissfully. Yet he was only rushing to the Schwanneke bar. It stayed open later than any other place. He had to have another drink! He was afraid to get sober. He conversed with the turn-signals and the shadows. He caressed the iron body like the flanks of a horse. Faster! Five more minutes and everything would be clear as day again: Anna's letter, Moritz's hints, the illness, the pills, old age, boredom, the watch, the main thing was the watch. . . . A glass, and make it snappy! . . .

Karl drove the car back to the garage and slowly walked home. His pocket held the wax-paper from the sandwiches: for tomorrow. At home, his pregnant wife was waiting, and an electric bill, and a piece of warmed-over pork, and sleep, sleep as empty, long, and useless as the five hundred streets he had crossed that day.

A fare got into Karl's taxi. He had no suitcase and no portfolio. But he breathlessly whispered: "Kaiserdamm 268." He wasn't able to sit calmly. He drummed his fingers on the glass. He propped his legs against the wall: He was urging on the lazy car. He was the most ordinary of passengers. Round glasses. A beige felt hat. He wasn't old or young, rich or poor. He was one of four million.

The car stopped at a crossing. The road was clear. No cars, no pedestrians. The passenger banged on the window. Karl didn't budge. Naturally the fare was in a rush. All fares are in a rush. That's what cars are meant for. But there was a red light. Somewhere an invisible authority pulled a lever, and suddenly, as though riven to the ground, excited cars stopped at various corners of various streets. The engine panted impatiently. Its breath mixed with the breath of the passenger. Then the green light flared up and the car zoomed off.

It started raining. The traffic-lights and the numbers wilted. Now a ruler slid across the windshield. It quickly wiped away the drops. It was fussy and exact: left to right, then right to left. A passenger's heart is not constructed as well. He took off his hat. He raised himself. He was very pale. Here was Kaiserdamm! . . . But how long this street was! Uneasily he peered at the numbers. Then, worn out, he closed his eyes. Karl stopped at the passenger's number. Karl waited for the passenger to thrust the warm coins into his hand. But now the passenger was in no rush. Karl stepped out on the sidewalk and opened the car door a little way. The passenger had fallen asleep. He shook him. He took his hand and instantly stepped back. The passenger's hand held the coins ready for Karl. After all, the passenger had been in an awful rush. But both the coins and the hand were cold.

Cursing, Karl went to the super's wife. She waved him off for a long time. Couldn't he see she was busy? If she left now, the milk would boil over. Finally, she went to the ill-fated passenger. He was sitting so peacefully with his soft hat on his knees. No, she didn't know him. He didn't live here. He had never even been here. Only proper people lived in this building. As she spoke, the woman thought that dying in a car was awfully unbecoming. It could get into the papers, and it was something like a scandal.

Karl took the passenger to the nearest police station. The passenger no longer drummed his fingers on the pane and he didn't wheeze like the engine at all the necessary stops. They took him out of the car, efficiently and quickly. The way they take out big trunks in railroad stations. The hat fell on the sidewalk. Karl gave the hat to the policeman, signed a statement, and stepped on the gas. He drove another passenger to the Skala Music Hall.

Then he stood once more at the corner of two streets. He didn't chew a sandwich. Unexpectedly for himself, he was thinking: Where had that passenger been rushing to? Yes, Karl did remember that he'd been rushing. He had even been tapping on the window. Maybe something extraordinary had been waiting in that building, number 268: an inheritance, a fiancée, or first prize in a contest. Why, the papers are always writing about different contests. . . . He must have died when they turned into Kaiserdamm. On Kantstrasse he was still tapping on the window. Now he hadn't made it after all. . . . Why do the passengers rush? . . . Karl made a face at this thought, but it was a long thought, as long as Kaiserdamm, and now a new fare was coming, and Karl instantly forgot about everything in the world except for the signals and the network of streets.

When he came home at night, he no longer thought about the tardy passenger. He chewed beef and softly reckoned up how much his wife's delivery would cost him. As always, he fell asleep amid a concatenation of streets, amid the fever of traffic-lights. He kept tossing and turning noisily because of the tiresome honking under the windows.

On July 28, 1928, the *Morgenpost* ran the following item: "Yesterday an unknown man died in taxi no. 6,817 of the Berlinia Company. No papers were found on his person. His hat had the initials A.O. His body is now in the city morgue. Steps have been taken by the police toward identifying the dead man."

Other newspapers didn't even mention the incident. It scarcely deserved notice.

Karl never again thought about the foolish matter. Karl didn't think. After all, he wasn't a herring fisher. He was a cabby for the Berlinia Company.

2

It's a small world. Everyone knows that: Deterding, Citroën, storks, tourists. And this tiny world has too many people. Once upon a time there was a deluge. Now Holland is drying out the Zuyder Zee. Once there was a plague. People got used to it and survived it. Laboratories prepare longevity like saccharine, and rejuvenated Methusalems giggle friskily. But the world isn't getting any bigger. It's crowded now, like a clearance sale at a department store. War's been done away with. People can only live by using their elbows.

But then the automobile came to man's rescue. It doesn't wait for any notes, it doesn't demand 14 points like Wilson. Meticulously and efficiently, it cleans the earth. All inoculations and all conferences are powerless against it. The body is quickly removed by truck, the car is carefully wiped, and the record is identified by a multi-digit number.

At first such things were known as "catastrophes." Now people speak of "accidents." Soon they'll stop speaking altogether. Silently they'll haul away the victim and silently write down the number.

Sentimental neighbors wipe their noses, of course, and philosophically minded people argue about the "new peril." Commissions discuss protective laws. But the automobile keeps right on doing its job. Sir Henry Deterding was destined to create an oil empire. Monsieur André Citroën was destined to turn out cheap cars. Karl Lang the cabby was destined to cross intersections. The automobile works honestly. Long before its birth, when it is still just layers of metal and piles of drawings, it diligently murders Malayan coolies and Mexican laborers. It is born in agony! It shreds flesh, blinds eyes, eats lungs, destroys minds. At last, it rolls out of the gates into the world which, before its existence, was known as "bright." Instantly, it deprives its supposed owner of his old-fashioned peace of mind. Lilac withers, chickens and dreamers dash away in terror. The automobile laconically runs down pedestrians. It gnaws into the side of a barn or else, grinning, it flies down a slope. It can't be blamed for anything. Its conscience is as clear as Monsieur Citroën's conscience. It only fulfills its destiny: It is destined to wipe out the world.

Johann Braeger lived in Leipzig. Leipzig is a commercial city. It prints manuals for young chemists, it produces costly furs, it puts on Socialist congresses. Needless to say, it has quite a lot of cars. Johann Braeger, of course, had no car. But on the other hand, Herr Stoss owned a marvelous Mercedes. In addition, Herr Stoss had an exemplary printing plant. He printed highly artistic labels for liqueurs, colognes, expensive cigarettes. He was the best label printer in the whole of Germany, and he certainly deserved his Mercedes. He had the right to honk proudly at all intersections. A true sportsman, he often drove the car himself. He lived outside of town and he loved speed—100 miles an hour. He loved speed in everything. His printing plant had the most perfect machines. The presses bowed obsequiously. Cutters glided. During a single year, Herr Stoss turned out over 800,000 labels. They showed Spanish women with fans or multicolored triangles. They praised the perfume *My Scent* or the liqueur *Mountain Cloister*. They were driven away on trucks. Herr Stoss drove away in his Mercedes. He understood what modern advertising is and what nonfading fast colors are. He was one of the men rebuilding Germany. Leipzig is a commercial city. Leipzig is justifiably proud of Herr Stoss.

But even in irreproachable Leipzig, the experienced eye of the proofreader can detect an occasional misprint. What was Johann

Braeger occupied with? Was he useful to the reconstruction of Germany? He didn't build Zeppelins, he didn't make aniline dyes, he didn't even produce sausages. He was busy with a ridiculous thing: He studied the old songs of various nations. He collated them. He was writing a book on the unity of themes, the primacy of the East, the identity of feelings with the identity of crafts. No one needed it. You couldn't turn that into records, or entertaining novels, or manuals for traveling salesmen who wanted to know the psychology of the countries that buy cars or aniline dyes from Germany. After all, Braeger was studying songs that no one sings anymore. He was learning languages that no one speaks anymore. For instance, the incantations of the Lusini. Instead of dumb songs, those upright Germans had been whistling Berlin foxtrots for some time now.

Some peculiar people had given Braeger a grant: 110 marks a month. Braeger ate potatoes without fat and deliberately wrote in a small hand to save paper. He had a patched-up suit. He had anemia and tuberculosis in the right lung. Nevertheless, he kept working. He didn't know what the Treaty of Locarno was. He didn't know there was such a thing as Mercedes cars. He didn't even know that Germany was being reconstructed. All day long he sat working in his shirt-sleeves so as not to wear out the elbows of his jacket. In the evening, he would visit Elsa Brecht, who sold *My Scent* perfumes. He spoke to her helter-skelter about Indian mythology, Serbian vampires, and the Arabic influence on the imagery of Castilian poetry.

At that time, Herr Stoss was at a party in the Astoria, listening to the latest charlestons. Next to him, a snub-nosed blonde was yelping softly. Herr Stoss was sticking her with his tiepin. The girl was blissful. She knew who was sticking her. At the entrance, the Mercedes was dozing under the watchful eye of the doorman. The blonde girl's bliss was justified: Herr Stoss had received a gold medal at the Cologne Fair. The previous year he had made 860,000 marks. His picture had lately appeared in the magazine section of the biggest newspaper in Leipzig. When a man like that is having fun, everybody around him is blissful: the servants, the girls, the saxophones. Why, after all, Herr Stoss was helping to rebuild Germany.

Today Johann Braeger had chanced upon an old Celtic song: "Yves plants an appletree. When there's no rain, he waters it with water from the well. The well is far away and Yves is patient. He waits for years and years. Then the tender appletree blossoms. Then the wind swoops down and tears out the sapling. Tell me, my darling, which would you rather be: patient Yves or the swift wind swooping from the sea? No, answers the maiden, no, I wouldn't want to be patient Yves or the swift wind. I would only like to be the tender appletree. It grows and grows. It blossoms. It is quickly destroyed when the wind swoops down. . . ."

Braeger was in high spirits. Just like Herr Stoss when he unexpectedly received an order for 500,000 tricolored labels. The Celtic song was amazingly similar to a sixteenth-century song from Estremadura and two much later Slovak songs.

That evening, as usual, Johann went off to Elsa's home in Wilhelmstrasse. He was going to tell her about his lucky find. He walked along, repeating: "Then the appletree blossoms. . . ." People barged into him. They had finished work and were rushing home. They had spent the day at printing presses or shop counters, sorting foul-smelling hides. They wanted to ease their swollen feet into soft felt slippers, don their earphones, and, like Herr Stoss, listen to the hit charlestons. Naturally, they bore along the right side of the pavement, furiously barging into Braeger: That creep didn't even know how to walk down a street! . . .

Johann crossed a square. "The the wind swooped down. . . ." What a remarkable song! Elsa would love it! Johann comically dragged along in his worn-down shoes. He didn't hear the horns. He didn't see the warning hand signals, which were purple and bloodshot. He didn't see the enormous, all-devouring eyes. He mumbled: "I just want to be the tree. . . ." And then came something that people rightfully call an "accident."

Johann Braeger's body was taken to the police station. Herr Stoss was indignant. His Mercedes wasn't hurt or anything. But he had to lose a quarter of an hour with the formalities. He had to show his papers, as though his name counted for nothing! He had to sign two interminable statements. He worked hard enough all day to have the right to rest in the evening. Tonight he wanted to have a good time at the Astoria. If that man had been deaf, why hadn't he looked at the signals? If he'd been blind why hadn't he had a seeing-eye dog? He was probably crazy: His papers said he was a Ph.D. Oh well, a philosopher! One of those people who count stars and steal oranges from fruit-stands. What was wrong with the Leipzig police anyway!?

Johann Braeger's book, which was to come out soon, according to the April issue of *Philological News,* would never be written. Instead, other books would be published. There were lots of presses in Leipzig. And Elsa would never find out about the Celtic song. But, frankly, she had had enough of those lamentations. Willi from the

Dresden Bank knew songs that were a lot more interesting. For instance: "Jim and I met in an elevator. . . ." That was fun and it had oomph! You could really dance to that. . . .

The Mercedes snorted in triumph. The chauffeur meticulously washed the lacquered fenders. The eyes were wide open. They pierced the dark street. Johann no longer existed. Karl and Willis jumped aside. Liqueur bottles delicately shone in the windows of nocturnal taverns. Somewhere high in the heavens, the name of a new cologne blazed up. Herr Stoss was touched: A solid order, 300,000, a Japanese girl in a kimono, a gold edging. His blonde was waiting at the Astoria. Today he would crush her like that. . . .

The Mercedes engine and Herr Stoss's heart throbbed in tandem. Both were powerful and both were beautiful. At every spin of the wheels, their kinship strengthened.

An hour later, after polishing off a bottle of champagne, Herr Stoss honked like a horn: Beep, beep! The girl blanched devoutly. In his chest, Herr Stoss had a forty-horsepower engine. His eyes were voracious and dreadful. Two headlights. Their gape had seen Johann Braeger die.

3

Benito Mussolini lived in Rome. He dreamt about a grand Italian empire. He inspected troops, gave speeches, and wiped out his enemies. Matteotti also lived in Rome. That was a mistake. Rome wasn't big enough for both of them. Matteotti hated the grand empire and every day he made fun of the militaristic monologues. Mussolini believed in the triumph of Italian industry and in a truce between workers and bosses. The owners of the Fiat auto works didn't mind. They knew what this truce meant. Mussolini was in command. The black-shirts yelled: "Eia! Eia! Alala!" The workers worked.

But while working, the workers nevertheless did not dream about the grand empire. They smiled in approval when they read Matteotti's mordant articles. After all, they were ordinary workers, hardly any different from the workers at Opel or Citroën. Matteotti himself was an ordinary Socialist. In arguing with his opponents, he cited the resolutions of international congresses. He just didn't understand that Italy is Italy and that Mussolini is Mussolini.

Mussolini directed high politics. He was the *duce* and he couldn't deal with economic trivia. That was for his assistants. Some of them had ministerial portfolios, others just party cards and subsidies. Dumini was in charge of wiping out enemies. Signor Filippelli published the newspaper *Il Corriere Italiano*, which wrote daily that Benito was marvelous and immortal. Signor Filippelli's work was a lot cleaner than Dumini's, and the hand that Signor Filippelli banged on the marble tabletop in the caffé was a tender and pudgy hand.

Matteotti wrote another article. He gave another speech in the Chamber of Deputies. Workers somewhere agreed under their breath. Dumini realized it was time to act. Dumini wouldn't stop at anything. He began thinking about how to get rid of Matteotti. He conferred with experienced black-shirts. With care and concentration, he prepared for the decisive day, just as Benito Mussolini had prepared for the March on Rome. Dumini knew his job very well.

He sat and thought. He was seriously worried. Matteotti had quite a lot of supporters, and he was known abroad. Here it was hard to ignore the public. All at once, Dumini's face lit up. He remembered: There was such a thing as cars. Of course, Mussolini loved to heap praises on the tiller of the soil and bucolic poetry. But Mussolini was not a foe of machines. He knew that without big industry there would be no grand Italy. Rome had a Colosseum and an airport, curiosity shops with imitation antiques, and chemical laboratories that turned out the finest gases. Rome had a place for everything. Mussolini honored the Capitoline Wolf. He honored Fiat engines as well. By blessing the automobile, Dumini was not committing any heresy. He was an orthodox black-shirt. They would have had to slip some powder into his great-grandfather's wine or, covering their faces with a cape, steal through back streets at night. Dumini blessed the new age. Only now did he understand the full beauty of Marinetti's verses. On the outskirts of Rome there was quite a lot of empty space, for instance Quartarella, and Signor Filippelli had a marvelous car.

Signor Fillipelli waved his pudgy hand by way of agreement. Benito's enemies had to be wiped out! His car would be praised by posterity like the ancient quadriga. But of course he wasn't Dumini. His work was clean. He would wait for Dumini at the newspaper office. He gave him his white, tender hand: "Have a good drive. . . ."

A scorching June day. The fortunate Romans were dashing in cars to the hills of Albano or the shores of Ostia. Those remaining in town drank lemonade and sighed loudly. As usual, profiteers spoke about the lira and a shipment of foreign stockings, Englishwomen sketched the Vestal temple, drivers at the crossings of narrow streets cursed lazily, and homeless cats, forgotten among splendid ruins, howled heartrendingly. Opponents of the grand empire sought comfort in cheap ice cream. The heat interfered with their thinking. The Fascists didn't lag behind. With the same dreaminess, they languished by the ice cream stands. They had black shirts on. They certainly loved the Italian sun, but they sweated buckets. They couldn't even shout "Eia!" They were too drowsy.

Benito Mussolini despised both sleep and ice cream. He thought about his empire. His thoughts were much wider than the narrow streets and the narrow peninsula. He thought about Savoy, Tunis, Dalmatia, Malta. Yes, he was destined to rebuild this land of picturesque ruins and demanding magicians! He would transform any coral vendor into an ancient legioneer. Rome was one, and this was Rome.

Mussolini's dreams were huge and swaggering, like the arches of ancient emperors. He saw himself under such an arch. Of course, he was in an open car, not a chariot. After all, he had speed in his hand now. What had taken the builders of Rome centuries to do, he had to accomplish in a few years.

Signor Filippelli's car nosed its way through the narrow streets. Dumini was sitting in it with four devoted Fascists. One was at the wheel. They had to leave the chauffeur at home. He was an ordinary chauffeur and, who could tell, he might have nodded in agreement when reading Matteotti's articles. Signor Filippelli's car was approaching Lungo Teveredi Michelangelo. It stopped. It was a large, good car, painted red, which, naturally, testified not to Signor Filippelli's political views, but only to his uncommon joie de vivre.

Matteotti, like Mussolini, worked despite the heat. He was supposed to be leaving soon to spend a few days in Austria. They had finally issued him a passport. He was thinking about the tactics of European workers. In Germany, the revolution was lost. In Italy, there was Mussolini. But England was waking up. Matteotti weighed the chances of both sides. What would the unification of heavy industry bring? What would be the effect of increased efficiency? The fate of the Fiat workers seemed closely linked with the fate of Europe. His thoughts, like Mussolini's, weren't restricted to the narrow peninsula. He laughed at the triumphal arches. Hadn't the impoverished members of a tiny sect in enslaved and ignorant Judaea turned out to be more powerful than those bronze demigods?

Matteotti was preparing a new speech. He was going to show where Mussolini was taking the country! . . . He wrote, smoking one cigarette after another. At one point, having finished a page, he reached for the box and then frowned. There were no more cigarettes. He told his wife: "I'll be right back. . . ." He strode quickly along the deserted bank. He kept thinking about his speech. He had to hurry: In another few weeks, Mussolini would abolish the Chamber of Deputies, shut down the newspapers, gag all mouths. The day after tomorrow, he was going to do a critical analysis of the latest financial legislation. . . .

Matteotti was surrounded by unknown men. They weren't wearing black shirts, just ordinary lustrine jackets. They grabbed Matteotti and shoved him into the red car. The man at the wheel evidently knew the way. He zoomed full speed ahead. The engine cheerily snorted.

The rare passers-by glared enviously at the whizzing auto. They didn't doubt that the red car was taking some lucky people to the country, toward mountain coolness or ocean breezes. The car enveloped them in honking and dust. Mournfully, they shook it off.

Inside the car, however, a battle raged. It didn't last long. Matteotti suffered from consumption and was very sickly. His hand could wield a pen but hardly squeeze a throat. Nevertheless, he tried to put up a fight. He even managed to clutch the door handle. Now Dumini pulled a knife. Dumini was not Signor Filipelli: He was a master at everything. Matteotti couldn't shout. They had instantly rammed a handkerchief into his mouth. Noiselessly he dropped upon the carpeting. Only the cushion showed traces of blood. The car with the happy vacationers raced out of the city.

Here was Quartarella already! There were no tourists here, no passers-by, no shepherds. Just low thorn-bushes and sunshine. Silently, the men dragged out the body, silently they lugged it off to the side, far from the road. Here! . . . They started digging a hole. It was a sublime labor, worthy of praise from Mussolini and all the poets of the *strapaese*, the "super-rustics." After all, it was akin to tilling the soil. But digging a hole is a lot more trouble than killing a man. The earth was dry, the earth was hard, and the setting sun was still pouring its unbearable heat on their heads. The hole was narrow and shallow. To get the corpse in, the men had to bend it together and trample it. They broke its spine. Then they convulsively shook themselves and mopped their wet faces.

The red car raced back to the city. The happy passengers were imbued with the country coolness. One after another, the killers vanished in narrow alleys. Dumini drove up to the editorial offices of the *Corriere Italiano*. The reporters and typists had long since gone, only

Signor Filippelli was anxiously waiting for Dumini.

Heavily breathing from the close air and his fatigue, Dumini told him the whole story. Generally, everything had gone well . . . except for some bloodstains on the seat. Also, some women had been standing on the drive by the river. Maybe they had noticed something. . . . After all, Matteotti had struggled. . . .

Signor Filippelli frowned. The seat could be cleaned, of course. Tomorrow, the *Corriere Italiano* would write that Matteotti had gone to Austria without even telling his wife. Well, that's Socialist habits for you! But what about the witnesses? The opposition newspapers hadn't been shut down yet. Those smart alecks, for all he knew, might start inquiring. . . . For the time being, he would have to remove the car, and as far away as possible.

Signor Filippelli drove the red car to a tiny garage. Let it stay there. Perhaps for a week. Perhaps even for a month. The garage-man smiled obligingly. The signor had a luxury automobile, the signor certainly wouldn't be stingy with gratuities. The man was right. Signor Filippelli was very generous this time.

Dumini washed, changed his shirt, and headed for a caffé. He drank a lemonade.

Beneficial night descended on Rome. The people came to life. The ruins came to life: Once again there were baths, a circus, a temple. The people who had been talking about stockings fell silent. They stared at women's legs. A bat circled smoothly. The Englishwomen no longer sketched, all they had before them was the moon, the big, slightly doltish moon, it's always the same one, both here and in cool England. Cab drivers played cards. Everything was a-jumble in Rome: the Vestal temple and the Caffé Aragno, the black shirts and the bronze of the centaurs, the marble and the asphalt, the melancholy and the greenish dust. Everything was quiet and serene.

But in a high, empty room one man was still working. If you want to create a grand empire, the oaths of legioneers aren't enough, you need exports. Italy was getting on its feet again. The automotive industry was already competing with France, even America. Mussolini beamed at the columns of figures. The workers were working. The truce was triumphant.

Rome was indeed black, tender, quiet. Matteotti was no longer here. Now and then, a faint screech resounded in the night, but it was either the meowing of a cat or the honking of a tardy automobile.

4

They hunted the missing broker for a long time. He had vanished with diamonds belonging to other people and with Monsieur Sostère's money for a short-term note. They hunted him in all-night taverns and steamship offices. No one, of course, looked for him in the forest. What could an embezzler be doing among ravines and trees? They couldn't find the broker. But in the forest of Armainvilliers, they stumbled upon charred bones and the rags of a jacket. Human bones are all the same. Jackets, however, are different. These were the rags of the jacket the ill-fated broker had been wearing when he disappeared. The gendarmes questioned the local inhabitants. A few people had seen an expensive chocolate-colored automobile.

Now they started hunting the car. Automobiles are all different, like jackets. They found a chocolate-colored car in a garage owned by Pasaine in La Vallière. It belonged to the Paris jeweler Charles Mestorino. But Pasaine told the police that on the day the broker had disappeared, the chocolate car had not left the garage.

They interred the broker's bones. Days and nights went by. During the day, Charles Mestorino looked at cut gems through a magnifying glass. At night, he tossed and turned and screamed in his sleep. His wife asked him:

"Are you sick?"

"No. I'm not sick."

He fell asleep again and screeched again. He couldn't forget the chocolate car. This went on for sixteen nights. Then they arrested him. When Sergeant Mougel walked in, Mestorino's wife knelt down before her husband and screamed:

"Charles, forgive me!"

No one could understand why she had screamed. After all, Mestorino's wife was innocent.

Charles Mestorino was Italian, but he wasn't anything like Dumini. He didn't think about a grand empire. He didn't receive subsidies and instructions from on high. He was just your average jeweler with a beautiful wife and unpaid notes. He dealt in diamonds in Paris.

The fate of thousands and thousands of people depends on these tiny gems. Blacks work in the South African diamond mines. They work for many years. They work till they die. The mines are surrounded by an electric fence. A high-tension current. Human bones bleach in the sun all around the deadly fence, for the edification of possible runaways. Then the stones are sorted and weighed. Then they are sent to Amsterdam. Here we have the diamond exchange of the world. The lackluster stones pass from hand to hand. They enrich some, they impoverish others. They are transformed into forty-horsepower automobiles or a dismal seventh-class bier without speeches or wreaths. Then the stones come to a factory. Here they are polished with diamond dust. They are polished by grimy, bearded Jews with Old Testament melancholy and festering eyes. All day long they never leave the magnifying glasses. In front of them they have stones costing 10,000 florins a piece. A polisher earns six florins a day. It takes a month to polish a good stone. The weak eyes shed tears, and the value of the diamond grows with each tear. Then the stores are bought by a wholesaler; he sells them to jewelers. The blood of tormented blacks, the delirium of the stock exchange, the pus of the polisher are turned into rings or necklaces. This one—the scalps of ruined competitors on the fleshy neck of Mrs. Jensen, whose husband owns a department store in Göteborg. This one—information on the social standing of Madame Teresa Terri: the little ring is meant to testify that she is really close to the director of the Phoenix Insurance Company. This one—a bucolic sparkle on seventy-year-old Lady Haines, who smells of Chypres, camphor, and the grave. They are the starry firmament of any *soirée*. There they are, admire them: The Cassiopeias of oil, the Pleiades of iron, the Vegas of rubber!

Charles Mestorino bought small diamonds of a mediocre water. Naturally, he didn't sell them to Lady Haines, but to the red-handed spouses of building contractors or stars at the Folies Bergéres. One carat. . . . Two carats. . . . One or two thousand francs profit. . . . He was able to buy a chocolate car. But he couldn't buy his beautiful wife a necklace worthy of her.

Mestorino's wife had the tender name of Lili. They had met a long time ago, before the war. That was at the ball in the Moulin-de-la-Galette, among Nana chignons and sentimental cancans. Mestorino chose Lili, but Lili chose a rich Brazilian. It was like a prewar torch song; but it was just a commonplace life story. Lili happily got married, and Mestorino went to Italy—to fight the Austrians. When the war was over, he came back to Paris. He had remained true to Lili, and Lili appreciated it. She exchanged the rich Brazilian for the modest but devoted Charles. From her first husband, she had rings, bracelets, necklaces. She had also gotten used to easy and carefree living.

Mestorino the jeweler loved his wife and he tried to become as rich as the Brazilian. But diamonds didn't bring him luck. Perhaps he didn't understand jewelry. Perhaps he didn't understand life. Within a year he lost 85,000 francs. He was forced to pawn Lili's valuables, somewhat to her surprise. He lived from day to day. Diamonds sparkled before his eyes, bombastic and supercilious. He tried to fathom their brilliance. His life became dreary and full of petty worries. He plunged into a maelstrom. He borrowed from one man to pay back another. He hated this life, but he couldn't change it. Charles Mestorino wasn't a philosopher, just a small jeweler.

He bought a stone worth 35,000 francs from Monsieur Sostère. He paid with a promissory note. He planned to resell the diamond at a good profit. But he needed money, and two days later he sold the stone for 25,000 cash. He did settle with a few creditors. But Monsieur Sostère still had his note. The deadline came, and Monsieur Sostère commissioned a broker named Truphème to collect the 35,000 from Mestorino.

Gaston Truphème came with the note early in the morning. What could Mestorino answer him? He said:

"I don't have the money. Come back in a few days."

"But the money was due today."

Mestorino made a helpless gesture.

"Well, then come back later. I'll try to raise it somewhere."

When Truphème left, Mestorino didn't hurry to his banker. He didn't even go over to the telephone. He didn't start asking jewelers he was friendly with to come to his rescue. He knew very well that no one would give him money anymore.

Then Truphème arrived and demanded the 35,000. Mestorino silently leaped upon Truphème and began choking him. He was stronger than the broker and dealt with him quickly. Truphème's briefcase contained diamonds belonging to other people. Truphème screamed:

"Take it all! Just leave me alone! . . . You can't kill a man for a few thousand francs!"

Gaston Truphème had seen a lot of things in his life. He had lived through the war. He had been wounded at Verdun. He should have known how easy it is to kill a human being. But he wanted to live and he screamed at Mestorino:

"You can't kill me! You can't! . . ."

All this happened during the day in Mestorino's office. On the other side of the wall there were workers and clerks. All of them could hear, but none of them came to help Truphème. Employers have their accounts to settle. The employees got small monthly salaries and understood nothing about diamond prices, promissory notes, or Lili's caprices.

Mestorino paced up and down the room, he went over to the window, he pushed a chair aside. He called his sister-in-law. He asked her something, received bills, gave orders. But he was dead, as dead as Truphème. He was dead from fear. He saw the flashing of carats before his eyes, Truphème's bared teeth, and the blade of the guillotine.

Then he remembered the chocolate car. His unraveled face tightened and hardened. He called one of his employees:

"Go to the hardware store and get me some sackcloth. About six or seven meters. Better make it seven. And rope—about twenty meters."

Mestorino was dry and businesslike now. First he wrapped Truphème's corpse in a thick woolen blanket, then he packed it in the sackcloth. He dragged this heavy load down from the fifth floor. He dragged it alone. He put the sack in his chocolate car. He drove home to La Vallière. There all three of them spent the night: Mestorini, Truphème, and the car, amid silence and the barking of dogs, under the sweaty, agitated moon.

In the morning, Mestorino drove to Brie-Conte-Robert. There he bought four cans of gasoline. Then he turned off in the direction of Armainvilliers.

It was early spring. In the forest, last year's leaves were rotting and the first chestnut-buds were painfully swelling. The forest smelled of dampness and childhood. Charles Mestorino had once walked in these woods, picking strawberries. That was long, long ago—before diamonds and before Lili.

The chocolate car stayed on the road. Mestorino dragged the corpse into the thicket. He poured gasoline over it and set it on fire. He gazed at the flame in horror and hope. He was ready to worship the all-purging fire. At last, Gaston Truphème was gone!

Mestorino went to Pasaine the garage owner. Truphème had vanished Monday. Mestorino asked Pasaine:

"If anyone asks you, say that my car was in the garage from Saturday to Tuesday."

Pasaine had a bright, raspberry-colored face and a bulging chest. He playfully giggled:

"Intrigues, Monsieur Mestorino, intrigues! . . ."

Mestorino didn't answer. He took 13,000 francs out of his wallet, all the money he had left, and silently he gave it to Pasaine. The man instantly stopped laughing, and silently put the money in his pocket.

And what about the clerk, that little Boyar? After all, Boyar could blab. However, yesterday, Mestorino had left his briefcase with several diamonds in the car. Today he noticed that two small ones were missing. He didn't have to talk to Boyar. The man had priced his own silence at so and so many thousands.

Mestorino calmed down a bit. He went to the office. He even tried to work. In Truphème's briefcase, he found lots of gems, about 50,000 francs' worth. But Mestorino's finances didn't straighten out. He sold only two stones. He gave the money to Pasaine. As before, the day was filled with debts, bills, calls from creditors. And at night—Truphème's bared teeth, the forest dampness, the chocolate car, and dear Lili's eyes, uncomprehending and widened in terror.

Some draymen had already found the shreds of the jacket. All the newspapers now wrote about one thing: the chocolate car. Detectives poked about, the laboratories examined fingerprints, police-dogs nervously sniffed the air and pawed the ground. The chase was on. The chocolate car! It had to be repainted—was there even one neighbor who didn't know that Mestorino the jeweler owned a chocolate car?

Mestorino no longer looked at stones. He picked up the magnifying glass only when visitors came. When he was alone, he read newspapers. All newspapers: morning, noon, and evening editions. Every hour another paper came out in Paris, and every hour Mestorino turned paler. He could already hear the footsteps of detectives, the panting of hounds. He stopped talking. He seemed to have stopped breathing. He no longer existed. Instead of him, there was a chocolate car. The car kept growing and growing. It turned into a black maria. The prisoner Mestorino was inside it. The crowd was hooting nastily. It was dark inside. There was only the snorting of the engine. He, the other man, in the blanket and the sackcloth, was silent. . . . The car was still growing. Now it was a huge van. Its door opened. Out stepped a properly dressed gentleman. He was extremely courteous. He smiled. He took baggage out of the van. But it wasn't a trunk, it wasn't a basket. Mestorino shuddered. He realized what the van had brought. The crowd was already at his door. Girls, photographers, jewelers. A blade glistened. The proper gentleman set up the guillotine. Mestorino covered his face with his hands. No one could save him, not Lili, not his sister-in-law, not Pasaine! . . . He had burned up the broker. He had dragged himself to the burial of the charred bones. He had given Pasaine 13,000 francs. But the car, the chocolate car! It came closer and closer. It wheezed. The engine. . . . Detectives. . . . Hounds. . . .

Mestorino stretched out his hands to the door. In walked Sergeant Mougel and put brand-new, shiny handcuffs on the outstretched hands.

There was a throng at the door. Hispano-Suizas and Rolls-Royces drove up. Inside there were supercilious, clean-shaven chauffeurs, flat-nosed Japanese puppies, and ladies, smartly dressed ladies. Scalpers were hawking tickets. Someone screeched: "It's an outrage! They only reserved two seats for me! . . ." "Hurry up, René, or we'll be late! . . ." The puppies were left with the chauffeurs. The ladies hurried into the auditorium. They greeted one another in passing:

"Why Lucie, of all people! I didn't recognize you in that throw! How *did* you get the tickets? Charles, I bet. You little vixen! . . . It looks like it's going to be lots of fun today. . . ."

"Yes. Charles said it's going to be a big day. Just look, even Bonnet is here. All of Paris!"

It wasn't the Diaghilev Ballet and it wasn't the dress rehearsal of a Giraudoux play. It was a dreary courtroom. But today Charles Mestorino was on trial. Could Lucie or Madame Bonnet pass up such a show? . . .

Mestorino's sister-in-law was crying. The presiding judge shouted: "You'll have to cry afterwards!" The spectators laughed. Mestorino's wife had tried to poison herself with gardenal. The spectators shrugged: "Who's she fooling?" And they laughed again. The district attorney exclaimed theatrically: "I shall be obliged to demand his head." And the spectators applauded.

The ladies, of course, were wearing diamonds. These stones were not stolen. They had been given at a wedding or a name-day celebration. The ladies hadn't killed anyone. They had such good hearts! Lucie couldn't even beat her dog. And the Africans? And the electric current? And the blind polisher? But that's all politics, after all! Ladies don't go in for politics. These ladies are for tender feelings and ordinary morality. Along with the district attorney, they demanded the murderer's head.

At the dock, Mestorino was hunched together. He was a lump of fat, dressed and combed. Now and then, he mumbled something inarticulate. Policemen pulled him up. He had dragged Truphème's corpse down the steps of the winding staircase. Now he was a corpse himself. But they weren't burying him. They were trying him.

Here was the president of the Association of Parisian Jewelers. He was indignant at Mestorino's commercial baseness. Death! Here was Monsieur Sostère. He hadn't gotten the 35,000 for the promissory note after all. Death! Here was Truphème's mother. A life for a life. Death! Here were the assistant prosecutors. They wanted 100,000 francs and a head in the bargain. Here was the district attorney. He reminded the court that Truphème had shouted: "You can't kill a man!" Ergo: They would have to kill Mestorino. The businesslike basses of the jewelers, and Lucie's charming soprano, all fusing into one chant: Death, death, death!

The courtroom was filled with the stuffiness of a June midday and the tender fantasy of female heads: a shaven neck, a glass of rum, a black maria, Monsieur Deibler, the sharp glint of a blade. And cars at the gates. Cars of all colors: ash-gray, slate, yellow, indigo, brick-red, and chocolate. Yes, there were chocolate cars among them. That was an entirely respectable hue. The cars waited for prey. Here was a new broker with a promissory note in his briefcase. Here was a new Mestorino hurrying out of town with a heavy sack. The crowd was screaming: "His head! His head!" Desperate people tested their guns, mixed powders, whetted knives. They cut up, hacked up, chopped up warm flesh. Murderers fled in cars. Monsieur Deibler drove through happy France in a car with his gleaming baggage. Kill faster! Cut heads off faster! Faster! After all, life is so short.

5

Boris Ignatyevich K., despite his youth, had an important position. He worked at the Oil Syndicate. He sometimes took business trips abroad. Once he even had a chance to speak with Sir Henry Deterding. First they spoke about the London fog, then about a five-percent discount. K. proved to be a fine diplomat. Sir Henry both smiled and frowned.

K. once even went to America. He brought back a complicated apparatus known as a "dictaphone" and some excitement. He enthusiastically talked about the Ford factories, about perfect bath equipment and rational bookkeeping. He added:

"Naturally, we have to change the content, but we ought to learn the method. . . ."

In his department, he organized everything in the American way. He reduced the number of workers, specified each one's duties, simplified the clerical work. He hated endless meetings and thick reports. He demonstrated that you can work without flies in inkwells, long lines of visitors in the waiting room, or discussions. He was humorously nicknamed the Yankee from Arbat. He wasn't offended. He had no time to take offense. Petroleum was the basic wealth of the Soviet Union. You had to know how to extract it. You also had to know how to export it.

Few of his colleagues knew anything about K.'s private life. He wasn't reclusive. He was simply busy. He hardly ever spoke to anyone about anything but his work. He received a large salary, but he lived modestly. He never caroused, played cards, or followed fashions. He did dress well, in foreign clothes, but he brought them all from London or Berlin: wide jackets, wide trousers, wide boots. K. never wore a hat, even in the worst frost; but he did shave every morning, which fairly embarrassed all the co-workers in his department.

Comrade K. had a venerable but well-preserved Ford at his disposal. How could he have managed without a car? He had three or four meetings each day, and all of them at different ends of town. K.'s schedule was worked out many days in advance. He was never late. He was proud of this punctuality; not his, but the Ford's. He drove it himself. The car was his relaxation as well. Sometimes, on holidays, he drove to the country. The wheels got stuck in the mud and K. groaned as he tried to rock the car out. He cursed Russian roads and Russian laziness. He drove as far as Tver, daydreaming about scattering factories, tracks, and grain elevators across the frozen fields and frightening the innocent cows of Russia.

How did this man get to Moscow, among the ragged coats of coachmen, tea drinking, and arguments about the new way of life? But he wasn't from out of town. He was an old Muscovite. He had grown up in Arbat, more precisely on Nicolo-Peskovsky Lane. On one side stood a lumberyard, on the other a beer hall, where students, belching from beer, argued on and on about whether Leonid Andreyev had justified Judas or not. K. was a little boy then. He was doing percentage problems and hurling tightly packed snowballs at girls.

By the time he began growing up, the war broke out. Everything around him was reeling. He couldn't get used to anything. As a result, the revolution didn't surprise him. It wasn't his doing, but it instantly became his life.

K. was slightly scornful of everything that had preceded the revolution, such as antediluvian cars in the guise of carriages or dresses with trains. Of course he remembered the Cossacks whooping and driving a crowd apart, and the poems of the Decadents, and the whisper: "Tolstoy has written against capital punishment. . . . " But all that seemed silly and trivial now that there were such things as petroleum, export, America, and a desk notebook divided into hours and even half-hours.

One of his desk drawers contained, among newspaper clippings and American magazines, a half-faded photograph. It showed K.'s parents. They had had it taken at their wedding. High, stiff collar, bouquet, the woman bashfully smiling, and on the table a book opened by the photographer.

Every time K. chanced upon this picture, he grinned: "Hihihi!" The book was probably by Mikhailovsky or Lavrov. They would read aloud about the community and then, between chapters, swear eternal love to one another. K.'s father was a *Narodnik*, a Russian populist, he worshiped the muzhik, and then, when the estate of barristers was abolished, he promptly turned sour and began waiting for some mythical generals or other. Well, as for the mother, she devoured Bashkirtsova's diaries and always spoke about love: Was it real or not real? Her husband went off to gypsy-girls and carried on with chambermaids. She wept, then she forgave him and only asked: Was it real or not real? K. grinned: Funny people! Old Fords. No, even more comical: Orlov trotters straight out of an old song!

K.'s life was orderly and secure. He never experienced disappointments, tears, or depressions. First he had fought the Poles, now he was organizing the oil export. He scarcely thought about the fate of the revolution. That was a far more interesting topic, of course, but K. didn't have the time: He was *working* for the revolution. Let others think about it. Once a week he went to the movies. He liked American comedies. They were out-and-out silly, and, watching them, he could avoid thinking altogether, he could simply laugh, the way horses neigh or roosters crow. Why think at the movies? They're a relaxation. Once a week, one-and-a-half hours. He had to think during working-hours, and not about some old woman who foolishly turns her son over to the police, but about business, that is to say, petroleum.

In K.'s office, frightening visitors, stood the American dictaphone. When the work day was over and K. was alone, he had long conversations with the stillness in the deserted offices. He would dictate a report or an article for *Economic Life* or the current correspondence. In the morning, the typist, Comrade Yegorova, sat down at the Underwood and put on the transparent headphone. She heard the even, slightly mocking voice of Comrade K.: "This also bears upon our negotiations with Spain, where, as we know, a state monopoly on oil now exists. Period. New paragraph." K. meanwhile was far away, in Sadovaya—another urgent meeting. . . .

But man is imperfect, even a man like K. He too had a foible which his colleagues didn't suspect: He liked women. He liked them simply, grossly, not just some specific woman, no, all women, he liked them to the point of sudden woolgathering during a meeting, fits of melancholy, migraine headaches. He made all sorts of efforts to get rid of this shameful ailment. Some two years ago he had up and married, on the spot, wasting no time on how or who. Just marry and live with a wife. That's what all men do. It's easier and faster. But his wife turned out to be a philistine who dreamt about French cosmetics and kept a volume of Romanov under her pillow. They soon separated. Now K. consulted a doctor he knew. The doctor, after tapping his knee, prescribed cold showers and bromide. But the treatment didn't help. K. was in agony. Sorry, comrades, but he had absolutely no time for affairs with Soviet girls. A hooker in Tverskaya? That simply did not accord with his views. What did rubles have to do with it? He wasn't a hero in Leonid Andreyev, after all. He was a new Soviet man.

Now K. was in luck. Recently, at the truck tests, he had met Musya G. She was a clerk at the Amo car factory. She had blue eyes and freckles. It really didn't matter though. She was a woman.

He knew one thing. All women, even those in favor of technology and sport, even knee-socked members of the Communist Youth and the League for Saving Time, have to be worked on for a long, long time. There's nothing you can do. True Communism is still far away and for the time being you've still got to pay for everything. The one from Tverskaya costs a ten-ruble note; this one, a few mindless words that are sickening and embarrassing, like tears in a trolley-car or a violin in a restaurant during burps and meatballs. You can't change yourself. He didn't talk to Musya about his feelings. He didn't read Yessenin's poems to her. He hadn't reached that point yet. Nevertheless, he had to invest five or six evenings of preparations. In his memo-book there was a huge, agonizing M. He went to Sokolniki, where Musya lived, and he labored till two in the morning. He talked to Musya about everything except the thing they should have talked about. He talked about the wonders of America, about hoisting-cranes that looked like giraffes, about skycrapers, even about jazz bands at bars in Harlem, that smell of rotten pineapples, black sweat, and raw brandy. Musya's blue eyes gaped and grew dim.

On the sixth evening, having finished talking about Jack Dempsey, K. asked courteously but businesslike:

"Musya, how about it? . . . ."

That night, he came home very late, it was almost morning. The car was eyed by militiamen, northern stars, and trolley workers with little lanterns as mysterious as fireflies. K. didn't see the lanterns or the stars. After three hours' sleep, he took a cold shower and chuckled contentedly several times. He wasn't late to work, of course. He worked well as usual. He didn't think about some girl with freckles and foolish questions: "Tell me, are you happy? . . ." No, he thought about business, that is, petroleum.

A tiny room. A tiny cot. On the table, breadcrumbs and Lermontov. Two blouses, an illustrated magazine, lipstick, and heavy breathing. K., maneuvering a mirror fragment, was knotting his motley Oxford tie. Musya avidly followed his hands.

"Are you leaving?"

"Of course."

"Borya, why don't you stay! . . . I have to talk to you. I just can't go on like this! . . ."

K. wasn't annoyed. He smiled, rather goodnaturedly: He pictured the faded photograph. Here it was: True or not true! . . . Then he looked at his watch.

"I still have five minutes. Ask me anything you like. Go ahead."

"I can't go on like this. Just forget about your watch for once! Can't you see how unhappy I am?"

"You're not thinking. I've got so much work today. I have to dictate the annual report."

He absentmindedly fondled her cheek, which was covered with freckles and tears, and then left.

Half an hour later, he picked up the dictaphone mike and began: "56,000 tons to France, 42,000 tons to England. . . ."

Musya G. was a very ordinary girl. Outside of K., she liked portraits of leaders and silk stockings, although in summer she wore knee-socks, assuring her girlfriends that they were a lot more pleasant: silk stockings were expensive, and Musya made only sixty rubles a month. Musya correctly registered the outgoing documents. She knew the manufacturing cost of an automobile, the number of cars produced, and their distribution. Even before meeting K., she had understood that automobiles were now a lot more important than Lermontov, and that she was taking part in a big and weighty task. She devoted herself to primary political education, as well as German and swimming. Her days were filled. But there were still a few free moments left: in the morning when she took the trolley to work or in the evening, before going to sleep, in the tiny room with the breadcrumbs. At such moments, Musya didn't think about car manufacturing, or interim stabilization, or Shura, who could stay underwater longer than anyone else. She thought about love. She even kept a diary. Naturally, she didn't say anything to K. about it. He would only have grinned. But on April 17th, the day they were testing the new cars, when she had met him for the first time, she had written: "There were a lot of other guys there. And besides, he's not good-looking at all. He's got buckteeth like a horse. What's wrong anyway? . . . I'm just not a good judge. At any rate, this is stupid and sentimental. You have to know how to get along with everyone, like Lyolka, or else just not give a damn about anyone, like Z. . . . But I still felt that beyond naked instinct there is something that is deep and even unintelligible to science. . . ."

Entry of April 26th (after K.'s first visit): "It's hard for me to write, I'm *so* happy. He's amazing. I'm so grateful to him. It certainly contradicts Lyolka. He's not a creep. He's truly a new kind of man, he's been everywhere, he's a marvelous worker, and yet he doesn't see the matter in such simple terms. He's looking for something else. I can sense that he is attracted to me as a woman. But he talked to me like a good friend. Which means he needs a wealth of feelings. Of course I'm not as smart as he is, but I suddenly became more adult, and then, this is a matter of the heart, not the mind. Maybe I'll be able to give him something."

Then Musya neglected the notebook. For about two weeks, she made no entries. When she remembered the diary, she started in with poetry:

"May 9th. Shura loves Mayakovsky's poems. She's always reciting them. I've written them down to remember them. There's one that goes like this:

Who cares
That—"oh the poor guy!"—
That he was in love
And felt so lousy?. . .

That's very malicious. I admit he's right, and K. is right, and Shura, and simply everyone. But my feelings are totally different. I find that Lermontov's poetry is no worse. He says, with true suffering:

They loved one another so long and so tender,
With deep melancholy and wildly rebellious passion.

Now that we have a new kind of life and the building of Socialism, why can't we have tenderness, for instance? Today Borya sat here a quarter of an hour for politeness' sake and then ran off. Obviously he only needs my body. The pig! I told him as much. I told him it would be better if he didn't come anymore. But he just talked about his work again. I'm starting to hate his watch, his car, even his petroleum. . . . The worst thing is I can't live without him now. If it turns out he really doesn't love me, I'll die.''

Entry, undated: "Borya, my darling! My beloved! My only one! I shall never send you this letter, but I want to have a long talk with you about everything. You understand—I am now your slave. I only live for when you come. But you always run off right away. Aren't my lips enough for you? But they're just an outward thing. You could just as easily go to another woman. . . . I have so many tender words for you, why don't you want to hear them? You're big, strong, you know everything, but I do love you. With all that's happened, I've as good as become your wife. I'd like to know what you think about when you're silent. Do you have a secret? Who else would you tell it to if not me? I can understand everything. When you left yesterday, I was ready to throw myself out the window. It's embarrassing to admit, but I don't control myself the way I used to. I'm completely in your power. And you, you aren't free either. Borya, just tell me this one thing: Who is bossing you around?''

Entry, May 19th: "He left as usual. He spent exactly twenty-five minutes here. I deliberately looked at the clock. I didn't even ask him to stay, I just lay there like a log. Now I feel like beating my head against the wall. There's no way out. I'm not Lyolka. For me it's forever. Absolute solitude. I can't work. All I think about is—death. Shura's sending me to the doctor. But I won't go. Either I'll be able not to give a damn, like in her Mayakovsky poem, or else I'll die. . . ."

On May 23, around ten PM, K. was driving to Musya in Sokolniki. He had been delayed by the conference, and his habits notwithstanding he was terribly late. Could Musya have already gone to sleep?

He raced along, increasing his speed. What if Musya had gotten angry and refused to open? Damn it all! He had managed to get involved with her! She was a drag with all that mush about the soul! But you can't find a woman without that. In any event, he had gotten her to stop asking him to stay. She had finally understood that he wasn't a loafer, he had a responsible job. That was the main thing. He could put up with the rest. Otherwise, she was just what he needed. He didn't even dream about other women now. He'd be willing to get a license any time. But he was so late! . . . What if she didn't open? . . .

It's good driving on Bogorodsky Boulevard, especially late at night: A smooth, straight road, no cars, no wagons. K.'s car zoomed as though he were in America and not Sokolniki. The headlights shone on a quivering swarm of midges and on the even graveling. Suddenly, they struck a shadow. The siren howled furiously, but the shadow didn't move. K. swerved off to the left. The shadow hurled itself to the side and sprawled upon the road. K. was jolted out of his seat. He leaped out of the car. He shouted:

"Yes! Help!"

Some guy came up and stupidly bleated:

"Tired of life, I guess! Heehee!"

With great difficulty, they managed to drag the crushed body out from under the car. K. turned away. And the guy was still bleating:

"What a fool!"

He reeked of vodka. K.'s hands were bloodstained. He tore open the blouse and pressed his ear against the familiar breast. He listened for a long time. But the breast was still. No mush about the soul, no contractions of the heart muscles. They put the corpse in the automobile. The engine breathed loudly. The Ford was a fine fellow, it hadn't suffered.

The whole next day, K. worked with great concentration. He studied the reports of the Paris delegation of the Oil Syndicate. "The orders of the naval department form a solid foundation for our export to France. . . ." He worked on till late at night. He looked through thin slips of paper covered with lilac spirit, jotted down figures, made notes. Then he began dictating. He spoke as usual, in an even, dispassionate tone. All at once his face screwed up in a cramp. He screamed. He himself seemed alarmed at this scream. He was alone in his large office, among files and diagrams. He could picture dim eyes, a slightly open mouth, dripping blood. He stood there, pressing his face against the wall so as not to see anything. He was gasping for air. A few minutes went by. Then he pulled himself together. He unbuttoned his collar, paced up and down, and got to work again. He mustn't think of Musya. Musya no longer existed. Period. Paragraph. Only one thing existed: his work, petroleum—and for all time.

The typist, Comrade Yegorova, was typing up the next report. She wrote: "The condition of the French market is subject to fluctuations, which can be explained in part by the emergence. . . ." Suddenly she pulled her hands back from the keyboard and tore off the headphone: Instead of Comrade K.'s normal voice she had heard a desperate, bestial shriek. Her neighbor asked:

"What's wrong? . . . You're so pale! . . . Maybe we should open the door and let in some air. It's so stuffy here. . . ."

Yegorova murmured:

"No, no, it's all right. . . . I just thought I. . . . I'm just overworked. It's a good thing my vacation's coming. . . ."

She put the headphone on again. Comrade K.'s voice kept going: ". . . explained by the emergence of Rumanian and Polish oil. . . . The voice, as usual, was even and dispassionate.

—The End—

Written in Paris
February-June 1929
*Translated in New York
September-October 1975*

Glossary

ANDREYEV, LEONID (1871-1919), Russian realist writer who turned to more metaphysical themes. An anti-Bolshevik, he emigrated to Finland after the Bolshevik accession to power.

ANNAM, historical region and former state in central Vietnam.

AXELROD (Akselrod), Pavel Borisovich (1850-1928), a Menshivik leader.

BACON, FRANCIS (1561-1626) English philosopher and statesman. His greatest work, *Novum Organum*, is an exposition of innovative and experimental scientific method.

BACON, ROGER (c. 1214-1294?), English philosopher and scientist. He predicted automotive vehicles.

BAKUNIN, MIKHAIL (1814-1876), Russian revolutionary and leading exponent of Anarchism.

BARRAS, Paul François Jean Nicolas, vicomte de (1755-1829), a French revolutionary and Jacobin. By consenting to resign from the Directory during Napoleon's coup, he contributed to Napoleon's success.

BRETON, ANDRÉ (1896-1966), French Surrealist writer and one of the first to publicize Freud in France.

BRIAND, ARISTIDE (1862-1932), French statesman, lawyer, Socialist, who advocated a United States of Europe.

BUISSON, FERDINAND EDOUARD (1841-1932), French educator and ardent pacifist.

CACHIN, MARCEL (1869-1958), French Socialist politician. He helped bring the Socialists into the Third International in 1929.

CAPET, HUGH (c. 939-966), king of France, first of the Capetian dynasty.

CÉZANNE, PAUL (1839-1906), French Post-Impressionist painter. His geometrization of object-forms prepared the way for Cubism and pure abstract painting.

CHAMBERLAIN, (Arthur) NEVILLE (1869-1940), a Conservative member of the House of Commons; he was Chancellor of the Exchequer, 1923-1924.

CHAMFORT, NICOLAS-SEBASTIEN ROCH DE (1741-1794), a French moralist writer in the aphoristic style.

CHEKA (VChK), Extraordinary Commission or Struggle Against Counterrevolution, Sabotage, and Speculation; the secret police agency established by the Bolsheviks after the victory of the revolution in late 1917.

CLÉMENCEAU, GEORGES (1841-1929), French political figure, twice premier. His harsh measures against strikers caused his final break with the Socialists.

DECADI, tenth day of the ten-day week in the French revolutionary calendar.

DEMOSTHENES (384?-322 B.C.), Greek political orator.

DENIKIN, ANTON IVANOVICH (1872-1947), Tsarist general; led one of the anti-Bolshevik (White) forces during Civil War, 1918-1920; emigrated.

DETERDING, HENRY (1866-1939), first managing director of Royal Dutch Shell petroleum companies, unified the group and gave it worldwide interests.

DIRECTORY, group of five men who held executive power in France after the Revolution. *See* Barras.

DUCLOS, JACQUES (1896-1975), French Communist Party leader.

FOUCHÉ, JOSEPH (c. 1749-1820), French revolutionary and Minister of Police.

FRANCE, ANATOLE (1844-1924), French writer whose work was slanted to political satire after Dreyfus Affair.

GAMBETTA, LÉON (1838-1882), French lawyer and politician; leader of Republicans and ardent patriot; helped establish the Third Republic after the downfall of Napoleon III.

GARIBALDI, GIUSEPPE (1807-1882), revolutionary nationalist and military leader. Led his "Thousand Red Shirts" in the conquest of "Two Sicilies" in the cause of a united Italy (1860).

GIRAUDOUX, JEAN (1882-1944), French author and playwright. Gained reputation as writer of irreverent comedies; after World War I, wrote a number of disillusioned, anti-war plays.

GUITRY, SACHA (1885-1957), Russian-born French actor and writer of witty dramas.

HERRIOT, EDOUARD (1872-1957), French statesman, politician and writer; leader of Radical Socialists; served as premier in mid-twenties.

ISTRATI, PANAIT (1884-1935), Rumanian; wrote adventure novels in French about Balkan life.

JACOBINS, political club of the French Revolution, formed in 1789. They eventually grew more radical, adopting many progressive ideas while adhering to orthodox economic principles. They instituted the Reign of Terror, but the fall of their leader Robespierre meant their own downfall.

KRASSIN, LEONID BORISOVICH (1870-1926), Soviet diplomat.

LAVROV, PETER (1823-1900), Narodnik (Populist) leader and writer. Believed in the need for a "civilizing minority" of dedicated men characterized by intellectual development and moral integrity.

LERMONTOV, MIKHAIL YUREVICH (1814-1841), Romantic Russian poet and novelist with Byronic overtones.

LEVASSOR, ÉMILE (1844?-1897), see Panhard.

LIEBKNECHT, KARL (1871-1919), German Socialist; leader of the Spartacus League; killed by reactionaries along with Rosa Luxemburg.

LLOYD GEORGE, DAVID (1863-1945), British statesman; headed Liberal Party; prime minister, 1916-1922.

MAKHNO, NESTOR (1889-1934), Russian Anarchist; leader of a guerrilla band that fought against both Bolsheviks and Whites during Civil War.

MARAT, JEAN-PAUL (1743-1793), French revolutionary stabbed to death by Charlotte Corday.

MATTEOTI, GIACOMO (1885-1924), Italian Socialist leader, the outstanding opponent of Fascism. His murder triggered a crisis which Mussolini overcame by tightening police control, thus beginning his dictatorship.

MIKHAILOVSKY, N. K. (1842-1904), outstanding theoretical leader of the *Narodniki* (Populists).

MILLERAND, ALEXANDRE (1859-1943), French politician, first Socialist to serve in a bourgeois cabinet (1899-1902). Sharply criticized for antilabor decisions, he ultimately became a rightist nationalist.

MIMI, character in Henri Murger's *Scènes de la vie de Bohème*. The consumptive flower-maker was immortalized by Puccini's opera *La Bohème*.

MOSSUL (MOSUL), an oil-rich area in what is now northern Iraq.

MUSSET, ALFRED DE (1810-1857), French romantic poet and dramatist.

OBREJÓN, ALVARO (1880-1928), Mexican general and president (1920-1924), carried out a revolutionary program, nationalized oil deposits, quarreled with Church. Assassinated by fanatical Roman Catholic.

PANHARD, RENÉ (1841-1908), French engineer and car manufacturer. In 1891-1892, he and Levassor produced the first vehicle with an internal combusion engine.

PHÈDRE, title character of Racine's drama, based on Euripides' *Hippolytus*.

PITT, WILLIAM (1759-1806), British statesman. Despite early liberal policies, he harshly opposed radical agitation in England and condemned the French Revolution.

PLEKHANOV, GEORGI VALENTINOVICH (1856-1918). Marxist philosopher and historian, became a Menshevik leader; refused to support Bolsheviks in their successful struggle for power in 1917.

POINCARÉ, RAYMOND (1860-1934), French statesman, regarded the Treaty of Versailles as too lenient. President of France, 1913-1920.

RACINE, JEAN (1634-1699), French classic dramatist.

RAKOVSKY, CHRISTIAN (1873-1942?), a prominent Bolshevik; president of Ukrainian Soviet (1919-1923); later ambassador to France.

ROMANOV, ruling Russian dynasty from 1613 to 1917.

SANDEAU, JULES (1811-1883), popular French novelist of the period.

SAN MARTIN, JOSÉ DE (1778-1850), South American patriot, general, and statesman. Won independence for Chile and Peru from Spain.

TAGORE, SIR RABINDRANATH (1861-1941), Indian author and guru. Coined word "togetherness."

TALLIEN, JEAN LAMBERT (1767-1820), French revolutionary, fell in love with Thérèse Cabbarus, a political prisoner.

TARDIEU, ANDRE (1876-1945), French statesman and journalist.

TAYLOR, FREDERICK WINSLOW (1856-1915), the father of scientific management.

THERMIDOR, eleventh month of French revolutionary calendar. The coup d'état of the 9th of Thermidor marked the fall of Robespierre and the end of the terror.

THIERS, ADOLPHE (1797-1877), French statesman, journalist, historian.

VALÉRY, PAUL (1871-1945), French poet and critic, follower of the symbolists.

VOROSHILOV, KLIMENT YEFREMOVICH (1881-1969), close associate of Stalin from Civil War days; later became Commissar of Defense.

YEAR VIII of the French revolutionary calendar: 1800.

YESENIN, SERGEI ALEXANDROVICH (1895-1925), Russian poet. The most popular poet of the early Revolution, he ultimately rejected Soviet policies.

ZAHAROFF, SIR BASIL (1850-1930), financier and munitions manufacturer.

OTHER BOOKS FROM PLUTO

A LONG WAY FROM HOME
CLAUDE McKAY

In this rich and rewarding autobiography,
Claude McKay, the Jamaican-born poet and
novelist, remembers the Harlem Renaissance,
the labour movement in Britain, meetings with
Radek and Trotsky in post-revolutionary USSR
and a formative trip to Africa.

McKay writes about meetings in the 1920s
and 1930s – with Frank Harris, George Bernard
Shaw, W.E.B. Du Bois, Isadora Duncan, Charles
Chaplin, H.G. Wells, Sinclair Lewis and many
more. He also describes his life among black
dock workers and sailors in Marseilles and
among Africans in Morocco, where he lived
until his return to the United States in 1934.

Throughout this book, McKay voices a
militant black consciousness that shocked bien-
pensant society of the day. Today's reader will
warm to this early expression of 'Black is
beautiful'.

Claude McKay went to New York from
Jamaica in 1912. His novels *Banjo* and *Banana
Bottom* and his poems, including *Harlem
Shadows*, were central to Harlem Renaissance
in the 1920s. He died in 1948. *A Long Way From
Home* is his autobiography.

384 pages
0 7453 0082 0   £4.95 paperback

NOTES OF A NATIVE SON
JAMES BALDWIN
With a new introduction by the author

Notes of a Native Son is James Baldwin's first non-fiction book. Since its publication in 1955, Baldwin has established himself as one of America's foremost writers. These essays on life in Harlem, movies, the protest novel and Americans abroad are as relevant today as when they were first written.

'A straight-from-the-shoulder writer, writing about the troubled problems of this troubled earth with an illuminating intensity that should influence for the better all who ponder on the things books say.' Langston Hughes, *The New York Times*

192 pages
0 7453 0059 6   £3.95 paperback

THE HISTORY OF THE RUSSIAN REVOLUTION
LEON TROTSKY

Trotsky's finest literary achievement and the most authoritative, impassioned and superbly written account of the Russian Revolution ever published.

'[Trotsky's] crowning work, both in scale and power and as the fullest expression of his ideas on revolution. As an account of a revolution, given by one of its chief actors, it stands unique in world literature.' Isaac Deutscher

1296 pages. Index
0 904383 41 5   £12.50 paperback

1985
GYÖRGY DALOS

Big Brother is dead. Massive sectarian struggle
rages between his widow, Big Sister, and
various revolutionary cliques.

György Dalos's sequel to George Orwell's
1984 is a 'historical report' written from exile in
the year 2035. Though Dalos's figures were
created by Orwell, his political commentary is
not so constrained.

György Dalos is a Hungarian poet, influenced
by his political experiences in post-1956
Hungary. *1985* is a novel which is witty, lively,
ironic, politically sharp – but deeply
pessimistic.

128 pages
0 86104 720 6   £2.95 paperback

KINO-EYE
The Writings of Dziga Vertov
*Edited and introduced by Annette
Michelson*

In post-revolutionary Russia, Vertov was a
prolific film maker – *The Man with the Movie
Camera* is now a classic. *Kino-Eye* brings
together his agitational writing, extracts from his
notebooks and proposals for creative projects.
Spanning a period of 30 years (1922-52) *Kino-
Eye* portrays Vertov's trajectory from film
maker of the revolution to non-artist in the dark
years of Stalinism. His writings reflect the
commitment of a generation of artists to
revolutionary change in form and content. Their
first appearance in English is a major
contribution to film studies.

344 pages. Illustrated throughout
0 86104 767 2   £19.95 hardback

Pluto books are available through your local
bookshop. In case of difficulty contact Pluto to
find out local stockists or to obtain catalogues/
leaflets (telephone 01-482 1973).
   If all else fails write to:

Pluto Press Limited
Freepost (no stamp required)
105A Torriano Avenue
London NW5 1YP